The writing partnership of John Francome and James MacGregor got off to a cracking start with *Eavesdropper* (1986) and *Riding High* (1987), both bestsellers. The authenticity of the novels is reflected by the backgrounds of the two authors: John Francome has been Champion Jockey seven times and is regarded as the greatest National Hunt jockey ever known. James MacGregor is the pseudonym of a practising barrister, who also has an avid interest in racing.

'Splendid racing scenes and a tight storyline. Gripping stuff . . . a must for all racing fans and a fun read for others' John Welcome

'A thoroughbred stayer . . . cracking thriller' *Independent*

'An entertaining tale of skulduggery in turf and law' *The Times*

'A racy thriller about the Sport of Kings' *Daily Telegraph*

D0042637

Also by John Francome and James MacGregor

Eavesdropper
Riding High

Declared Dead

John Francome and
James MacGregor

HEADLINE

Copyright © 1988 John Francome and James MacGregor

First published in 1988
by HEADLINE BOOK PUBLISHING

First published in paperback in 1989
by HEADLINE BOOK PUBLISHING

10 9 8

ISBN 0 7472 3251 2

Typeset in 10/12½pt English Times
by Colset Private Limited, Singapore

Printed and bound in Great Britain by
Cox & Wyman Ltd, Reading, Berkshire

HEADLINE BOOK PUBLISHING
a Division of Hodder Headline PLC
338 Euston Road
London NW1 3BH

Declared Dead

Chapter 1

My hands were shaking so much I could hardly hold onto the reins. Pulling that horse in a seller at Fontwell had been bad enough, but to throw the Gold Cup in front of a crowd of forty thousand enthusiastic racegoers was a desperate and terrifying prospect. I could feel the goose bumps rising on my skin from a mixture of nerves and guilt. I patted Cartwheel on the shoulder and talked to him in a forlorn attempt to calm myself down. I just kept wishing that this whole business was a bad dream from which I would awake any moment, but the bark of the starter, telling us to get in line, brought me sharply back to reality.

Cartwheel was itching to be off and I had to tug hard on the reins to restrain him. He loved his racing and I wasn't even that confident he would go along with my plans. He was an old hand at jumping these Cheltenham fences and if I kept mistiming my take-offs to get him in close to the bottom of them, he was just as likely to think it was all a game and outwit me

1

by standing off a stride and putting in a long one. That way I would be gaining ground instead of losing it.

The starter had a quick look across the field to make sure we were all ready and then screamed, 'Right!' as he pulled down on the lever to release the starting tape. Immediately a huge roar of anticipation and excitement went up from the enclosures and grandstands ahead of us. For the first few yards Cartwheel led the way and I let him skip over the first fence as he wished. I had absolutely no intention of doing anything suspicious in front of the packed grandstands – I had chosen the tricky downhill fence on the second circuit for my 'accidental fall'. By the time we reached there I'd make certain we were on the outside and therefore less likely to be galloped on after we had hit the ground. More importantly, we would be out of the full view of the television cameras and most of the spectators.

If I'd been riding almost any other horse, the chances were, if I tried hard enough, I would be able to get it to fall at one of the twenty-six fences; but Cartwheel had a firmly placed instinct for self-preservation. He was a handsome liver-chestnut who planned to stay that way and liked to handle all the intricacies of take-offs and landings himself. He was never going to be another Arkle or Mill House, but he was as good as anything that had run that season and had been favourite for the Gold Cup since skating home in the King George at Kempton in December.

If I took a chance that he might just not be good enough on the day, it would be sod's law that he'd win pulling a cart. There was no alternative; I'd just have to fall off him and try and make it look as though I had been unseated.

I had only ever seen one jockey jump off a horse deliberately before, and that had been at Devon and Exeter when, for some reason, the animal he was riding in a two-mile hurdle race suddenly went off the racecourse and bolted towards a wood. I'd always remember the jockey coming back into the weighing room saying it was the most terrifying and unnatural thing that he had ever done.

As we jumped each fence on the first circuit, his words echoed in my ears as I mentally went through the motions of what I had to do. The more I thought about it, the more frightened I became and the less confident I was of being able to go through with it, and yet I knew I must.

For the first time since I had started racing I looked down at the grass speeding by below me and imagined what damage I might do to myself. It was the ultimate irony. Here I was with the chance of realising every jump jockey's dream by winning the Gold Cup and I was committed to throwing it away. I'd be lucky if I ever got another ride after what I was about to do, never mind have a chance like this again.

At this stage my foremost task was to ensure that we stayed in touch with the leaders for the first part of the race. I had at all costs to avoid alerting any kind of suspicion. As we galloped up the hill and round the top bend towards the second fence, I looked for our principal rivals in the betting. Out front, five lengths clear and blazing the trail, was the grey, Stonepicker. He had already won the Hennessey Gold Cup earlier in the season and was a natural front runner. Just ahead of me and hugging the rail I could see the backside of Eamon Brennan, the champion Irish jockey, aboard Pride of Limerick. The big chestnut, a strapping son of Deep Run, was carrying the hopes of Ireland and, I suspected, most of its ready cash. The Irish had so far enjoyed a bumper festival and had backed their champion as if it was simply a case of putting the money down, returning to the bar, and calling back a few minutes later to collect their winnings.

Brennan was a brilliant horseman who was not averse to a bit of chicanery if the situation demanded it. His catch phrase of 'nothing personal' as he squeezed you for room on the inside rail, or took your ground before a fence, was a standing joke in the weighing room, although it was not so easy to explain to an irate trainer or owner who had seen his horse's chances apparently blundered away by an incompetent jockey.

Finally, at least as far as the ante-post betting market was concerned, there was the most dangerous rival of them all – the mare, Melodrama. She was trained in the North of England by Dick Walker, one of the shrewdest men in racing and also one of the most fearless gamblers. When he put his money down, it was strictly on temporary loan. Because of her sex Melodrama was entitled to a five-pound weight allowance and if her last two races were anything to go by, she was as tough as nails and didn't need it. On both occasions, she had been off the bridle a mile from home and looked to have no chance, but the further she went the better she seemed to go. She had all the stamina of a bookie counting his winnings. As for the rest, they were all good-class steeplechasers, but on form none had the beating of the four of us.

For the first circuit everything went smoothly. Stonepicker was setting a very decent gallop and even though Cartwheel was putting in a string of good jumps, we remained several lengths adrift in the middle of the first chasing pack. We were now only three fences away from the downhill fence and I told myself to keep calm. To anyone watching I was riding an intelligent and sensible race, giving Cartwheel every chance. Nobody would ever realise that I had no intention of getting him to the finishing line. As we passed the stands to start the second and final circuit, everyone in the crowd seemed to be shouting at the top of their voices but Cartwheel appeared wholly unperturbed. A couple of fallers had left us in second place, although I knew that Eamon Brennan and Pride of Limerick were jogging along half a length behind us. There was no sign of Melodrama, although she must have still been with us. When the favourite falls in any race, news of it soon spreads through the field of jockeys; and this was the Gold Cup.

Much too quickly for my liking, we now turned away from the stands and were galloping left-handed towards the tricky fence before the water. This was it. I felt nervous and desperately uncertain. Falling off a horse and making it look like an accident is not quite so simple as some punters seemed to think. The field was beginning to close up behind me and for the first time I caught sight out of the corner of my eye of Melodrama, or rather more accurately of her sheep-skin noseband. Her head was already set with determination as she fought to keep up and I had no doubt she was going to be right in there at the finish.

Three strides away from the fence, I moved my feet back in the stirrups so that only the tips of my toes were touching. I then snatched one final deep breath and held it. 'Here we go!' I thought. 'God! I hope I don't hurt myself.' Just as Cartwheel was about to take off, I put my head down by his shoulder and let myself go limp.

But then I quickly sat up again: I couldn't do it. I was frightened, but more than anything I knew that I wanted to win, and I was sick of betraying all those people who had placed so much trust in me. This time I was going to win and to hell with the consequences.

I immediately concentrated hard on setting a good stride and Cartwheel duly obliged but, just as I squeezed my legs against his sides to make him go in and jump, Stonepicker, ahead of us, hit the fence hard and swerved out to the right where we were due to land. Steve Rampton, his jockey, performed a miracle to stay on board, and if he had only been able to keep a tight hold of the reins everything would have been fine. But he couldn't. Stonepicker lost his balance as he hit the ground and crumpled up in front of us, leaving Cartwheel with nowhere to put his feet as he landed. If I now pulled one way and he decided to go the other I would bring him down for certain. I decided to leave him alone and just sit tight as he dodged instinctively to the right. For a split second I thought we had got away with it. Instead I shot up his neck as his back legs became entangled with those of Stonepicker, who lay kicking wildly on the ground. By some miracle we stayed up but were brought almost to a standstill. From going well and not trying in second place we were now desperate to win but out at the back with the no-hopers.

Within seconds the water jump was upon us and we only just managed to reach the other side. The sight of Brennan's motionless backside, ten lengths ahead, said it all. By the time we reached the next, the third open ditch, we were on an even keel and once we were over I had time to take a breather at last, look up and assess the situation. We were a good fifteen lengths adrift of Melodrama, who had now pulled herself into the lead. She was followed by a couple of others I didn't recognise; then, travelling easiest of all, was Pride of Limerick.

7

There was less than a mile and a half to go, and although it wasn't impossible to win from where we were, it was frankly unlikely. At least we had the conditions on our side. The rain, which had started falling on the first day of the festival, two days earlier, had come just in time and the deep mud underfoot put a premium on stamina. Cartwheel was an out and out stayer and could be relied upon to do his best in the last half mile of the race. But were we now too far behind to make use of it? Clearly there was no time for caution and I kicked Cartwheel into the next fence and steered him towards the inside.

We flew the next three fences before reaching the top of the hill, and began racing left handed towards the long downhill run. He was in top gear now and eating up the ground. Gradually we were beginning to make an impression, and the lead had been cut to about eight lengths as we raced towards the third last. There was no doubt by now which of us was more tired. My legs felt like jelly and my lungs were burning. I desperately wanted Cartwheel to put in a short stride at the next, so that he would take more time to recover and I would be able to snatch a lungful of air. But he had other plans. We stood off the fence a whole stride too soon and landed just as far over the other side, with Cartwheel's neck stretched out, heading for home. His only concern was winning.

I was now so exhausted that I was little more than a passenger. It was Cartwheel, not me, who forced us between the running rail and another tiring horse in his effort to reach the front and as he galloped up relentlessly towards the second last, every muscle in my body was straining at the effort. I just wished to God that I could summon up the assistance he deserved. He jumped the last two fences with ridiculous ease and then began the long gallop up the famous Cheltenham hill.

Ahead of us and locked together were Melodrama on the standside and on the inside, being driven along, Pride of Limerick. With fifty yards to go we passed Melodrama, who was rolling in the mud and going nowhere, and drew alongside Pride of Limerick. Brennan was arched over the chestnut with his whip in his left hand, striking him repeatedly. Responding to his jockey's exertions, Pride of Limerick fought like a terrier to match strides with us. As the two horses joined battle I could feel Cartwheel edging towards the chestnut as the strength in his legs began to give out. I couldn't bear losing now. With one last desperate effort Cartwheel forced his head in front as we passed the line.

The judge would have to call for a photograph but I knew we had done it.

The stewards had other ideas. We had pulled up and I was accepting the congratulations of my fellow jockeys when the announcement of an enquiry came over the tannoy. I looked quizzically over at the rider of Melodrama to see if he had any idea what it was about; he merely shrugged his shoulders and told me not to worry. That was easier said than done. It would be ironic if, having decided to be honest, I should now lose the race in the stewards' room. Ralph Elgar came running out to me as the lad led us towards the winners' enclosure and I could tell from the worried look on his face that he was none too happy.

'Do you think you'll keep it?' he asked anxiously, his voice still hoarse from shouting Cartwheel home.

I felt angry at his lack of confidence. 'What do you mean? I've done nothing wrong.'

He shook his head ominously. 'I hope you're right. It certainly didn't look too good from where I was watching. Brennan definitely had to stop riding, you know.'

My heart sank. Cartwheel had beaten Pride of Limerick on merit but it was beginning to look like the loser's jockey may have outwitted me. The outcome would hinge upon the head on film and the mood of the stewards.

We reached the winners' enclosure to a tumultuous reception – at least the other half of the Cheltenham crowd appeared to have backed us – and as I dismounted I turned to Cartwheel's owner and apologised.

'I'll have none of that,' replied Angus Knight, beaming with pride and apparently unflustered by the unfolding drama. 'He ran a great race and you gave him a great ride. Now go and make sure you do as well in front of the stewards.'

I patted Cartwheel on the neck and pulled the

saddle off before turning and walking across the grass towards the weighing room. Trainers, jockeys and racing journalists shouted congratulations as I passed. I only hoped that they were merited. Just before I reached the steps one of the stipendiary stewards stopped me and told me to come to the stewards' room as soon as I'd weighed in.

I was terrified. Twenty minutes before, I'd been set on losing the race and now here I was praying that it would not be taken away from me. I had no doubt that Brennan would lie through his teeth if he thought it would give him half a chance of winning the Gold Cup and, to be honest, I was certain I would do the same in his position. The Irishman was already waiting outside the stewards' room when I arrived, his riding silks splattered with mud and his cheeks still flushed from his exertions. He sneered at me malevolently and through the gap in his front teeth hissed the magic words, 'Nothing personal'.

As soon as the stewards had finished watching the re-run of the race, we were summoned into their presence. The three of them were seated behind a beautiful antique beechwood table, whose four legs were carved like the hind legs of a rearing horse. In the middle sat Brigadier-General Allsopp and on his right, much to my despair, Sir Arthur Drewe. He was a great friend of my father-in-law – I think they were at school together – and had gone out of his way to be rude to me ever since I had turned professional. What's more, I'd already stood before him on a couple of occasions, and both times I'd lost. He was in his late fifties, with grey hair and a moustache, and his face bore testimony to many years of exposure to the good life, and in particular to vintage port. Unfortunately he had once ridden the winner of a point-to-point, which in his mind had made him an authority on everything connected with racing. The fact was that he could have passed on his entire knowledge in under a minute and replayed it on his video, too. I did not recognise the third member of the triumvirate, who was considerably younger and gave me what I hoped was a sympathetic smile. The stipendiary steward, who was standing beside the table, was the first to speak:

'This is Pryde, the rider of Cartwheel, and this is Brennan, the rider of Pride of Limerick.' He then formally introduced the stewards to us. I could tell immediately from the acid expression on Drewe's bucolic face that the best I could hope for was a majority decision.

The Brigadier-General, as chief steward, began by asking each of us to give an account of what happened on the run-in. I went first, but was shaking so much that the words came out hesitantly and without conviction. Brennan, by contrast, had attended more enquiries than he had confessionals, and gave a virtuoso performance of a jockey wronged. He claimed that Cartwheel had crossed him on the run-in to such an extent that he had had to check and stop using his whip.

'I can honestly say, sir,' he concluded, 'that without that interference I would certainly have won.'

We then watched a re-run of the race on the video, both side and head on, and when that was over we were asked if we had anything further to say. Fortunately the head-on film had shown that Cartwheel was not the only culprit and I decided that I couldn't let Brennan's comments go unchallenged. Nothing personal, of course.

'Only this, sir. You'll see that although we did come together it wasn't all my fellow's fault. They were both very tired animals and . . .'

'And because of your failure to steer a straight line, Brennan was unable to use his whip.' Sir Arthur's interjection was as savage as it was demoralising. I so much wanted to answer back, but decided to keep my mouth shut. My only hope was that his fellow stewards disliked him as much as I did, and had taken a different view of the film.

The Brigadier-General told us to leave the room and wait outside while they reached their decision. Brennan was grinning away confidently and I waited for him to repeat the usual sentiment. I chose to ignore him and paced up and down the corridor, cursing myself for letting Cartwheel drift off a straight line and then for making such a fool of myself during the enquiry. How was I going to face Ralph and the owners and tell them that I'd blown it?

The wait seemed interminable, but in fact it was no more than five minutes before we were recalled. As we entered, the stewards' secretary rushed out holding a pink ticket in his hand with the announcement to be given to the operator of the tannoy system. It would either say that the placings remained unaltered or give the details of the corrected result. His stony face gave nothing away. It was left to the chief steward to deliver the verdict.

'Jockeys, we've looked at this film and heard what you both had to say.' He coughed and reached for a glass of water, at least I presumed it was water, in front of him. 'Get on with it,' I muttered impatiently under my breath.

'We have decided that there was interference,' – I swore to myself as he paused – 'but that in no way did it affect the result. The placings remain unaltered.'

I couldn't stop myself smiling and victory was made all the sweeter by the apoplectic look on Sir Arthur's face.

Outside, Ralph Elgar was waiting for me with a smile as big as Bechers. He had heard the result over the tannoy and for all his sixty years was in a state of uncontrolled boyish joy. It is every National Hunt trainer's dream to win the Gold Cup and he was certainly no exception. Although not one of the biggest or most fashionable trainers, he had sent out a steady stream of winners for the last thirty years and had the support of a devoted band of enthusiastic owners. What's more, he had given me a retainer when everyone in the racing world, from fellow trainers to racing tipsters to punters, had told him he was crazy. Now at last I had repaid that trust, although my shameful conduct over the past few months had far from merited his continuing support.

Seeing Ralph's excitement brought me back to reality. The original decision to pull the race had not been taken for fun. I had agreed to do it, just as I had those earlier races at Fontwell and Worcester, because at the time there had seemed no other option. At least, that's what I had told myself before each of those races, and how I consoled myself afterwards. The only trouble is that once you've sold your soul, you can't buy it back at any price. What I had achieved today was a part penance. The original instigator of my sin still remained and was likely to become even more demanding, if not threatening. I just had to hope that I could negotiate more time to think of a way out.

One thing at least was clear. I had to give up my retainer with Ralph. He had done so much for me and I couldn't go on cheating him. Today may have ended well, but I knew I couldn't give any guarantees as to my future conduct. I decided to tell him immediately after the presentation of the winning trophy, and I was still working out what to say when I was collared by a man from the BBC and asked to give an interview. It was the last thing I wanted to do but Ralph patted me on the back and pushed me forward:

'Go on with you. It's not every day you're a piece of history.'

Ten minutes later, having enthused about the race in front of the cameras, I made my way across the paddock towards the changing room. The area was almost deserted as the runners for the next race had already gone down to the start and would shortly be off. I was looking forward to changing out of my silks and having a few minutes to myself before meeting Ralph and the owners in their box for a victory drink. For once, I was glad that I didn't have a ride in the last two races.

I was so buried in my thoughts that I barely heard my name being called. I hesitated for a second and then turned round, just in time to catch the full force of a clenched fist in my mouth. I staggered back for a moment and then, as much from shock as from the blow itself, fell to the ground.

'I hope you're bloody satisfied!' screamed my attacker as he rushed away in the direction of the tented village.

Within seconds a crowd had formed and all I could see as I tried to focus was a muddle of faces peering inquisitively at me. No wonder babies scream so much. Soon a very kind St John's ambulance woman arrived and cradled my head while another went off for bandages and dressings. I told them that it was nothing and I was fine, but they were not going to miss this moment for anything. I looked up to see the anxious face of a uniformed policeman.

'I saw it, officer!' shrieked an hysterical middle-aged woman clutching a couple of tote tickets, and pointing in the direction of the tented village. 'He was in his early thirties, I'd say. He ran off in that direction.'

'Are you all right?' the policeman asked, ignoring her and kneeling beside me. 'Did you get a good sight of him?'

I shook my head. This time lying came easy. Of course I knew him. I'd recognise my husband anywhere.

Chapter 2

Half an hour later I was on the road back home to Lambourn, leaving a bemused police officer and a posse of journalists behind me. The courts, or for that matter the front pages of the tabloids, were the last places I wanted to air my troubles. It wasn't the first time Edward had assaulted me, but it was certainly going to be the last. Now, looking back over the past few months, I still found it hard to believe that our marriage had deteriorated so dramatically. But there was no point pretending we could get back to normal after this.

Edward had never had a job since I'd known him, but always seemed to have plenty of ready cash, which he claimed was an inheritance from his grandfather. Then gradually the money seemed to be lasting for shorter and shorter periods as his gambling increased and he'd begun to drink heavily.

He refused to tell me how much he owed but the quantity of whisky he was putting away each night

made me think that the situation was becoming serious. Luckily for us, I was now beginning to get some
decent rides and had taken over paying all of the bills.

Then one night, he came home drunk and calling
me all the names under the sun. We hadn't had an
argument, so there was no reason for his bad temper
and, at first, I thought it was just one of his stupid
pranks and that a few of his mates would follow him
in and begin laughing. But then suddenly he lashed
out with his fist and caught me on the cheek,
knocking me to the floor. I was terrified and tried to
scramble to my feet but as I did so he walked over to
me and kicked me twice in the stomach. As I dropped
back to the floor, completely winded and gasping for
air, he swore at me a few more times and went
upstairs.

I'd had plenty of falls whilst I was riding and I
thought I was pretty tough, but being beaten up by
my own husband shocked me more than I thought
possible.

As I got my breath back and pulled myself onto a
chair, my legs turned to jelly and I began to tremble. I
sat wondering what to do. My first instinct was to go
upstairs, collect our little boy, Freddie, and leave. Go
anywhere; I didn't know where, but just go. The only
problem was where could I go with a child at eleven
o'clock at night without everybody knowing what
had happened?

My mother lived over sixty miles away, at
Wincanton, and anyway she had enough worries of

her own without me adding to them. Since I'd left home to become an apprentice jockey, after a brief period as a cub reporter, nothing had gone right for her. First of all, my father had run off with another woman and left her to manage the farm on her own, but that had probably been a blessing. He had treated her like a skivvy for years. Then her eldest sister had been paralysed in a car accident that had killed her husband. Mum insisted on nursing her at home herself even though it hadn't been easy for her, and although I had sent money home for her every week, I knew that she struggled to make ends meet. I was an only child and felt guilty that I hadn't given up my apprenticeship and gone home to help her, but I was just beginning to get a few rides. I'd also just started going out with Edward. He was tall and well built, with jet black hair brushed straight back and the darkest eyes I had ever seen. He was also very amusing and, so he was always boasting, very rich. His father was Sir Gerald Pryde, one of the most able High Court judges presently sitting on the Bench, and the man tipped to become the next Lord Chief Justice.

Edward and I had met at the annual Jockeys' Dance at Newbury. I'd gone with James Thackeray, an old friend and a journalist for the *Sportsman* newspaper. He had introduced me to Edward just after the meal had ended and we'd spent the rest of the evening together dancing and talking. We didn't make love that first night but it hadn't been through any lack of trying on Edward's part, or wanting on mine. It was just a matter of nice girls not doing that sort of thing.

All of this happened on a Saturday evening and my 'niceness' lasted until about three o'clock the following afternoon, when, after having had a good lunch in a local pub, we spent the rest of the day in bed in Edward's cottage. From that moment on, we had been inseparable and were married six months later on Derby Day.

Unfortunately, Edward's parents disliked me intensely. It had been perfectly all right for him to go out and sleep with an apprentice jockey – even his mother accepted that her darling son would need to sow some wild oats – but to marry one and then father a child was beyond the pale. Still, at least we'd had a boy.

In the end, after that first assault, I decided to stay. I went upstairs and got into bed with Freddie but slept fitfully.

The following morning I crept out of bed and went to ride out for Ralph. My jaw was still sore, but it was a Tuesday and a work morning for the horses and I knew I would be needed.

When I returned Edward was already up. As I walked through the kitchen door, he rushed towards me holding something behind his back and I stood frozen in terror. As he brought his arm forward, I had never been so pleased to see a bunch of daffodils in my life. Edward put his arms around me, begging

22

my forgiveness. But I would not be able to forget what he had done and knew things could never be the same between us again.

I told him it was time he found a job and pulled himself together, and for a little while he really did try. He didn't find a job as such, but at least he made an effort to help in the cottage, and cut out the drinking completely. Even Mrs Parsons, who came up from the village to look after Freddie for me while I was riding, commented on how much happier everything seemed.

Then one afternoon I came home from visiting my mother with Freddie and found Edward slouched in the chair with an empty bottle of whisky by his side. He immediately began shouting at me and Freddie clutched my skirt and began to cry. I told him not to worry and tried to send him upstairs, but he refused to go.

'You're going to help me out with my little problem,' Edward slurred, pointing his finger at me.

'It's not me you need, it's a doctor,' I replied, but he carried on. He saw my recent riding success as a way of getting 'out of bother' as he so delicately put it. I reminded him that jockeys gave notoriously bad tips and I was no exception but he just laughed and told me to wait and see.

I didn't have to wait long.

Three days later, just as I was getting dressed to go and ride out for Ralph, Edward called me over to his side of the bed. I was surprised to hear his voice as he usually slept to mid morning.

'I don't want you to win today,' he commanded.

'What are you on about?' I answered, trying to keep my voice down so as not to wake Freddie.

'I don't want you to win,' he repeated, grabbing my wrist.

'Thanks for your support, but if you don't mind, I do!' I tried without success to pull my arm free from his grip.

'Listen to me, you silly bitch.' Edward now sat up in bed, pulled me down towards him and started slapping me about the face.

'I want you to lose. Get it? Is that clear?'

His breath was foul with a mixture of alcohol and nicotine from the night before and his voice had taken on a menacing tone.

'This horse of Ralph's you're riding this afternoon at Worcester is going to be well backed but if you so much as look like winning I'll give you a hiding you'll never forget.'

He stopped hitting me and pushed me away. His eyes were wild with anger. Terrified of waking Freddie and afraid of being beaten further, I tried to reason with him.

'Don't be so stupid. If the stewards catch me and I lose my licence what the hell do you think we're going to live on?'

'Don't worry about the stewards. They're taken care of. It's about time you did your bit to help me out of my present difficulties.'

He grabbed me again and hauled me onto the bed.

He no longer made any attempt to restrain his temper.

'You're going to do as I say. If Fainthearted wins today I'll not only give you a good hiding but I'll leave you and take the kid with me, and then apply for custody in the courts. After that, you'll have to leave the cottage. I don't somehow think that the word of a woman jockey, who spends every day at the races and leaves the upbringing of her child to a middle-aged cleaning woman from the village, would prevail over that of the son of a High Court judge when it comes to a decision about custody.'

Before I could reply, Freddie came in crying. As I picked him up and looked at him, I realised that for the moment I had no option.

I will never forget that afternoon at Worcester and the very first occasion in my life when I actually stopped a horse winning. Even then, it so nearly didn't go according to plan. Coming to the last and ignoring all my efforts to discourage him, Faint-hearted was only a length behind the leader. To make matters worse, I was sitting with a double hand-ful and I could have won almost without moving a muscle. Desperate measures were called for. I pushed him into the hurdle and really asked for a big one and then at the last moment deliberately changed my mind. He was completely confused and fell through the hurdle, breaking the top two bars and losing his balance with his back legs as he landed. I did nothing to help him and let the leader go as far away as I could before giving the impression to everyone in the stands that I was making a heroic effort to get back up to win. In fact we failed by a length.

Far from suspecting that I had been up to no good, Ralph was full of praise for the way I had managed to stay on board and comforted himself with the reflection that Fainthearted was nailed on next time out. The punters were less sympathetic. They had backed the horse down to 5–2 favourite and I had to listen to the usual cracks about how female jockeys ought to stick to the kitchen sink and bringing up children. If they had only known the real reason they had lost their money, they would have lynched me, woman or not.

It was now three months since that race and in the meantime my relationship with Edward had deteriorated even further. For the first time in years he had become interested in how I spent my day, cross-examining me in detail about whom I had seen and what I had done. Sometimes I felt he already knew the answers and was just trying to catch me out. One thing was clear. This sudden curiosity was not born of any desire to make our marriage work, as he took endless pleasure in ridiculing my friends and belittling my performances in the saddle. I had become a caged bird – to be played with and taunted with no chance of escape.

As I drove down the tricky Hungerford Hill into Lambourn my elation at winning the Gold Cup had given way to a profound sense of foreboding. However

I viewed the future for Freddie and myself, it was shrouded in gloom. Edward was not going to forgive this afternoon's betrayal. Since that Worcester race he had made no secret of the fact that I now had to do what he ordered and each night before I had a fancied mount I went to sleep dreaming that I would wake up to be given the instruction not to try. In fact it had only happened on one other occasion, and I had duly caused the nominated horse to fall in a novice chase at Fontwell.

Little had I suspected that he had been saving up for the Gold Cup, the one race that every jockey dreams of winning. I could hardly believe my ears when he had casually mentioned the subject the night before as I turned off the light beside the bed. I had begged him not to make me do it, offering to cheat as often as he wanted in the future, but he just shook his head and laughed.

'I'm sorry, old girl, it's no good. You see, this is the big one, when I solve all my financial problems at a stroke. A touch of genius, I'd call it.'

'But why the Gold Cup?' I asked despairingly. 'I can't see how it makes any difference to you when I throw a race.'

'You wouldn't, would you? Think of all those greedy sods who'll be backing Cartwheel, believing he's going to win, and only you, me and one or two friends of mine knowing that it's the one certainty in the race that won't finish.'

'Who are these so-called friends? They're bookmakers, aren't they? I get it. They can afford to offer generous odds on Cartwheel if they know he's bound to lose. It's a licence to print money. I won't do it.'

If I didn't lose, he said, the game was up. He would expose me and take Freddie away. When I countered by saying that he would also be exposed, he roared with laughter.

'You're bloody naive, aren't you? There's nothing to link me to your dishonesty, but plenty to nail you. I took the precaution of paying a thousand pounds cash into your post office account after both Fontwell and Worcester. When, acting out of public duty, I tell my friends at the Jockey Club about the money, and they then take another look at the patrol films of those races, you can wave goodbye to your licence and that darling son of yours. Freddie!' he called out.

'Shh! What the hell do you want to wake him up for?' I asked angrily.

'So you can look at him for the last time. I'm sure my mother will be delighted to let us stay with them pending the court proceedings.'

'You're mad. He's your son as well, you know. Don't you love him too?'

'I suppose so, but to be honest I love myself a great deal more.'

I arrived home from Cheltenham at about six-thirty, to find Freddie still finishing his tea. He was so excited to see me that I put aside my fears and threw myself into playing games with him for the next hour.

We were building a space station with his Lego set when the phone rang. It was a man's voice on the line, one I didn't recognise, flat and very matter-of-fact. He asked for Edward Pryde.

'I'm sorry, he's not back from Cheltenham. Can I give him a message?'

There was no response at the other end.

'Hello? Is anyone there? Who is this?' I wasn't in the mood for an obscene phone call or a practical joke.

'My name's not important. You must be Mrs Pryde. I thought you rode a very gutsy race today. A great shame, though, about the result. Could you just tell your husband there are one or two very upset people around who'd like a word with him?'

The line went dead. The vultures were beginning to gather.

The proposed carcass did not arrive home until the early hours of the morning. After putting Freddie to bed I had been inundated with phone calls from friends congratulating me on my victory and journalists trying to obtain further information on the attack in the paddock after the race. I just blamed it all on a disgruntled punter, which in one way of looking at it was true, and said that as far as I was concerned the incident was closed.

I had been in bed for well over two hours, going over the race in my mind again and again to stop me thinking about the confrontation ahead, when I

29

heard the sound of Edward's Jaguar pulling up outside. Through the crack in the curtains I saw the
headlights go out. My heartbeat began to quicken as
the key turned in the lock of the front door. He
usually poured himself a nightcap before coming to
bed and I listened for the sound of his footsteps as he
walked to the dining-room where the whisky was
kept. Only this time there was silence, save for the
tick of the alarm clock beside the bed. Edward was
down there all right, but where and what he was doing
I had no idea. I slipped out of bed and tiptoed to the
door, opening it gently, just a little. The light was on
in the kitchen and I could hear the kettle puffing as it
boiled. Presumably he was making himself a cup of
coffee to sober himself up. I went back to bed and
waited.

It must have been a good ten minutes before he
came up the stairs, taking each step deliberately as if
he was afraid of falling over. I thought of getting up
and pushing him back down again in the hope he'd
break his neck. Death by misadventure they would
call it. I just didn't have the courage. He came to a
halt outside the door and paused for what seemed an
eternity. I could bear it no longer.

'Edward. Is that you?' I asked pointlessly.

He responded by throwing open the door and
hurling a pan of boiling water towards me in the
bed.

I was lucky he was so drunk. Most of the water hit
the wall behind, although some splashed on my

shoulder and neck and part of my forehead. I screamed in pain and rushed past him into the bathroom and locked the door. Heart pounding, I listened to see if Freddie had woken up but fortunately there was no sound from him. For the next ten minutes I stood under a cold shower cooling off my shoulder and wondering what I should do next. I decided my only option was to sit on the floor and wait there until Edward had fallen asleep.

About half an hour later, I could make out the sound of snoring. I tiptoed into the spare room, took his shotgun from under the bed and loaded it with two cartridges from the ammunition belt he kept above the wardrobe. I then returned to the bedroom and sat down in the rocking chair beside the window and watched him. If he woke up and threatened me or Freddie I was going to blow him away.

It seemed unlikely to happen. He was out to the world. He lay there in front of me on his back, still in his checked racing suit, his mouth open, occasionally muttering incomprehensible half sentences punctuated by the odd tobacco-inspired cough. It was strange, almost unbelievable, to think that once upon a time I had thought him beautiful and wanted no more than to caress his soft skin and run my fingers through his thick dark curly hair. All I could see now, as I rocked back and forth, was a countenance ravaged by greed and deceit, rounded off by a lascivious mouth, which was about as sensual as an adder's tongue. And I just wished I had enough courage to pull the trigger and shoot him dead.

Despite my attempts to stay awake, I dozed off to a barrage of disjointed dreams and woke up at seven with the loaded shotgun balanced precariously across my knees. Edward was still lying comatose on the bed and at least that meant I could avoid any further scene for a few hours. I certainly didn't delude myself that the boiling water would be his final gesture of frustration and anger. Luckily, I had agreed to school some horses over at Wantage and three quarters of an hour later, after dressing Freddie and leaving him with Mrs Parsons in the village, I arrived at Tom Radcliffe's yard. It was, as usual, bustling with activity and Tom himself was waiting to greet me.

'Hail the conquering hero!' he shouted. 'We were worried that now you've ridden the winner of the Gold Cup you might consider schooling a couple of novice chasers beneath your dignity.'

I grinned. 'Well, I must admit I was tempted to go back to sleep after the butler served me breakfast in bed, but then I thought I'd better help out a poor struggling trainer.'

Tom grinned and hugged me and as he did so I almost burst into tears. He was big and slightly overweight but as strong as an ox, and after what Edward had done I suddenly needed to feel safe.

In fact, Tom was anything but struggling. In the five years he had held a licence he had sent out a continual stream of winners and was now one of the top trainers in the country. What's more, he had achieved his success without the backing of rich parents or social connections.

He'd had a few rides as an apprentice jockey but by his own admission was never very good and had soon given up. It was then he was offered a job as travelling head lad to Ron Cox, who trained over a hundred horses on the flat in Newmarket, and Tom had never looked back. He'd been blessed with a gift for understanding horses and knew exactly what distances and going they preferred but, more importantly, he could tell to the minute when they were right.

In no time at all he had made quite a lot of money by backing Cox's horses and word of his success soon spread around the small world of the racing industry. He then found that he no longer had to risk his own money. Punters were actually putting money on for him in return for information. In his first flat season Tom had won or earned over £15,000 from betting, but his success was beginning to cause friction between himself and his boss. Word was going around that if you wanted to know how one of the horses from Ron Cox's was likely to run, you asked Tom and not the trainer.

The situation came to a head the following spring in the first big flat race of the season, the Lincoln Handicap at Doncaster. Ron had entered a four-year-old bay colt called Tuneful, which Tom had been riding out at home throughout the winter. He could tell that the horse had grown much stronger during the off-season and had been backing it through his punters since early February, when the horse had begun to work well at home. Tom calculated that he would win the best part of £100,000 if Tuneful did the business, but then two days before the race, Ron declared that the horse wouldn't run because he didn't think that it was fit enough. They had had a stand-up row in the middle of the yard and Tom had taken the liberty of telephoning the horse's owner and offering to refund his entry fee and all of his travelling costs if the horse didn't win. That had been enough to persuade the owner and the horse had duly taken his chance and won in a photo-finish from another Newmarket-trained horse.

Tom didn't wait to be given the sack. He handed his notice in and with his winnings moved to Wantage and set up as a trainer on his own. He knew that he couldn't afford to buy the type of horses needed to compete successfully on the flat, and for that reason had concentrated on the National Hunt game. He'd begun with twelve horses, owned mostly by his original band of punters, but now trained over seventy horses owned by some of the most respected people in the country.

Tom stood for everything Edward most resented, although perversely, it was Edward who had been one of the first to recognise his ability. And at a time when he had been flush with money, he had been one of the initial owners to send Tom a horse. The horse had been a novice hurdler called Without Prejudice and had won his first three races by a distance. It looked as though he might one day be good enough to run in the Champion Hurdle, and Edward was offered a lot of money for him, but after much debating Tom had persuaded Edward to keep the horse. It was sod's law that on his very next run the horse had broken down and Edward had, of course, blamed Tom. Poor Tom. He had understandably felt guilty about what had happened and had waived six months' unpaid training fees, but Edward had still remained convinced that somehow he'd been cheated. Thereafter, he'd devoted himself to bad-mouthing Tom around the racecourse, happily to no avail, and Tom had continued to give me rides.

'Hey, what's this?' Tom had noticed the marks on my neck. 'I read about the cut to your lip, but how did this happen?' He eyed me suspiciously as if he already knew the answer.

'It's nothing. A silly accident last night when I was frying some chips,' I lied clumsily.

'Frying chips? Who are you kidding? I know you don't have a weight problem and that rosy complexion hasn't come from eating greasy food. You never eat chips and you know it.'

'They were for Edward.'

'What? Do you mean that he didn't even have the decency to take you out to dinner to celebrate? Typical. Or perhaps he had nothing to celebrate. I saw him in the Mandarin bar immediately after your victory

and he didn't look best pleased. Sick more like. That
husband of yours couldn't back the winner of a
walk-over and there's a rumour going round that he
really is in bother this time. That kind of talk doesn't
do you much good either.'

'What do you mean?'

'Gambling debts breed crooked jockeys.'

I looked at him and wondered whether he knew
more than he was letting on. I decided to change the
subject. 'Where are these horses I'm meant to be
schooling?' I turned to walk towards the boxes and as
I did so Tom grabbed hold of my arm.

'Hey, Victoria, not so fast.' He pointed again at
my neck. 'He did that, didn't he? Don't answer then.
And all this stuff in the papers about a disgruntled
punter attacking you. That was him as well, wasn't
it? I'm beginning to think this has gone on long
enough. If I get my hands on that bastard I'm . . .'

The tears began to well up in my eyes.

'Please, Tom, don't. I can't stand any more trouble at the moment. If anyone is going to have the
pleasure of killing Edward, I want it to be me.'

I turned round to see Tom's head lad, Jamie
Brown, standing there with a riding helmet in his
hand. I had no idea how long he had been listening
and frankly, in my present mood, I really didn't care.

After an hour's schooling, I was desperate for something to eat and readily accepted Tom's invitation to
breakfast. He'd had a couple of steady girlfriends but

had so far managed to escape marriage, largely due to a middle-aged Scots dragon called Mrs Drummond. It was rumoured that she terrified everybody in the yard, including even the head lad, and she had certainly succeeded in driving away a number of girls who fancied turning Tom's stables into a love nest. Because I was married, and happily so far as she was concerned, Mrs Drummond always gave me a warm welcome. That my grandmother also came from Inverness was an additional factor in my favour.

We sat down to an enormous helping of bacon and eggs and Tom tried hard to make me laugh by reading out loud from the morning's edition of the *Sportsman*. Staring out from the front page was a picture of yours truly, grinning in her racing silks, and beside it the banner headline proclaimed: 'PRYDE'S VICTORY COMES BEFORE A FALL'

'What a dreadful pun!' said Tom. 'I can't believe they actually pay someone to write this rubbish.'

'It's probably one of James Thackeray's. He loves that kind of thing.'

Tom chuckled. 'That clown! The only literary thing about him is his surname. Listen to this piece of purple prose:

"Yet again the Blue Riband of racing produced a sensational climax to the festival meeting. Under an inspired, if not always elegant, ride from dashing professional Victoria Pryde, Cartwheel put his nose in front on the line to rob Irish hotpot, Pride of Limerick, of victory. But the drama didn't end there. No sooner were they past the post and disappointed Irish punters heading for the bar, than a stewards' inquiry was announced. Thousands of anxious racegoers held their breath and their betting slips for what seemed an eternity as the stewards, led by Brigadier-General Allsopp, decided whether Pryde should keep the race and earn herself a place in the history books as the first woman to ride the winner of the Gold Cup. Irish maestro Eamon Brennan, rider of Pride of Limerick, was confident that the placings would be reversed, claiming that Victoria's inability to keep a straight line had cost his mount the Cup. The stewards thought otherwise, and all those who snapped up the generous 5–1 on offer on Cartwheel were soon celebrating their good judgment. Unfortunately for Victoria, her joy was short-lived. Returning to change after being interviewed on television, she was struck to the ground by an unidentified man and, as a result, left the course nursing a cut lip. The police are investigating the assault, which they believe to have been committed by a disgruntled punter.''

'Disgruntled punter!' Tom put the paper down and snorted. 'On that basis, there must be at least two million suspects. I'm surprised to see that Cartwheel started as long as 5–1.'

'I suppose it must have been because of all that

money on Pride of Limerick. You know how the Irish pile in when their blood's up.'

Tom nodded. 'I suppose so, but even then you don't tend to find the bookies being that much more generous about the opposition. Sometimes I think we're in the wrong business. Let's see what the betting report says.' He turned to one of the inside pages of the paper, which always carried a short summary of the betting on every race. 'Here, look at this. "One of the features of yesterday's race was the generous odds laid on Cartwheel. One rails bookmaker is rumoured to have laid the horse to lose over a quarter of a million pounds." There's one person, then, who doesn't have you as his pin-up.'

I smiled nervously and wondered whether there could be any connection between that unnamed bookmaker, my less than happy husband and the previous night's phone call. It was a subject that for the moment I wanted to put out of my mind.

I had been booked to ride a novice chaser for Ralph Elgar that afternoon at Lingfield and with the heavy overnight rain there was a chance he had decided not to risk him. I asked Tom if I could give Ralph a ring and find out what was going on.

He waved me to the phone: 'It's all yours. Tell him you've decided to spend the day with a real trainer.'

Ralph answered almost before the tone had rung out. 'Victoria?' he boomed. 'Thank God! Where the hell are you? I've been trying to get hold of you all morning. Your husband claimed to have no idea

where you were and gave me an earful for waking him
up so early.'

'I'm sorry. I'm down at Tom Radcliffe's, doing a
bit of schooling.'

'It's Edward you should be schooling, in some
manners.'

I chose to ignore the jibe. 'Is Lingfield still on?' I
asked.

'The racing is, but Mainbrace isn't running. I've
checked with the Clerk of the Course and as the
going's so heavy we're allowed to withdraw without
incurring a penalty. I've discussed it with the owner
and she's not prepared to take the chance. That
means you've got a day off and if you want my
advice, and you're going to get it anyway, you won't
spend it with that rascal Radcliffe.'

'Don't be so cruel. He's very nice really. In
fact, I'm going off any minute to see a friend in
London.'

'London? That's the last place you'd catch me
spending a free day. Ah well, it takes all sorts. Make
sure you look after yourself: you know you're my
favourite girl jockey!'

'I know, and I'm also your only girl jockey!'

I put the phone down and smiled at Tom. 'Good
old Ralph. I owe him so much.'

'Dirty beast. I reckon he's got a soft spot for you.'

'Who, Ralph? Don't be ridiculous! He's twice my
age.'

'When's that ever stopped anybody? By the way,

who's this friend you're going to see in London? Is he anyone I know?'

'That'd be telling. But for your information, it's a she.'

I drove to Didcot station and took the next train to town. An hour and a half later, I was sitting in the lounge of the Waldorf Hotel in the Aldwych having coffee with Amy Frost, an up and coming solicitor and old school friend. Even though she had been against my marrying Edward and studiously avoided his company ever since, Amy had remained loyal and supportive to me and if anybody could help me now it was going to be she. I told her the whole story, beginning with the Worcester race and ending with the previous night's attack with the boiling water. She listened impassively, even making the occasional note on a jotting pad perched on her shapely crossed legs.

'So there it is,' I concluded. 'My husband's a vicious and egotistical lunatic who is knee-deep in debt and it seems I can't leave him without losing custody of my child. Is he really right when he says the courts would prefer him to look after Freddie rather than me?'

Amy picked up her coffee. 'It's not quite as simple as that. I suppose you've seen the announcement in this morning's papers?'

'No, why? I read the *Sportsman* on the train and planned how I could do away with my husband without being caught. Weedkiller ought to do the trick.'

'I'll treat that as a joke. It's your beloved father-in-

41

law. He's just been appointed Lord Chief Justice, probably the most important legal job in the land.'

'Is that as bad as it sounds?'

'From your point of view, it couldn't be much worse. I can't somehow see the Lord Pryde, as he will now be called, sitting back and watching his son lose custody of the heir to the family name.'

'Nor can I. I can just picture Lady Pryde turning up in court to say what a decent loving chap her son has always been, forced to stay at home and care for Freddie while I gallivant about the country riding racehorses.'

'Hold on, Victoria, it's not that hopeless. There is some justice in this world. However impressive Edward's pedigree, it'll end up being your word against his and if you can show him to be an outright scoundrel you'll win custody even if his father's the Pope, if you know what I mean.'

'Isn't that a bit of a problem – and I'm not referring to the Pope! I'd have to come clean on all this horse fixing business and surely the courts aren't going to be that attracted to a self-confessed crooked jockey?'

Amy looked genuinely worried. 'I'm afraid you could be right. What's more, if that found its way to the Jockey Club you'd lose your licence and in the present climate might even end up on a conspiracy to defraud charge. I'm sorry I'm not being very helpful.'

'It's not your fault. I didn't expect any miracle

solution. What about divorce? Would my position be any different?'

'It could be if you were the complaining party. These days, though, they go in for the consent approach, trying not to talk about blame.'

'There's no way Edward would ever consent. What about unreasonable behaviour?'

'You mean other than the race fixing? You'll have to keep a record from now on every time he hits you and any other disagreeable piece of conduct. Do you still sleep together?'

'He insists on it. Sexual relations, as they say, are virtually non-existent although he hates the idea of anybody else touching me.'

'And have they?'

'Do I have to answer that one?'

She gave me a quizzical look and continued. 'Well, tell me when you feel ready. You see, the courts aren't too keen to find irretrievable breakdown when the husband and wife are still cohabiting. They do sometimes, but it's pretty unusual.'

'So in a nutshell, my position *is* hopeless.'

'You make me feel terrible. I'm sorry, I just wish you had told me about this earlier. I could see you weren't happy but I didn't want to pry or do the "I told you so" bit.'

'You're the last person I can blame. To be honest, it's an even bigger mess than it seems. Do you mind if I keep in touch? It helps so much, being able to tell someone.'

'You must tell me,' said Amy firmly. 'And something may just turn up.'

'And I thought an optimistic lawyer was a contradiction in terms! Aren't you meant to be back at work? You said something about a meeting at twelve-thirty.'

Amy glanced at her watch and rose to leave. I kissed her, paid the bill and hurried back by taxi to Paddington. All I wanted to do now was see my little boy.

Chapter 3

I arrived back in the early afternoon and gave Mrs Parsons the rest of the day off. During the National Hunt season, I didn't have a lot of opportunities to play with Freddie and I wanted to make the most of having his undivided attention. We were playing hide and seek when he discovered the diary. He had hidden in his father's huge mahogany wardrobe which, apart from the bed, took up most of the spare room. Edward usually kept it locked, but for some reason had forgotten to take away the key when he had gone out at lunchtime. Freddie handed me the diary as if he had discovered the crown jewels.

'Do you think it's special? Will daddy be pleased with me?'

'Let mummy have a look at it, and then we'll decide.' I gave him some toys to play with and, curiosity getting the better of me, sat down beside the fire and went through it. It was a small, well-worn pocket diary in black leather with Edward's initials embossed on it in gold. It was five years old and to my disappointment the calendar entries merely recorded his appointments or lunch dates and contained no chronicle of his innermost thoughts. I had hoped that I was going to learn something new about my husband.

I flicked through to the back and to the pages intended for addresses and telephone numbers. No names were listed, only sets of initials and against each a figure. Some of the initials had been crossed out and the different coloured inks suggested that the list had been added to and amended over the years. I wondered whether it stood for his investments on the Stock Market or even the bookies to whom he was indebted and decided to make my own list to try and decipher the code when I had more time. I was just going to fetch a pen and paper when Edward returned. It was obvious from his unsteady gait that he had been drinking and I thought I noticed his right hand shaking as he tried to hang up his coat. He kissed Freddie and, ignoring me, moved uncertainly towards the stairs. I decided to go on the attack: 'You had a phone call last night. Some man who wouldn't give his name. He just said that my victory had upset a lot of people. Your bookie, I presume?'

Edward went visibly grey. 'What did he sound like?'

'There was nothing particularly distinctive about his voice. Very flat and matter-of-fact. I didn't get the impression he was best pleased.'

'Did he say anything else?'

'Nothing significant. I'm sure he'll call again.'

'Don't you bloody sneer! You've got me into this mess and now you're going to help me get out of it. If you hadn't tried so hard yesterday, my problems would be over now.'

'I suppose you backed Pride of Limerick, then?'

'There's no need to be so smug. Because you weren't meant to be trying, my bookie laid the world and his wife against Cartwheel winning and was nearly trampled to death in the rush. You could at least have thrown the race in the stewards' room but, oh no, you had to go and claim that Pride of Limerick had taken your ground.'

'How do you know that?'

'None of your god-damned business. I also know it was a majority decision and it was only because you smiled so sweetly at that fool Allsopp you got away with it. You've really done it this time. This particular bookie means business. No one likes dropping a quarter of a million pounds and on top of that he'll expect me to come up with the hundred grand I owe him.'

'A hundred thousand! How the hell have you managed that?'

'Mind your own bloody business.'

'Don't pay. Gambling debts aren't enforceable, you know. The worst they can do is report you to Tattersalls. Although I suppose being warned off wouldn't be good publicity for the son of the Lord Chief Justice.'

'What do you mean?'

'Haven't you heard? Daddy's got the big job.'

'Has he now?' A wicked gleam came into Edward's eyes. I could see he was already plotting something.

'That's the first bit of good news I've had today. Anyway Tatts is out. Those bets are all illegal; I don't pay tax even though they're made off course.'

'So they can't even embarrass you into paying?'

'Don't be so naive. People like this aren't interested in social graces when it comes to collecting. They'll use any method that produces a result. I can see a little holiday is called for.'

He ran up the stairs, only to return two minutes later.

'Have you been nosing around in my wardrobe?'

'No, of course not.'

'Are you sure?' His voice had become markedly more aggressive.

'You know I never . . .' At that moment Freddie came out of the kitchen where he had been playing.

'Daddy! Has mummy told you about the book we found in your cupboard?'

Edward looked at me and smiled.

'Really darling? How clever of you. I'm sure mummy was just about to hand it over, weren't you, mummy?'

His outstretched hand waited menacingly for me to surrender the diary. Reluctantly I took it from my pocket and handed it over.

'I suppose you couldn't resist reading it,' he snarled as he snatched it from my hand.

I nodded and countered: 'And I suppose you're not

going to tell me what the entries at the back stand
for?'

He stared at me for a few seconds before replying. I
suspected that too much drink was going to loosen his
tongue and prompt an indiscretion or a display of
vanity. He never could resist an opportunity to show
how clever he was.

'Why not? Since you've become my partner in
crime there's precious little you can do about it and
after all, married couples aren't meant to have any
secrets from each other, are they? Freddie darling, go
and play in your bedroom for ten minutes will you,
whilst I have a little chat with mummy.'

He beckoned me to sit opposite him by the fire
while he fingered through the diary. Without showing
the slightest trace of embarrassment or regret he
started explaining: 'As you've no doubt already gath-
ered, the last few pages are the most interesting. Each
of these initials stands for what I call one of my investors, and the figure against his or her name, the
amount of their monthly investment.'

'What do you mean, investors? What, for God's
sake, are they investing in?'

He grinned mischievously. 'My silence. A very precious commodity indeed.'

I leant over and grabbed the diary from his hand. It
was still open at the relevant pages.

'You mean, you're a blackmailer, and these are
your victims? You bastard!'

'Cut out the moralising. I can do without lectures

on that front from a crooked jockey. I'm only telling you all this to let you know that we're not the only people who do things they shouldn't.'

I looked down the list, and tried to decipher the initials. 'Who is A.D., who presumably pays you one hundred pounds a month?'

'That, darling, is your favourite steward, Sir Arthur Drewe.'

'Drewe?'

'One and the same. Who'd have believed it of him? For our purposes he has the added advantage of standing at Worcester and Fontwell.'

'I follow. So that's why you were so confident there would be no problems with the stewards in those races. Does that also explain why Drewe was so intent on taking the race from me yesterday?'

'And he very nearly did so. If only those other oafs hadn't been so susceptible to your confounded smile.'

'And what was Sir Arthur's crime?'

'A little bit of indiscreet adultery, spiced with a desire for the odd burst of flagellation. It was just bad luck for Arthur that I know the young lady in question. And of course old Lady Drewe is not an understanding shrew. That's rather a clever rhyme, isn't it?'

I ignored him and looked down the list again. 'And who's M.C., who pays you thirty pounds a month? What's his sin?'

'Ah, M.C. Michael Corcoran.'

'The one who works in Tom Radcliffe's yard?'

'Yes. I don't charge him much because now and

again he provides useful information about what's happening there, and I don't just mean about the horses.'

I was speechless. Michael Corcoran had come over to work for Tom Radcliffe when he first started training. A good-looking Irish boy, now in his late twenties, he had failed to make the grade as a jockey and had stayed on as a stable lad. I recovered my composure and resumed my questioning. 'What have you got on Corcoran then? He's a single man, so it can't be adultery. Which of the other ten commandments has he broken?'

'The eighth, as it happens. Do you remember all those years ago when the wages were stolen from Radcliffe's office?'

I remembered it well. About two thousand pounds had gone missing which, at that time, Tom could ill afford. They never caught the culprit, but the police were certain it was an inside job.

'Well . . .' Edward continued, 'that was Michael's handiwork. He had got himself in bother with the bookies and took the easy way out. He made the mistake of confessing to me as one of Radcliffe's most respectable owners at that time, and asking my advice.'

'And this is how you repaid his trust?'

'Precisely. I told him not to say a word about it to anyone, and he's been indebted to me, literally, ever since.'

'What if he just upped and left one day?'

'I've considered that, and told him if he ever entertained such an idea I'd send an anonymous letter to his mother in Ireland. One thing these Irish boys hate is the idea of family disgrace, you know.'

'And who are these others – E.F., D.T., T.C., A.P.B. What have they done?'

'They're nobody you know. Pillars of society who have committed minor peccadilloes which they would prefer not to be made public. I don't charge them any more.'

'E.B.?'

'Eamon Brennan. He's my most reliable payer, although after his performance in front of the stewards yesterday, he may have to increase the size of his investment.'

'And his error of judgement?'

'Greed. When he accepted that retainer last year with Rhodes he insisted on a cash payment on top. Only he forgot to tell the Jockey Club about it. Rhodes spilled the beans to me one night when he was in his cups.'

I looked over the list again. One set of initials was particularly faded.

'And G.P. Who's that? Not our local doctor?'

'Much funnier than that, darling. Have a guess.'

I went through in my mind all the racing people we knew and then other acquaintances who might fit into the venal category.

'I give up. What has he or she done that earns you two hundred pounds a month?'

'That's the present figure, but with today's news I think an increase is clearly called for. G.P. stands for Gerald Pryde.'

'What! Your own father? I don't believe it! Nobody could sink to that.'

'Really? I found it pretty easy.'

'And his crime?'

'A touch of professional dishonesty. I was in my last year at Oxford when it happened. My father was then still at the bar, and although very successful and famous, as a criminal lawyer was not earning the big fees you now hear about. Unfortunately he had inherited the Prydes' gambling streak and managed to lose a bundle on the Stock Market. He's too afraid of my mother to go and ask her for a loan so he used another means to find the wherewithal.'

'What other means?'

'Do you remember the Lorenz murder trial?'

I nodded, although I wasn't certain I did.

'My father was conducting Lorenz's defence on legal aid. In fact, Lorenz was as rich as Croesus through his drug and prostitution business, but it wouldn't have done to declare that to the Inland Revenue. My father, in his desperation, agreed to accept an additional ten thousand pounds for acting for him.'

'What's wrong with that?'

'Only that you're supposed to be paid solely by the legal aid fund and any other payment would be regarded as highly improper. Somehow, I don't think he told his clerk about it, let alone the tax man.'

'How did you find out about it?'

'Pure luck. I came across the letter from Lorenz setting out the arrangements in the old man's desk drawer one weekend when I was looking for some spare cash. I thought it was well worth keeping, just in case.'

'And your father goes on paying you?'

'We call it my allowance. I just let him know one day that I was sympathetic to the predicament he had found himself in, and suggested casually that he kept my allowance on. After all, his money will be mine one day anyway.'

I stared at him in disgust and revulsion. He was even baser and more corrupt than I had believed possible. I shuddered at the thought I had once loved him.

'Is that it, then?' I asked, making no attempt to disguise my contempt.

'Not quite. Have a look over the page.'

I turned over to what was the back page of the diary. There was a single entry with only one set of initials, and no figure against them.

Edward grinned.

'Recognise them?'

'How much were you intending to charge me for my investment?'

'I thought about a hundred pounds a month. That would be fair, wouldn't it?'

Chapter 4

The telephone rang before I could make any further comment, and Edward walked across the sitting room to answer it. Whoever was on the other end of the line soon had him breaking into a sweat and the hitherto complacent tone in his voice rapidly gave way to one of panic.

'You know that's impossible!' he shouted. 'It's not my fault she disobeyed her instructions.' He kept shaking his head as the caller dominated the conversation. 'Don't do that,' he pleaded, when at last given an opportunity to talk. 'Just give me time. I guarantee I'll come up with some of it and I can assure you she won't make the same mistake twice. That's all I need, one more chance.' The call ended abruptly and he was still shaking as he put the receiver down.

I wasted no time in making my position clear. 'If it's me you're referring to, it was no mistake that I won yesterday, and I have absolutely no intention of doing your dirty work again. From now on, you can sort out your own mess. I'm leaving you, Edward, and I'm taking Freddie with me.'

'And leave me at the mercy of these people? No, you silly bitch, you're not going anywhere! You're going to stay here and next time, when I tell you to lose, you'll do just that.'

His first blow caught me just above the eye and I fell backwards onto one of the armchairs by the fire.

'Now will you realise that I'm serious?'

The noise attracted Freddie, who came running down to the bottom of the stairs. I shouted at him to go and get help. The next thing I knew Edward had leapt on top of me and started to throttle me with both hands. The pain around my neck was excruciating and soon spread to behind my eyes as I fought with increasing panic for air. At least my left arm was still free and I felt desperately along the top of the coffee table for something to grab and hit him with. The maniacal look in his eyes left me in no doubt that he was mad enough to kill me. I had no desire to die and leave my son alone with this monster as a father. With one final lunge I managed to pick up the silver ash-tray, a present from his mother, which was on the edge of the table. Lifting my left arm and mustering all my strength, I hit him repeatedly on the side of the temple. He ignored the blows and tightened his grip. By now my head felt as if it was about to explode and all I could see was a warm red glow like a harvest moon. I was done for.

Suddenly Edward groaned, his hands went limp and he slumped down like a dead weight on top of me. I looked over his shoulder to see Freddie standing there, crying, a bronze statuette of a horse and jockey in his right hand. The head of the horse was covered in blood. The boy was hysterical.

'Mummy, are you all right?' he sobbed.

With considerable effort, I managed to push Edward off me and onto the floor.

'Is daddy dead?' Freddie asked, shaking with fear.

I gazed down at the motionless figure slumped against the side of the sofa. He was still breathing, if in a somewhat laboured fashion, and I felt for his pulse. It was regular. Mild concussion, I reckoned, which would give us about twenty minutes to get out. I reassured Freddie that daddy would soon be all right and rushed him upstairs to help me pack a few things. Five minutes later, we were in my car heading I knew not where, but at least as far away from Edward Pryde as wheels could take us.

When I'd calmed down, I thought of driving straight over to Tom's but on reflection I decided against it. I couldn't trust his reaction to seeing us in this condition. Instead, two hours later, after driving aimlessly round the country, we pulled up at Ralph Elgar's yard in the Cotswolds.

I kept looking in the rear-view mirror expecting to see Edward's Jaguar, but there was no sign of it and as soon as I'd pulled up and stopped the engine, Freddie and I darted inside the house.

Ralph jumped up from his chair as we ran into the kitchen.

'Whatever's the matter?' he exclaimed.

I began crying as I blurted out what had just happened, including how Freddie had saved my life.

By the time I had finished and had drunk a cup of tea, I felt much better.

'So that's it. I just wondered if we could both stay here for a few days until I can get things sorted out.'

'You know that you're both welcome to stay as long as you want,' said Ralph. And then added, 'If I were you, I'd call the police.'

I disagreed. As Freddie and I were both all right, and I had finally had the courage to leave Edward, I decided to let the whole thing resolve itself on its own. Once the police knew, then the press would get to hear about it and the story would be on the racing page of every daily paper in the country.

Freddie was still in a state of shock, and repeatedly asked if his father would be all right. About an hour after I had put him to bed, he came back downstairs crying, saying that he had had a nightmare, and he spent the rest of the evening asleep in my arms.

'He'll be a long time forgetting what's gone on today,' said Ralph.

'I know, and he's going to miss having Edward around, but I certainly won't. My main worry is what will happen when Edward finally comes looking for us. It may be that the battle's only just begun.'

*   *   *

During the next two weeks, much to my surprise, Edward made no attempt to contact me. I expected him to turn up at the races and accost me or try to follow me home. I couldn't believe he would give up Freddie that easily. When the boy kept asking me where his father was, I told him that Edward had fully recovered and had gone away on holiday. I thought it was the most likely explanation, although when I had telephoned Mrs Parsons on the Monday after the attack, to say that Freddie would be away for a short while, she told me that our bed had been slept in and there was no sign of any of Edward's clothes missing. We agreed that she would take a paid holiday until Freddie and I returned.

Not surprisingly, my riding began to suffer amidst the uncertainty of my position. I found it difficult to regain my usual enthusiasm and managed to get beaten at Stratford on a certainty trained by Tom Radcliffe. Coming to the last I was two lengths ahead of my flagging rival and had only to jump it clear to win. Instead of settling my horse down to take it comfortably in his stride, I gave him a kick in the belly and asked for a long one. The stride I'd seen was a lot longer than I thought and the horse brushed the top of the fence and pecked on landing. I fell off him like a bad seven pound claimer and had to walk back to the jockeys' room through a jeering crowd of irate punters.

Fortunately, Tom was sympathetic, but we both knew that I was to blame. On the way home he asked me about Edward. I hadn't told him about our fight or, for that matter, that I had walked out. I was still anxious not to involve him at this stage if I could help it, fearing what he might do if angered.

'Do you know that I saw your husband on the Saturday night after the Gold Cup?'

'No. Whose idea was that?'

'Mine. I know I promised not to get involved but I couldn't go on letting him behave like that towards you. He's a bully and there's only one thing that kind of person understands.'

'Where did you meet him?'

'I phoned him up on the Friday evening and asked him to come for a drink at the Crown and Anchor on the Marlborough Road. I thought I'd choose a pub where no one was likely to recognise either of us.'

'And so?'

'It all turned rather nasty. I won't bore you with the details. I must have drunk too much as I woke up in the early hours of the morning in the car park with a splitting headache.'

'Is that all that happened, Tom?' I asked anxiously, although fearing to probe too far.

'All you need to know. I wish you'd reconsider your decision, Victoria.'

'Just be patient, please, that's all I ask.'

Another week went by and there was still no sign of Edward; I began to wonder whether I should report him missing to the police. I decided against it for the time being. I couldn't really pretend to be the caring wife; in fact I wouldn't have minded at all if his disappearance became permanent. It was just the uncertainty that was beginning to unnerve me.

Everything changed on the Friday, when I received a phone call at Ralph's from Amy Frost. I had kept her informed about everything that had happened and her advice had been to stay put and do nothing. Apparently, if Edward could be shown to have deserted me, it could in time be grounds for a divorce and would be very important in the question of custody. She didn't waste time with any niceties.

'Have you seen today's *Sportsman*, page seven?'

I had to admit I hadn't. Amy loved horse racing and gambling and must have been the only solicitor in London who started her day by reading the racing paper cover to cover.

'Well, you'd better go and get a copy. I'll hang on.'

I walked over and picked up the paper off the kitchen table, found the right page and returned to the phone: 'Fire away. What am I meant to be looking for?'

'Just below tomorrow's racecards. Look at the notice headed ''Official Scratching''.'

I found what she was referring to and read it. It couldn't have been more succinct. **'Official Scratching. All Engagements. Mr Pryde (dead).'**

'Amy, do you think this is some kind of a joke?'

'I don't know. Is there a horse called Mr Pryde?'

'Not that I'm aware of,' I replied. 'But who the hell would want to put this in, unless . . .'

'Unless,' interjected Amy, 'somebody wanted to deliver a very tasteless message.'

'To declare Edward dead, you mean?'

'Exactly.'

I ended the conversation with a promise to be in touch if there were any further developments. The announcement in the paper could just be a mischievous trick and I wondered how the *Sportsman* had been duped into carrying it. I made a mental note to ask James Thackeray when I next saw him, because apart from working on the paper, he was an enthusiastic amateur rider. I also realised that the time *had* come for me to report Edward missing. After all, the last person to have had any contact with him was Tom Radcliffe, and that was almost three weeks previously. I thought about it for a while, and decided that if something had happened to him, it would look pretty strange if his wife had kept quiet in the meantime.

I had been booked to ride a horse in the opening race at Hereford, an unreliable no-hoper who regarded each fence as a launching pad to send his jockey into orbit. If still in one piece, I resolved to drive over to Newbury police station later on in the afternoon, and then go on to the cottage and collect some more clothes.

I survived the race and reached the police station just after three-thirty. The officer on duty could not have been more charming and sympathetic. He suggested that a constable should come over to the cottage in a couple of hours' time to take down further details and collect a photograph of Edward for circulation. I couldn't very well refuse, and he reassured me that, apparently, disappearing spouses were not at all uncommon and advised me not to become over-concerned. It was arranged that the make, model and number of Edward's car and other details of his description would be logged on the police computer and circulated round the country.

Feeling that I had at least done something positive, I plucked up the courage to return to the cottage. It was cold and strangely forbidding and I found difficulty in believing that for six years this place had been the family home, and that Freddie had spent the whole of his short life here. It was like reading an old love letter when the affection once felt is at best an unreal and distant memory.

The cottage was much as I had left it that Friday and that alone created a sinister, depressing atmosphere. To keep myself occupied, I lit the fire and sat down to watch the television and catch up with the racing results until the police arrived. I was still uncertain just how much to tell them about the relationship between Edward and myself. I had no doubt they would pursue that line of questioning, as to the outsider matrimonial discord was the most likely explanation for his disappearance.

I decided to be economical with the truth. I could see no advantage in coming clean about my involvement in Edward's attempts to clear his gambling debts and, equally, I could see no virtue in exposing him as a blackmailer. It was hardly in Freddie's interest to have his father's evil personality revealed to the public glare, and anyway I had no independent evidence to support it. Nor, I reasoned, would it be fair to name Edward's 'investors' as he called them. Indeed, even if I did, how did I know the authorities would believe me? It would take a pretty brave or foolhardy policeman to go and ask Lord Pryde if he had been paying out hush money to his son! I resolved to play the role of the concerned wife.

At six o'clock the door bell rang. A uniformed police constable was accompanied by a man of striking good looks, over six feet tall and dressed in a surprisingly well-cut dark grey suit. All in all, he looked a class above the popular image of his profession. I put him in his mid to late thirties and made a note to be extra careful in what I said, for fear that, in the time honoured phrase, it might one day be used in evidence, and even worse, against me. Inspector Wilkinson introduced himself and asked if they could come in. There was no milk in the refrigerator, but five minutes later we were all seated by the fire drinking black coffee, the young constable poised knowingly and breathlessly over his notebook. I was determined to give the impression of being relaxed and in control, and as the Inspector seemed in no rush to begin questioning me, I took the initiative.

'I'm sure there's really nothing to worry about, but he has been gone for three weeks now, so I thought that it would be only sensible to notify you.'

Inspector Wilkinson said nothing and just looked at me expectantly. I obliged by going on.

'He's never gone away like this before; without even a telephone call or a card.'

He muttered something incomprehensible and then asked: 'You have a son, don't you?'

'Yes, Frederick. He's five.'

'Same age as my eldest.' He looked around the room. 'Is he here with you?'

'No, well, you see we – I mean Freddie and I – we haven't been staying here for the last three weeks. We've been staying with friends.'

'Trouble between you and your husband?' he enquired, trying to appear sympathetic.

For some reason I hesitated before replying. 'I'm afraid we had a row.'

'About anything in particular?'

'Nothing specific really. You know the kind of thing.'

He appeared to understand. 'Perhaps he's taken a holiday to collect his thoughts. It does happen, you know, and then he'll come back full of remorse and seeking your forgiveness.'

I laughed to myself. The only remorse Edward knew was the horse of that name who had won the Triumph Hurdle two years previously.

The Inspector continued. 'Are any of his clothes missing? I suppose you've checked?'

'Yes, I did look, but nothing seems to be gone.'

'And are you sure he hasn't been here at all during the past three weeks? Popped in and out as it were?'

'I can't be absolutely certain. My daily, Mrs Parsons, has been on holiday. All that's definitely missing is his car.'

He looked over at the constable's notebook. 'That's a green Jaguar 4.2 registration REF 376X?'

'Yes, that's it. He loves his car.'

'Did your husband have any problems you were aware of, at work, say, or any debts perhaps?'

'He hasn't had a job for some time; we live off my earnings as a jockey and a little private income he has. As for debts, he did tell me he was in a spot of trouble with his bookmaker.'

'Do you know what sort of trouble?'

'I think there's quite a lot of money involved,' I answered, playing the innocent. 'We don't discuss that kind of thing, with me being a jockey.'

'How much is quite a lot? It would help if you were more precise, Mrs Pryde. Are we talking about hundreds or thousands?'

'Thousands, I'm afraid.'

The Inspector raised his eyebrows, and I noticed the constable underlining my answer in his notes.

'Your husband's father is the new Lord Chief Justice, isn't he?'

'That's right; does that matter?'

'Obviously, when the son of a very important person disappears, senior police officers have to become involved.'

'You don't think the IRA are behind this or anything?'

'Quite frankly, at this stage we don't think anything, nor for that matter do we discount anything. We're just being extra cautious. That's one of the reasons I'm here.'

'And the other?' I asked suspiciously. His relaxed and confident manner was beginning to unnerve me.

'Do you know the Melksham area well by any chance?'

'I know it's the other side of Marlborough and I've picnicked with Freddie on the downs there a couple of times; otherwise I can't claim to know it well. Why?'

'We've found your husband's car there. On the site of a disused chalk pit, set well back from the main roads. The car's been gutted, burnt out, and it's being examined by forensic experts at the moment.'

'You're not suggesting Edward was in it?'

'I'm not suggesting anything. Did he know that area well?'

'Not that I'm aware of. He came on one of the picnics, I think. When was it discovered? The officer at the station didn't mention anything at all when he fed the information I gave him into the computer.'

'It was only reported this morning. Your information wouldn't actually have found its way onto the computer until late this afternoon and then we got the word from Swansea.'

The telephone rang and I answered it. It was for the Inspector. His back straightened and his whole manner became increasingly alert and excited. What-ever he was being told clearly made interesting listening.

'Really?' he remarked to the caller after five min-utes without interrupting. 'In the boot? When will forensic know if they've got anything to go on? Tomorrow. Good. We'll have to tell the Yard and probably Special Branch as well. Any chance of keep-ing it from the press for the moment? I'll be here for another, say, ten minutes and then I'll come straight on over. We can go on to the site together. Excellent.'

He put the phone down and turned gravely towards me. I knew something was wrong and that despite his sombre expression he was secretly excited. The adrenalin was running just like any jockey's does before a big race.

'That was my sergeant at the station. I'm afraid I have some bad news for you. They've discovered the charred remains of some human bones in the boot of the car, and a pool of dried blood on the ground nearby. I don't want to distress you unnecessarily, Mrs Pryde, but I'm afraid your husband may be dead.'

I felt I ought to cry and I knew they expected me to, but I just couldn't. For a long time, I'd felt nothing for Edward but hate.

'Can I get you a glass of water -- or something stronger perhaps?' the Inspector asked solicitously.

I shook my head. 'No, that's all right, thanks.' I decided to feign shock and buried my head in my hands. I then genuinely began to cry, not for myself or for Edward, but for Freddie. He had lost his father and that was a terrible thing, however evil he may have been. I looked up to find Inspector Wilkinson seated opposite me again, analysing my reaction.

'I know this is difficult for you,' he started. I'm sure I detected a slight hint of cynicism in his voice. 'But can you think of anybody who might have wanted to do away with your husband?'

I shook my head. In fact I could think of a whole lot of people who would not mourn his passing, all those whose names were in that pocket diary, for a start, including mine. Presumably that had gone up in smoke with him.

'Think about it, please. Anybody with a grudge, for example. What about this bookmaker he owed money to? Do you know his name?'

I shook my head again. 'He never talked about his gambling to me, not in any kind of detail. He regarded it as his own private business, a gentleman's preserve.'

'I'll need a list of his friends, acquaintances, anybody who might be able to help us piece together his movements during the last two weeks.'

I knew of course that Tom Radcliffe had met Edward on the Saturday, the day after our fight. There was no point keeping quiet about it as everybody in the pub had probably heard their row, and anyway, Tom was the last person to lay a hand on Edward.

'He did see a friend of mine, a trainer, the night

69

after we had our row. His name's Tom Radcliffe and his stables are over at Wantage.'

'Mr Radcliffe? Well, that's a start. I'll have his address, if you don't mind, and we'll go and have a word with him. Anybody else you can think of?'

'No, nobody.'

'Do you have a photograph of your husband we can borrow, please?'

I went upstairs and picked one up from our dressing room table. It had been taken about two years before, at Newbury Races. I handed it to the Inspector who, in my absence, had picked up the bronze from the coffee table and was admiring it. To my horror, I could still see traces of blood on the horse's head. I'd had no time to clean it after Freddie had hit Edward, and Mrs Parsons, true to form, must have overlooked it the following Monday.

'Is this you?' he asked, holding it up in front of me.

'No, that's Arkle, you know, the great Irish horse, with Pat Taffe up.'

'Of course, I should have seen the jockey was a man.'

'This is Edward?' he asked, carefully putting the bronze back and taking the framed photograph from me.

'That's him. It was taken a couple of years back. He hasn't changed much; he's just a little bit fatter round the face and has a few streaks of grey in his hair now.'

'A fine looking man. He wasn't wearing this tweed

suit, was he by any chance, when you last saw him?'

I thought back to that Friday and of Edward lying on top of me, his hands round my throat. Sartorial observations weren't at that time my major concern.

'I think so, but I can soon find out by checking his wardrobe upstairs.'

'Would you mind taking a quick look?'

'If it will help. Do you want to come with me?'

He followed me up to the spare room. The wardrobe was still unlocked and there was no sign of Edward's favourite tweed suit.

'It looks like he was,' I said. 'It doesn't surprise me. There were times I thought he slept in it.'

The Inspector smiled. 'We all get attached to certain clothing. It's an unusual weave so the fibre might show up under the microscope, that is if any has survived the fire. Did he wear any rings or anything else that might help for identification purposes?'

'Not Edward. He hated what he called poof's paraphernalia and only wore a signet ring on the little finger of his right hand. He had inherited it from his grandfather.'

'What about his teeth? Do you know the name of his dentist?'

'He never went, not as far as I was aware anyway.'

'No gold fillings or anything?'

'None. He was very proud of his teeth, even though they were yellow from those cigars he smoked.'

'That's a nuisance. If you've only got charred bones to work on, teeth and jewellery can be very helpful when it comes to identification. I'm sure we'll find something.'

'Do you mean that otherwise you won't be able to tell for certain if it's Edward's body or not?'

He looked at me as if surprised by my question, and I felt myself going red in response. He took up the initiative. 'Do you have any reason to think that it might not be?'

'None at all. I just don't understand why he would want to kill himself and in such a horrible way.'

'You think it must be suicide then?'

'What else? You're surely not suggesting he's been murdered?' I said, in disbelief.

'At this stage, Mrs Pryde, I'm keeping an open mind. I'm just sorry to be the bearer of such bad news. Now, if you don't mind, I think I'd better be going.'

We went downstairs where the constable was reading through his notes.

'Right then,' the Inspector continued, 'I'll leave Garnier here to wait for the fingerprint boys. We'll need some of yours as well, of course, and Freddie's and your daily's, Mrs Parsons. Would you mind giving Garnier her address? Is there anything in particular your husband has recently had his hands on?' I instinctively thought of my neck.

'There're his binoculars in the hall. Will they do?'

'Perfect. We should get some very good dabs off them.' He turned to leave. 'I'll need to take a more detailed statement from you later. Let me say again how sorry I am that this has happened. I would prefer it if you didn't talk to the press and you might find it sensible to lie low for the next couple of weeks. You can give Garnier the address where you're going to be staying.'

I didn't feel any need to reply. He reached the front door then looked round as if to survey the room. 'Oh yes, one final thing, Garnier. Make sure the finger-print boys take the marks on that bronze and then bring it back to the station for forensic to have a look at. I'll be in touch, Mrs Pryde.'

Chapter 5

An hour and a half later, two fingerprint experts had grunted and crawled over the cottage. Edward's binoculars were greeted with whoops of satisfaction as they yielded apparently perfect specimens of the fingers of both his hands. My prints were taken and then they left to visit Mrs Parsons. I warned her by telephone that they were on their way to see her. Her involvement at this stage made any call to the press unnecessary. By midnight the whole of Lambourn would know that something serious was up in the Pryde household. I had already telephoned Ralph Elgar and told him the barest details of what was happening. He was shocked, and reassured me that Freddie was quite all right with him until I could get back. He insisted that we continued staying there until everything was cleared up. After the fingerprint men and Garnier had left, I telephoned Amy Frost in London. I was relieved when she answered the phone, as I thought she might be away for the

75

weekend. I recounted everything that had happened.

'Where are you now?' she asked.

'At the cottage. Why?'

'I'm coming down, if you don't mind waiting there for an hour or so for me.'

I looked round the room. It suddenly seemed extremely eerie. 'I think I'll be okay, but hurry up all the same.'

By the time Amy arrived, I had drunk a quarter of a bottle of whisky, and heard footsteps in every part of the house, except the downstairs lavatory. She was dressed in a leather cat suit. Amy wasn't classically good looking, but she made the most of herself and I think men were attracted to her because of her bubbly personality. She was almost three inches taller than I was and quite well built with dark hair and hazel eyes, her face liberally covered with freckles.

'Amy, I'm sorry, did I interrupt something?' I asked, grinning at her.

'Well, I was just warming up with some champagne when you called!'

'I'm sorry.'

'Don't apologise. I was beginning to have second thoughts anyway. Those barristers do know how to bang on about themselves! If I have to hear once more about what he told the judge . . .'

'At the rate I'm going, I'll be appearing in front of one myself, soon. What am I to do if those are Edward's remains in the boot of the car?'

'Co-operate and tell them everything you know.'

'Everything? Even about the fight and Freddie and the blackmailing?'

'All of it. They probably won't believe the blackmail bit and even if they do, there's no way they're going to drag old man Pryde into this.'

'Do you think they'll want to see me again?'

'They're bound to, and next time it won't be in the cosy warmth of your sitting room. Who saw you today, by the way?'

'An Inspector Wilkinson and a young constable. Wilkinson was a bit too smooth for my liking, but he's plainly on the ball.'

'I'll have him checked out. This is the kind of case that a policeman can make his name on. Identify the body, quick arrest, speedy trial and unanimous conviction. Result: instant promotion and gratitude of nation.'

'They've got to identify the body first. From what I could gather, they've only the charred bones to work on. And, oh yes, the Inspector mentioned a pool of dried blood near the car, too.'

'I don't know about the bones, but the blood will be enough to provide a positive identification provided they have something else to match it with.'

'Positive identification? I thought that all you could tell from blood was the individual's group, which could be the same as millions of other people's.'

'Haven't you heard of DNA?'

'Well, vaguely.'

'It's this new process that is revolutionising everything from the detection of rape to the determination of paternity. It works like this, or at least I think it does. Every one of us has our own individual blueprint. Once you have a piece of an individual's skin or some semen or blood for example, you can detect from that the chromosomal ingredients unique to that person, his or her blueprint, as it were. They can then be matched up to another sample of blood or semen or skin or hair root, it doesn't even matter which, and hey presto, you have positive identification.'

'So if I told you that there was still some of Edward's blood on that bronze they took away . . .'

'It would be a major breakthrough for them. If that pool of blood they found is human, they will now be able to tell you for certain whether it's Edward's or not. In other words, they'll have both halves of the jigsaw.'

I frowned.

'Do you think it might not be Edward's then?'

'No, not really. I'm just worried that if it is, suspicion's going to fall on someone I know.'

'May I ask who, and perhaps even more importantly, why?'

She looked extremely concerned when I gave her the answers.

I returned to spend the night at Ralph Elgar's. Freddie was fast asleep, still blissfully unaware of the tragedy unfolding around him. Not surprisingly, I couldn't sleep. I looked back on my life with Edward and tried to pinpoint a time when things had started to go wrong. There was no doubt that some of the blame for the failure of our marriage lay on my shoulders. I had become consumed by my ambition to make it as a jockey and expected him to understand that ambition too, as well as giving it his whole-hearted support. It never occurred to me that he might have different goals for himself; indeed he never gave any indication of having any goals. I suppose on reflection that we married because at the time we enjoyed going to bed together and liked having fun. Unfortunately, marriage requires a commitment of a different nature. And now Edward was dead.

I wondered what was going to happen, just how much was going to come out. I thought about what Inspector Wilkinson had said about lying low for a couple of weeks and rejected the idea. There would no doubt be a lot of gossip on the racecourse and no shortage of pointing fingers. On the other hand, if I gave up riding, even for a short while, it would seriously damage my prospects. After all, someone still had to pay the bills and the mortgage and buy Freddie's clothes. I compromised by deciding not to ride for a week and to do my best to shelter Freddie from the turbulence that lay directly ahead. If Edward *was* dead, I wouldn't be able to go back to riding six days a week as I had been. I would have to spend a lot more time at home with my son.

*　　*　　*

The police arrived to collect me just before lunchtime. I can't say I was surprised. I had tried to phone Tom earlier that morning, only to be told by Mrs Drummond that he had been taken away for questioning shortly after breakfast. She sounded perplexed and upset and said that the police had been extremely brusque in their manner.

It was a curious sensation sitting in the back of a police car with an officer on either side. Like ambulances, police cars may be part of our everyday life but somehow they always seem reserved for somebody else, never you.

After arriving at the station I was shown into a bleak and depressing interview room, which contributed even more to my sense of foreboding. The walls needed a good coat of paint and I could not help wondering what sordid details they had heard over the years. Waiting to greet me was Inspector Wilkinson and he in turn introduced me to an overweight, morose gentleman, a Superintendent Pale down from Scotland Yard. It appeared that Wilkinson was to conduct the interview under Pale's watchful glare.

'Firstly, Mrs Pryde, I must warn you that this interview is being recorded on video camera . . .'

I looked over and spotted the camera in the ceiling.

'. . . and that everything you say will be taken down and may be used in evidence. Is that clear? You are, of course, entitled to say nothing and if you wish, you may contact a solicitor.'

Neither course appealed to me. The last thing I

wanted to do was to appear in any way embarrassed or as if I had something to hide.

'No, thank you,' I answered. 'I'm perfectly happy to answer your questions.'

'Good. You told me yesterday that the last time you saw your husband alive was three weeks ago on Friday, that would be the nineteenth.'

'Yes, that's right.'

'You had a row, following which you walked out on him taking your son with you.'

I nodded.

'And since that time, you have had no contact with him?'

'Correct. That's just what I told you yesterday.'

'You know, of course, that Mr Radcliffe claims he saw your husband the next day, in the evening?'

'I've no reason to doubt Mr Radcliffe's word.'

'Can you remember what Mr Radcliffe said about that meeting?'

I chose my words carefully. 'Only that he had asked my husband to meet him at the Crown and Anchor pub on the Marlborough road, that they had a row and that the next thing Mr Radcliffe remembers is waking up in his car, still in the car park, in the early hours of the following morning. He was unable to explain why he had passed out.'

'And you have no idea why your husband and Mr Radcliffe met?'

I had a very good idea, but saw no reason to tell Inspector Wilkinson.

'Is it true to say that you and your husband didn't see eye to eye?'

'You might as well know, Inspector, that my husband didn't see eye to eye, as you put it, with a lot of people. He was capable of being very charming to some people and rather vicious towards others.'

'Didn't he and Mr Radcliffe fall out about a horse?'

'That started it, but it was all over years ago. Tom, I mean Mr Radcliffe, wasn't in the least to blame but you couldn't tell Edward that. He wouldn't hear a good word about him.'

'But you wouldn't describe your marriage as a happy one? Surely the truth is, Mrs Pryde, that your marriage was on the rocks, wasn't it?'

I saw no point in lying. 'Things were going very badly. You've probably heard it all from Mrs Parsons anyway. I no longer loved my husband, Inspector, and I very much doubt if he had the slightest bit of affection for me.'

'Did you consider divorcing him?'

'I did, but I was worried about losing custody of our son.'

'Did you fight?'

'Do you mean just argue, or actually come to blows?'

'Come to blows.'

'He often hit me. The cut above my lip was his work at Cheltenham races, as are these burn marks.'

'Do you know how the blood came to be on that bronze we found at the cottage?'

'It was Edward's. I hit him with the bronze on Friday.'

'Tell us about it.'

I told him about Friday's fight, embroidering it in such a way as to divulge nothing about Freddie's involvement.

'Are you sure your husband was only concussed that evening?'

'If you're accusing me of murdering him, you're wrong. If I had done, how could he have met Mr Radcliffe for a drink on Saturday night?'

'We've only Mr Radcliffe's word for that.'

'What about the landlord and anyone else who saw them in the pub?'

He didn't pursue that train of thought. 'Did you go and ride out at Mr Radcliffe's yard that morning?'

I nodded.

'When you arrived, did you have a long conversation with him in the yard before you started schooling?'

'Not that long, about five minutes.'

'What did you talk about?'

'My ride in the Gold Cup, that sort of thing.'

'Did you mention your husband, what had happened the night before?'

I could see where this line of questioning was leading. Tom's head lad, Jamie Brown, had a sour tongue inside a big mouth, as well as a great aversion to women jockeys.

'If you're referring to the end of our conversation,

when Tom said he'd like to get his hands on my husband, that was just talk. He wouldn't hurt a fly. Did
he also tell you I said I wanted Edward dead?'

This time it was the Inspector's turn to nod.

'Well I meant it, but that doesn't mean I killed
him.'

'Are you sure you don't know what your husband
and Mr Radcliffe discussed in the pub, why they
became involved in such a heated row?'

I shook my head. 'Positive.'

'They were discussing you. Your husband was telling Radcliffe to stop seeing you. Just how long have
you and Radcliffe been lovers, Mrs Pryde?'

'Can I see my solicitor now?'

Amy's appearance was a good deal more sombre than
the night before. Leather had given way to a conven-
tional black suit and she behaved more like a solicitor
than a friend from the moment she arrived. After a
brief discussion in private it was agreed that I would
continue to answer questions provided she was
present.

Wilkinson went straight back on the attack. 'You
don't deny, then, that you are lovers?'

I looked to Amy sitting beside me and she indicated
I should answer.

'I was, but am no longer, Tom Radcliffe's lover.
Our relationship began over a year ago and lasted for
about eight months, after which I put an end to it.'

'Were you in love with him?'

'Yes. But I realised that so long as I was still married to Edward I couldn't continue the affair, and that it wasn't going to make anyone happier in the long term. I was particularly worried that if Edward found out, he would use it as grounds for taking Freddie.'

'How did Mr Radcliffe react to your ending the relationship?'

'He was disappointed, but understanding. He thought I ought to leave Edward and fight him for custody.'

'And you didn't want to do that?'

'You know who my father-in-law is, don't you? What's more, that wouldn't have been in Freddie's interest. He would be the one to suffer most.'

'But you continued to see Mr Radcliffe?'

'On a professional basis only. He had always supported me as a jockey and he saw no reason to stop doing so.'

'Perhaps he hoped you would go back to him?'

'I made it clear that would have been impossible.'

'As long as Edward was alive.'

'If you're seriously suggesting that Tom killed Edward, you're making a grave error of judgement. It's ludicrous. You don't even know that it's Edward's body yet.'

'We're very confident that the blood found near the car will match the blood found on the bronze.'

'And if they don't match?'

'We still have a murder enquiry, and until he is found your husband becomes a missing person again.

But don't pin any hopes on it. That body is your husband's and what's more, we believe that Tom Radcliffe murdered him. What we don't know is whether you were in it with him. Were you?'

'Of course I wasn't. I was up all night looking after Freddie. I think you ought to know that there are many people who wanted my husband dead. You see, he was a blackmailer.'

I could have sworn the Inspector grinned.

'That's a very serious allegation to make, Mrs Pryde, particularly about a man who's in no position to defend himself.'

I proceeded to tell them all about the diary and our conversation that Friday afternoon. It was obvious from their reaction that they didn't believe me.

'Where is this diary, then?' asked the Inspector.

'I presume it was burned with him. I didn't know it even existed until the day we found it. He must have carried it about with him.'

'And why didn't you mention this before?'

'Because I hoped it wouldn't be necessary. It's not the nicest thing, you know, for my son to be brought up with his father's wrongdoings exposed in this way.'

'Very thoughtful of you. And also a very convenient explanation for what I regard as a seriously unhelpful attitude. Are you really asking us to believe that your husband was blackmailing his own father?'

'That's what I said.' I was beginning to become angry at his supercilious manner.

Wilkinson looked despairingly over at the Super-intendent, who now spoke for the first time.

'The initials JP2 weren't also there by any chance were they?' he sneered.

'I'm sorry, I don't follow you.'

'Pope John Paul the Second. Quite frankly, your allegations are ridiculous and do you no credit. If your motive is to help Mr Radcliffe, you're not going the right way about it.'

Amy intervened before I could let fly. 'There's no need to be rude to my client. I expect you to follow up this particular line of enquiry. Unless you intend to charge my client, I must advise her not to answer any more questions.'

The officers looked at each other and shook their heads. 'No, that's all right. You can go for the moment, Mrs Pryde, after you sign the statement that we'll now prepare. I must warn you not to talk to anyone about this case or to try and get in touch with Mr Radcliffe. We'll have to check up about Saturday night.'

'You mean, talk to Freddie?' I started to panic.

'Unless someone else can corroborate what you've just told us.'

'Ralph, Ralph Elgar. He got up a couple of times and asked if he could help.'

'That should be all right, then.'

'Can't I see Mr Radcliffe, just for five minutes?'

'That's impossible.'

'Where is he?'

'He's still here helping us with our enquiries.'
'Will he be released today?'
'I'm afraid I'm not in any position to answer that.'

That night Amy phoned to say Tom had been charged with Edward's murder. The dried blood found near the car had matched precisely the blood sample taken from the bronze. It seemed that DNA was a truly reliable form guide. As far as the police were concerned Tom had both motive and opportunity to kill Edward. Although they couldn't pinpoint the precise time of death – bones and blood yield no such clues – they firmly believed that Tom had killed Edward after leaving the pub and that his memory block was a convenient fabrication. The final irony was that as I had admitted we were lovers, the police were intending to call me as a witness for the prosecution. According to Amy I was lucky. I had been a short head away from joining him in the dock as an accessory or accomplice. She ended the call by telling me that in the morning the police were going to apply for a warrant to search the cottage.

'Is there anything you don't want them to see?' she asked.

'Of Edward's? Nothing I can think of. They're welcome to it all.'

I lay in bed and thought of Tom. When I was an amateur, and he first started giving me rides, I thought his interest was solely platonic, a kind of peace gesture in the light of Edward's antagonism towards him. Unlike Edward, he obviously enjoyed any success I had. He was fun to be with and I found his good humour and enthusiasm a welcome antidote to Edward's ever-increasing depression and short temper. Our affair just blossomed one day.

We had driven down to Devon and Exeter where I was riding a horse for Tom in a handicap chase. When we arrived at the course, there was thick fog and racing was abandoned. Tom suggested that we went for lunch in a nearby hotel just on the edge of Dartmoor. It was cold outside and there was an enormous log fire burning on one side of the restaurant. We both had a bit too much to drink, and during lunch, Tom reached across for my hand and told me how much he loved me. I hadn't really known what to say. I wasn't certain whether I loved him but at that moment knew that I wanted to go to bed with him.

Ten minutes later, after having booked a room, we were upstairs in a warm bedroom. As soon as the door was closed, Tom pulled me gently towards him. He then took my face in his hands and kissed me softly on the lips.

'I've been wanting to do this for months.'

I didn't say anything but pulled him back against me and we began kissing again. Our tongues darted in and out, exploring and licking. He then moved his hands gently down my neck and began to undo the top buttons of my blouse. Once he had undone them far enough, I almost stopped breathing with excitement as he moved his hands slowly inside. As he began caressing my breasts, he moved his head lower, his tongue exploring the inside of my ear, and then started to kiss my neck. From being almost breathless, I was now breathing heavily and my nipples began to ache as they hardened. I hadn't felt so good in ages, and moved my hand under his jumper and began to unbutton his trousers. As I slipped my hand under the elastic of his boxer shorts and started to run my fingers gently over his smooth skin, I could hear his breathing quicken. From then on, we had all but torn the clothes off each other and had made wonderful love on the carpet.

I hadn't felt any guilt at all, and after that we had made love as often as possible, and wherever possible, until I realised that it had to stop because I had been putting my own interests above my son's. If Edward found out, he'd make sure we both suffered: I couldn't live with myself if Freddie was hurt because of my infidelity.

I had at least kept Tom's letters and now and then I used to take them from their hiding place and recall our times together. The letters! I shot up in bed. They were hidden in the cottage and their contents would be extremely damaging to Tom if the police were to find them. I had no option but to go and recover them. I dressed and slipped out of the back door of the house.

It was well past two in the morning when I arrived at the cottage. I drove past to make sure the police weren't watching it and parked the car a hundred yards down the road. I was terrified as I pushed open the front door and tiptoed across to the stairs. I didn't want to turn on the lights and decided to fetch a torch from the kitchen. I then went up to the spare room. I put my hand up the chimney of the fireplace in the corner, which we never lit. There was a small alcove inset into the wall; I'd discovered it by chance a couple of years previously. I felt about for the small package of letters. It was a month since I had last taken it out. I fumbled around on the edge of the ledge but could not feel anything. Just as I began to panic, my fingers brushed against the package. I heaved a sigh of relief. I must have pushed it further back than usual on the last occasion. I shone the torch on the packet and opened it. One last nostalgic look through before I burned them. But instead of the bundle of envelopes, I found only a few newspaper cuttings and a photograph, taken on holiday some years before, of me – naked from the waist up. I was smiling at the camera but it was Edward who had had the last laugh.

Chapter 6

The next day the papers were full of the news. THE CHALK PIT MURDER screamed one headline; BODY IN THE BOOT another; and even *The Times* had TOP JUDGE'S SON IN MURDER RIDDLE. I sometimes wondered just how many top judges there were. The *Sportsman*, true to form, had its own angle on the story: TRAINER'S ARREST RUINS TITLE CHANCES it proclaimed, referring to Tom's attempt to become the season's leading trainer. That particular piece of genius had all the hallmarks of James Thackeray and I decided to give him a call later in the morning. I suspected I would need an ally in the press, particularly the racing one, and there was quite a lot of information he could find out for me.

To start with, I needed to know the name of the bookmaker who had laid Cartwheel so disastrously at Cheltenham, and also how the *Sportsman* had come to carry the announcement that Mr Pryde was dead. Whoever had put that notice in was either a murderer or a soothsayer, and I knew that Tom Radcliffe was neither.

That morning, Tom was remanded in custody at Newbury Magistrates' Court and, according to Amy, the committal hearing was due to take place the following week. Pressure from on high meant that the trial would probably be heard within a couple of months. I felt angry and impotent but realised that neither emotion would be of much use to Tom in his present predicament.

Accepting Amy's advice, I spent the week at Ralph Elgar's refusing to take any calls. That didn't stop a journalist from one of the tabloids calling at the house and slipping through the letter box a grubby piece of paper on which was scribbled an offer for the exclusive rights to my life story. He had even spelt my surname wrongly. When I didn't reply, it was taken as a signal that the money wasn't enough and an increased offer soon followed. Fifty thousand pounds, provided I gave full intimate details of my sex life and posed topless! Both letters ended up in the fire.

It was just as well I had decided not to ride for a week, as not one trainer had called wanting my services. Ralph told me bluntly that the gossip on the racetrack was that I'd been having an affair with Tom, and that when Edward refused to give me a divorce, I'd encouraged Tom to murder him. So the wrong person was on trial. Even Ralph was shaken when I admitted that Tom had been my lover. Suddenly it seemed everyone had at least one fond memory of Edward Pryde, whereas I was being written off as too ambitious for my own good. It was at times like these that wives rein in their husbands and no one could afford to be heard, at least in public, to adopt a forgiving attitude towards adultery. After all, that sort of thing could so easily become an epidemic.

I left it to Amy to keep me in touch with the latest developments in the police enquiries. I nurtured the forlorn hope that something at least might come of their questioning of the names in the diary, enough to establish that I wasn't lying and that other people had a motive for wanting Edward dead.

Unfortunately it only took a couple of days before I was relieved of that illusion. According to Amy's information, the police tried to interview Michael Corcoran in Tom's yard but to no avail. It appeared that he had failed to return to the lads' hostel after a day off and had not been heard of since. No one seemed unduly perturbed, as it was fairly common for stable lads to up and leave without any notice and my initial reaction was that Edward's death had given Corcoran the chance to start his life afresh. I can't say I blamed him really.

They had also approached Sir Arthur Drewe and Lord Pryde. According to Amy's source at Scotland Yard, they had both blown a fuse on being questioned, and Pryde had threatened to have Wilkinson kicked out of the force if he persisted in such an offensive and outrageous line of enquiry. Hardly surprising when you think about it: the death of a blackmailer must be a great relief to his victims.

Finally, they had carried out a cursory check on the records of all the major bookmakers, which had revealed only a handful of bets in the name of Edward Pryde. For some reason they had chosen to overlook the fact that, if I was to be believed, he was avoiding off-course betting tax and in such circumstances you would hardly expect the bookmaker concerned to record the wagers in an official ledger.

It was now apparent that I was the only person, other than his lawyers, who was prepared to work for Tom's acquittal and even then I was in the invidious position of being a potential witness for the prosecution. The problem was knowing where to begin. It was no use confronting the individuals named in Edward's diary, as in the absence of any material proof to the contrary they would just deny any knowledge or involvement. What's more, if one of them really was the killer I would be exposing myself to danger and I certainly had no desire to be a member of the honourable company of dead heroes. All this meant I had to tread carefully and cautiously and the only consolation was that I had plenty of time on my hands to do it.

Being a jockey was clearly going to be a part-time occupation for the forseeable future; the ground was beginning to firm up and Ralph had roughed-off most of his horses for the season and spare rides seemed to be few and far between. The only runners he had that week were a couple at Worcester on the Thursday and by happy coincidence one of them was Fainthearted, the horse I had pulled on Edward's orders on that very first occasion all those months ago. I could not waste this opportunity to redeem myself and to justify Ralph's continued support and I therefore decided to defer my sleuthing until after the day's racing was over.

It was the first sunny day of Spring and as Ralph and I drove to the course together we discussed the riding instructions for both the races in which he had runners. Ralph was his usual chatty self, doing his best to keep my mind off the whole business. It was clear that he was very keen on Fainthearted's chances in the first and he reiterated that I was to hold him up for a late run and if possible only hit the front just before the winning post. As an ex flat horse, Faint-hearted had the intelligence to pull up as soon as he was ahead and from a jockey's point of view there was nothing more sickening than hitting the front too soon, apparently full of running, and then finding yourself coming to a standstill as if the race was over. This time Ralph wanted no mistakes and, unusually for him, he kept on repeating how he wanted the horse ridden. I just sat back and listened. Judging from his uneasy manner and disregard for the other traffic on the road I was pretty sure that he was going for a major touch and with Fainthearted carrying only ten stone four on his back there was every reason for feeling confident.

Having narrowly missed at least two collisions I
was very glad when we arrived unscathed at the
course. As we walked into the members' enclosure I
noticed several people point at me and then turn away
as we drew closer. Even the man on the gate appeared
surprised to see me, as if I should be wearing widow's
weeds and not racing silks. I hated being the object of
such attention and for once was relieved to be the only
woman jockey riding that day. As soon as Ralph had
gone off to check that the horses had arrived safely at
the racecourse's stables, I hurried over to enjoy the
solitude of the lady jockeys' changing room. Not for
us the luxury of having a valet to help us dress like our
male counterparts. With the race only twenty-five
minutes away, I started to undress and put on the
brown and pink colours of Fainthearted's owner,
glancing in the mirror to check that I was presentable.
I was surprised at how suddenly I seemed to have
aged. My skin had lost its glow; my eyes looked dull
and soulless and I thought I could see the first grey
hairs in my blonde, bobbed hair. Sighing, I picked up
the saddle and went over to the weighing room to
weigh out. Ralph's travelling head lad was waiting to
take it from me.

'This is an absolute certainty,' he said as I handed it
over. He then looked me straight in the eye: 'Try not
to make a cock up at the last hurdle this time.' He
didn't give me time to answer, just turned and went
off to the saddling boxes. As I stood there wondering
whether he knew what had happened last time, a

couple of jockeys came up and said how sorry they were about what had happened to Edward.

'I know we take the piss out of you quite a lot, but seriously, if there's anything you want, just give us a shout.'

It's amazing how just a few words can lift you and I felt much better.

I returned to the changing room to collect the rest of my gear and stood for a few minutes, lost in thought, looking out onto the River Severn. I could see two crews of young oarsmen straining away in enthusiastic rivalry and at that moment I envied them the pleasure of true amateurism. A tap on the door from one of the racecourse officials brought me sharply back to reality. It meant I had four minutes to get ready. I tied on my cap, pulled my goggles over it and picked up my gloves and whip. Then, taking a couple of deep breaths, I wished myself luck and skipped down the wooden steps and on towards the weighing room. This was it and I had never felt so nervous.

As I walked along, several punters sidled up to me and asked if I thought we would win. I just smiled, said nothing and muttered to myself that we better had. I joined up with the other jockeys, gaily joking amongst themselves, and finally entered the paddock where I could see Fainthearted being led around by the lad. The good weather meant that none of the horses were wearing sheets or rugs and Fainthearted's neck was already gleaming with sweat. I pulled my half-fingered gloves on in readiness for a battle with a pair of slippery reins, knowing that if I lost it he would run away with me to the start and almost certainly cart me during the race itself.

The paddock was packed with excited and ever hopeful owners and trainers, some of whom were more on their toes than their animals were. The Topley Hurdle had attracted the maximum field of twenty-eight runners although I reckoned there were only four in with a real chance. One of those was to be ridden by Eamon Brennan and I made a mental note to stay well clear of him during the race. I soon spotted Ralph in the corner, chatting with the owners, and walked over. I had barely time to reach them and say hello before the bell rang for the jockeys to get mounted.

'I don't need to tell you how to ride him,' said Ralph. He could say that again! 'Just remember to take him down to the start last and be certain you've got him well and truly settled before you put him into the race.' I nodded and turned to make my way through the throng to where Fainthearted was pulling his lad round in a very small circle.

'And make sure you win!' Ralph called after me, with a distinct edge to his voice. I was beginning to wonder just how much he was having on this time.

The lad was sweating even more than the horse and was evidently relieved to see me arrive.

'I've never known him as strong as this,' he remarked as Ralph's travelling head lad checked the girths and helped me into the saddle. 'I bet you can't hold him today,' he added cheekily. I ignored the jibe and told him to take a right-hand turn to ensure we were the last to go through the iron gate which led out of the paddock and therefore the last to go down. The plan worked a treat and by the time we were out on the course and had turned right to parade in front of the stands, the early runners were already galloping down past us to the start. Fainthearted was dripping with sweat from head to tail and tried to take off after them. The lad just managed to turn him in a circle on the lead rein and then send him off in the right direction. I barely let him out of a trot as we made our way alongside the white iron railings and waited until the horse in front of me was far enough ahead before turning back down the course. With so much at stake I couldn't allow him to waste all his energy at this stage by chasing another runner. Again, the tactic worked and we reached the start without incident. While I was having the girths checked I called out to the starter, himself a former jockey, and explained why I would be lining up at the rear of the field and told him that he wasn't to bother if I was some way behind. He looked at the sweat on Fainthearted and smiled sympathetically.

'Okay, but don't be too far back or I'll end up with a rollicking from the stewards.'

In a couple of minutes he was on his rostrum and telling us to line up. I let everybody else position themselves in front of me and as the starter pulled the lever to release the tape, I turned Fainthearted's head to one side to prevent him sprinting off too quickly. There were a couple of front runners and with such a large field we went at a furious gallop.

I settled Fainthearted towards the rear as we jumped the first two flights before passing in front of the stands and round the long left-hand bend into the back straight. Even though he wasn't running away with me, he still wasn't properly settled and he only really relaxed once we had passed the racecourse stables half way down the far side. Three or four of the runners were already beginning to feel the strain of the fast gallop and were dropping back. By the time we had jumped the last on the far side, we were within striking distance of the leaders and I hadn't yet had to move a muscle. We were going to win, I could just sense it. There were still six furlongs to go, so I tucked him in on the rails and looked up at the field ahead to see who was travelling easiest, as that was the one I would track. Five lengths in front of me I spotted my man. Ben Stevenson was sitting motionless on Dock Brief, waiting for his time to pounce on the leader, and no doubt already counting his percentage of the prize money. As the runners made their way round the bend and into the straight the pace began to quicken and I went to move Fainthearted out from behind a tired horse to go with them. As I did so, Eamon Brennan suddenly appeared from nowhere on my outside, travelling equally well, but instead of going on he took a pull on the reins and proceeded to box me in. The Irishman appeared totally unconcerned about winning the race and as tired horses kept losing ground and taking me backwards with them he just slowed his horse down on my outside. From sitting pretty and planning when to make my move, I was penned in helplessly with the leaders going further away. I'd had enough.

'Let me out, you bastard!' I shouted over at him but he took no notice. Instead he ostentatiously waved his stick backwards and forwards as if trying to keep up, but I could see that his reins were held tight. I had plenty of horse under me but nowhere to go. Fainthearted simply wasn't big enough to barge his way out and I now had to sit and suffer until we straightened up for home and a gap finally appeared. Eventually it did and by then it was me and not the horse who was sweating. I was convinced it was too late. Fainthearted might have a blistering turn of pace but not even he could make up that much ground.

With only half a mile left, he flew the first two hurdles in the straight and he was going so fast that the horses ahead appeared to be galloping backwards. With one good jump, I thought, I might just do it. I threw everything into the last and now he responded, taking off twelve feet in front of the hurdle and landing, running, just as far the other side. He even passed a couple of other horses in mid air. Now there were only three runners ahead and we had four lengths to make up.

The nearest of them began to tire and we moved in

to third place, gaining distance with every stride but fighting a losing battle with the finishing post. The three of us passed the line together but there was no need for a photograph. We were beat and Ben Stevenson would collect that percentage after all. As we began pulling up I looked back for Brennan and stopped alongside him.

'What the hell did you do that for?' I demanded angrily.

'Nothing personal,' he replied, turning to gallop back to where the also-rans were unsaddled on the course in front of the parade ring. I made my own way back.

'What were you playing at out there?' screamed the lad as he caught hold of the reins and began leading Fainthearted back to the unsaddling enclosure in front of the weighing room. 'Nijinsky couldn't have won from where you left it.' I tried to explain but he made no attempt to listen. He had done his money and wasn't in the mood for excuses.

Ralph and the owners were waiting and looking just as upset.

'That was a disaster,' said a crestfallen Ralph, angrily, as I dismounted. 'How could you have left it so late?'

I could feel myself going redder and redder. I explained what had happened but Ralph insisted that I should have pushed Brennan out of the way.

'That's what you're paid for,' interrupted one of the owners.

A few of the punters had come over from the stands and were now shouting their opinion of my riding ability. Nothing speaks with more eloquence than a burnt pocket. Forlorn, I undid the surcingle and girth, pulled the saddle off and gave Fainthearted a sympathetic pat on the head. I only wished he could give evidence for me. Having apologised to the owners I muttered my regrets to Ralph and disappeared up the concrete steps into the weighing room. I just wanted to get to the changing room and beat the wall in anger but even that relief was to be denied me. As I sat on the scales to weigh in, the ominous figure of the stipendiary steward appeared out of the ground like a mushroom. Leaning over the wooden rails that divided the scales from the rest of the room, he informed me in a quiet yet authoritative voice that the stewards wanted to see me straight away. My heart sank. A premature confrontation with Sir Arthur Drewe was all I needed.

'Third, sir,' I called to the Clerk of the Scales, who looked up to check that I was within two pounds of the weight I had gone out at. He dismissed me with a sideways movement of his head and I dumped my saddle, together with my helmet and whip, in the corner by the number cloth deck and walked despondently to the stewards' room. The stipe who had spoken to me only a minute before came out just as I was about to knock on the door.

'Just wait here,' he commanded.

He left the weighing room only to return a couple of

minutes later bringing Ralph in his wake. The trainer raised his eyes to the heavens, as if to say what a right mess I had landed us both in, and all I could do was to say again how sorry I was.

'Follow me, please,' said the stipe, opening the door and ushering us inside. The three stewards were seated behind an old wooden desk. In the middle, looking as complacent as ever and a veritable model of self-righteousness, was Sir Arthur, flanked on either side by two much younger men wearing almost identical tweed suits. Having introduced us by name the stipe began the proceedings:

'Mr Elgar, will you please tell the stewards what your riding instructions were?'

Ralph was standing bolt upright, as if on regimental parade, holding his worn trilby behind his back with both hands. He repeated what he had told me in the car and paddock and added that he had never had any cause to complain about my riding before.

'I think she just lost her head and overdid the waiting tactics. Everyone makes a cock-up once in a while.'

I wanted to hug him. You couldn't put a price on loyalty and he had every reason not to stand by me. I had heard plenty of stories of trainers who were not so steadfast in their support of their jockeys in front of the stewards.

Drewe wasn't impressed by such loyalty or plain speaking. He launched into the attack. 'Are you seriously saying that you are pleased with Pryde's riding performance?'

Ralph did not suffer fools gladly and was livid at being asked such a ridiculous question.

'Of course I am not pleased!' he retorted. 'A blind man could see that the horse should have won, but that's racing.'

Drewe wasn't finished yet. 'There's no need to be offensive, Mr Elgar. Can you explain why Fainthearted opened as 6–4 favourite but by the time the race began had drifted out to 7–2?'

Ralph went through the roof. 'If you're suggesting that I'd stop a horse you're mad!'

The stipe intervened.

'Mr Elgar, we're not accusing you of anything. We're just holding an enquiry to establish the facts.' He then turned to me.

'You looked to leave far too much ground for your horse to make up. Could you please tell the stewards why?'

I fixed Sir Arthur straight between the eyes and told him that once I had managed to settle Fainthearted I was perfectly happy with my position until we had approached the final bend. It was then that I had got boxed in. Sir Arthur had no intention of letting me finish.

'So you're telling us you got penned in. That's almost unheard of in a hurdles race.'

'I know, sir, but Brennan was doing it deliberately.' I felt no guilt about blaming the Irishman. He owed me and I had absolutely no intention of earning a suspension on his account.

'You should be very careful before you make allegations like that, my girl,' snapped Sir Arthur. He turned to the stipe.

'Mr Pugh, could we please see the video.'

Mr Pugh signalled to the video operator to begin and told him to start at the last hurdle on the far side. The stewards' secretary, who had been seated all the while in the corner taking notes, rose to switch off the lights and draw the curtains. As the film began Mr Pugh pinpointed with a cane both Fainthearted and Brennan's mount. Unfortunately for me, the incident was at the furthest end of the course and not particularly clear. What could be made out, however, was Brennan using his stick and me sitting as still as a nun at prayer.

As the film played on and showed the runners turning for home, the head-on camera came into use. All it showed was the gap appearing and Fainthearted bursting through. They waited for the film to end, both head and side on, before turning the lights back on and pulling the curtains.

'Have either of you anything to say?' asked Sir Arthur.

'No sir,' we replied in unison.

'All right then. Kindly wait outside.'

The stipe opened the door and we left the room accompanied by the secretary, who was not allowed to be privy to the stewards' deliberations.

'That didn't look too good,' said Ralph gloomily.

'No it didn't, did it?' I replied dejectedly. 'Brennan really did fix me, you know. What do you think's going to happen?'

'You'll be fined for riding an injudicious race and I'll have to eat a large slice of humble pie in front of the owners. What really concerns me is why he drifted in the betting. It's as if someone knew what was going to happen. You don't think Brennan is in with the bookies do you?'

Before I could reply the door opened and we were called back in. Drewe could hardly conceal his pleasure.

'We've discussed what we've seen and what you've told us and quite frankly we're not satisfied. We're reporting this matter to the disciplinary committee of the Jockey Club at Portman Square and you'll be informed when you have to appear. That's all. Thank you.'

I couldn't believe my ears and nor could Ralph, judging from his stunned expression. We were barely outside the room before he let fly a string of expletives, casting doubt on the parentage of each of the stewards. 'I've got to go and have a very large drink,' he raged. 'This is absolutely disgraceful. This is nothing personal, Victoria, but do you mind if I put Stevenson up in the last instead of you?'

Of course I minded. No one likes being jocked off, even if it was in favour of the champion jockey, and it would inevitably lead to talk of a rift between us. I swallowed my pride. 'No, if you think that's right, Ralph, it's fine by me.' I tried not to let him see how close I was to tears.

'Good. You know how it is with these particular owners. Don't you worry, I'm sure everything will turn out all right at the Jockey Club. I'll meet you in the car park after the last.'

I wished I could share his confidence and I trudged back to the changing room before giving way to my sobs.

I was waiting for Ralph in the car park when I saw Brennan walk towards his brand new BMW. The opportunity to have a word with him was too good to miss and I wanted more than anything to wipe that complacent grin off his face.

'Eamon,' I called out from the passenger seat of Ralph's car as he passed by. 'Can you spare me a moment?'

He was far from pleased to see me and made on towards his own vehicle.

'Hold on!' I shouted, leaping out of the car and running after him. 'You owe me an explanation.'

'Piss off!' he retorted. 'I've nothing to say to you.'

'Thanks very much. It's no good playing the innocent with me, Brennan. My husband told me all about you.'

'He did, did he? Well what a tragedy it is that your husband's now dead and, as you no doubt know, dead men don't tell tales.'

'But living women do. And I've told the police

110

about why and how Edward was blackmailing you.'
He stopped trying to open the door of his car and
squared up to me menacingly.

'You have, have you? And what have you got by
way of proof to support these allegations?'

I ignored the question in the absence of a satisfactory retort. 'I just want to find out who killed my
husband and reckon you might be able to help me.
Who was the bookmaker who laid Cartwheel to lose
at Cheltenham? The same who paid you to fix me
today?'

'You're imagining things. I was trying today, just
like I always try.' His tongue was so far in his cheek I
was surprised he could get the words out. 'Your problem is you'd be better off riding rocking horses and
even then I wouldn't back against you falling off.' He
turned away and climbed into the driver's seat. I
wedged my foot between him and the door.

'Let me make one thing clear,' I said, doing my best
to sound calm and rational. 'I didn't know or approve
of what my husband was doing to you. What I do
know is that Tom Radcliffe is not a murderer and I
intend to prove it, and if that means exposing or even
implicating you in the process, then so be it. I just
wanted you to know.'

Brennan was unimpressed. 'You're not dealing
with the stewards, darling. If you go on talking like
that you'll be joining your husband, and that kid of
yours will be an orphan. And one final thing. How
can you be so sure your lover boy didn't do it? How

do you know that he wasn't also being blackmailed?'

With that he pushed me away from the car so violently that I stumbled and fell. He turned on the engine and, having made one last offensive gesture out of the window, roared out of the car park.

I picked myself up off the ground and walked back to Ralph's car. 'Nothing personal', I said to myself, had now become 'everything personal'. And just to add to my misery, Ralph's other runner won.

Chapter 7

That evening after dinner I sat in my room and worked out a plan of action. Brennan was right when he said that I had no proof that he was being black-mailed, or indeed of the reason why. The first thing I had to do was find out a lot more about the back-grounds of the names in the diary, and also the identity of both Edward's bookmaker and the bookmaker who had dropped a fortune laying Cartwheel at Cheltenham. It was better than evens that they were one and the same person.

Trapped in the Cotswolds I had no means of finding out the latest gossip in the legal and racing worlds and therefore the obvious answer was to enlist the help of those who did. My first call was to James Thackeray. There was an outside chance that he would still be at the *Sportsman*'s offices, putting his copy to bed and creating those dreadful headlines. I sneaked down to Ralph's office and used the phone.

My luck was in and I was put through to the man

himself: 'James? It's Victoria Pryde. Still slaving away then?'

'Certainly! We creative geniuses never pause, even for alcohol. I'm glad you called, Victoria, as I've made a few enquiries about those things you asked me last week. There's good news, and bad news, I'm afraid.'

'Tell me the worst.'

'The bad news is that nobody knows how that announcement of your old man's death got in. One of the subs thought he remembered it being phoned through by Weatherbys, but I've phoned them up and they vehemently deny knowing anything about it, got quite shirty with me too. The good news is that we know the name of the bookmaker who did his bo . . . sorry, nearly said it, lost a packet on the Gold Cup. My man on the rails tells me it was a fellow called George Musgrave; ever heard of him?'

'Never. What do you know about him?'

'Only that he's mean and very successful. Owns a chain of betting shops in West London and has only recently started betting on course. Wears cashmere coats and oozes charm to the punters, although I doubt if he's so genial when he does his money. Never known a bookie who was. Not in their nature, is it?'

'Hardly. Thanks a lot for the help. It was really kind of you. Can I beg another favour?'

'All right, I'm feeling generous today. I've napped three consecutive winners including the winner of your race at Worcester. Sorry, that's probably a bit of a sore subject. What did those brutes have to say to you?'

'That I wasn't trying and all that stuff. You know they've sent me to Portman Square?'

'I've heard. Are you going to be represented? I would if I were you, you know.'

'I hadn't thought about it. You're probably right, although I've got enough problems with lawyers at the moment.'

'Poor you. You're still certain Radcliffe is innocent then?'

'You know I am, and that's why I'm calling. You ready?'

'At your service. I'll do anything for a pretty face. You'll remember to give me first refusal on the serial rights after the trial?'

'You and the rest of Fleet Street! Got a pen handy? Right, could you find out everything you can – you know what I mean, family, clubs, interests, etcetera – about Sir Arthur Drewe and Eamon Brennan?'

'You mean the Drewe who stands as a steward?'

'That's the one.'

'I'll do what I can, although I don't see Eamon Brennan having many interests outside racing. He's the only jockey I know who wears blinkers off course.'

I laughed. 'Just do what you can, please. I'll be here all tomorrow if you call.'

'Blimey, you don't give a man much time! I'm not

going racing tomorrow, though, so you may well hear from me. In the meantime, Victoria, keep your pecker up.'

My next call was to Amy and she readily agreed to provide me with the legal low-down on my father-in-law, the Lord Chief Justice. That left just Michael Corcoran. In his case I decided that the best approach would be to visit Tom's yard, which reminded me that I still had a bone to pick with his head lad, Jamie Brown.

The next morning a letter arrived from solicitors acting on behalf of my parents-in-law. Judging by the weight of the notepaper, they had retained a top and no doubt extremely expensive city firm, whose partners' names had more barrels than a brewery. The letter itself made grim reading:

'Dear Madam,

We have been instructed by Lord and Lady Pryde concerning the well-being of their grandchild Frederick Clifford Pryde. We understand that Master Pryde is at present staying with you at the above address.

It is our clients' considered view that, in the light of the recent tragic events involving the death of their son, you are not a fit and proper person to have custody or care and control of the child. The purpose of this letter is to put you on notice that, following the hearing of the trial of Regina v Radcliffe, our clients will apply to the Family Division of the High Court to have their grandson made a ward of court. We hope that you will accept that such an action is in his interest which, as you will no doubt appreciate, is the paramount concern in such a situation.

We respectfully suggest that you show the contents of this letter to your own legal advisers.

Yours faithfully'

It was followed by an unintelligible signature.

With the greatest respect to Lord and Lady Pryde, and for that matter their solicitors, I had absolutely no intention of giving up my own child. Freddie was essentially a happy young boy whose father had been a skunk. I intended to make sure the rest of his life was carefree and secure. From what I knew about Lord and Lady Pryde, fun was in strictly limited supply. Still fuming, I took Freddie out riding and returned shortly before lunch to find a message to call Amy.

She had been as efficient as ever.

'Here you are, a layman's guide to Lord Pryde culled from a variety of sources – including *Who's Who*, a couple of friends of mine at the Bar, and my father, who it turns out was at school with him. All dad can remember is that he's a diabetic. Ready? Some of this you'll no doubt know.'

I picked up my pen. 'Fire away!'

'Gerald Clifford Pryde, sixty-four this year. Educated at Marlborough and Brasenose College, Oxford, where he won the Coltart Prize for Jurispru-

dence. Called to the Bar two years later. Member of
Lincoln's Inn. Became a Queen's Counsel after
enjoying enormous success, particularly in criminal
cases, where his grasp of detail and ability to master
heavy briefs in fraud trials was legendary. Became
Recorder of Bicester and Chancellor of the Four
Arches, whatever that is, a year later. Chaired the
Government Inquiry into the Rocamadour Takeover,
and is a member of the Committee for Legal Reform.
Author of *A Guideline to Sentencing of Juveniles and
Delinquents* – that sounds like a bundle of
laughs – and *The Origins of Latin Maxims*. Must
remember that one for Christmas! Appointed to the
High Court bench eight years ago. Three years later
became a Lord Justice. The rest, as they say, is history. Reputation for being a tough sentencer and an
arch conservative. Not that popular with Counsel,
who reckon that he forgets that he was once a barrister himself and ought to know that it's not always
Counsel's fault that things go wrong. Clubs: Garrick
and Athenaeum.'

'Remind me about family details.'

'Hold on a sec. Married Eleanor, née Grime. One
son, Edward. Aren't Grimes the cereal people?'

'Yes. She's the one with the money. Keeps a pretty
tight hold over her husband, which probably explains
that little slip on his part. Interests?'

'Theatre, but they all say that. Bridge, and
numismatics.'

'Coin collecting? I never knew that. Probably

started when he married old Eleanor. What's his address in London?' I knew that, in addition to their house in Oxford, the Prydes had recently taken the lease on a flat in one of the Inns of Court.

'It's in Lincoln's Inn. You'll have to ask the porter, and even if he tells you, there are bound to be security guards.'

'Don't worry, I'm sure he'll see his daughter-in-law when he hears what it's about.'

'Another secret?'

'No. I've received a letter from his solicitors threatening to make Freddie a ward of court. When I'm ready to see the old man, I'm going to use that as a pretext.'

'And your real reason?'

'There are some things I don't even want to tell my lawyer yet!'

I had no sooner put the phone down than it rang again. The second leg of the double had come up.

'James here. Pen and paper handy?'

I told him to let it flow.

'Well, let's start with Eamon Brennan. It's funny what you discover about these jocks. Born in Kilkenny and ran away from home at the age of fourteen to become a lad in Jim Hogan's yard. Became apprenticed to him two years later and at the ripe old age of seventeen rode his first winner under rules. From then on, never looked back. Champion jockey three times, then lost the job with Hogan after his performance in the Sweeps Hurdle, where it was rumoured he pulled the odds-on favourite. Since then has ridden freelance, until accepting a retainer last year in England with Colin Rhodes. Not renewed this season, apparently by mutual consent. Still based in England but frequently rides over in Ireland. A brilliant horseman who can't lie straight in bed, he's so crooked. Separated from his wife and has one conviction for possessing an offensive weapon. Will that do?'

'And Drewe?'

'Not a very nice man. Educated Eton and Sandhurst. Has a filthy temper and loves fox hunting. Has estates in England and Ireland, that's Southern Ireland – County Limerick to be precise. My chum on the Gloucestershire paper describes him as an upper-class brute who must have overslept the day they handed out brains. Wife's apparently a formidable dragon whose father was an Earl. The family's a pillar of local society – you know, front pew of the church every Sunday and twice on Christmas Day, and he's Master of Foxhounds. Stands as a steward at Worcester, Cheltenham and Fontwell. He's a very keen shot and, oh yes, one final thing; there's a rumour going round that he's going to be appointed Chairman of the Disciplinary Committee of the Jockey Club.'

I wondered whether Edward had picked up that piece of information; it would no doubt have called for an increase in Drewe's premium on his insurance policy. 'His address?'

120

'In England? Rivers Hall, Upper Wallop, Gloucestershire. Will that do?'

'It's more than I could have hoped for. James, I can't thank you enough.'

'Don't try. Just don't forget that exclusive interview after the trial. I've already written the headline: "HOW MY LOVER GAVE MY HUSBAND THE BOOT." Do you like it?'

'It's in very poor taste! I may not exactly be the grieving widow . . .'

'All right. I'm sorry. Go on. Prove Radcliffe innocent, but remember if you don't I'm still available.'

'James, I'm going to prove Tom's innocent if it is the last thing I do.'

'Well, just make sure it isn't.'

I don't know why I gave the impression of being so confident. If Sir Arthur or Brennan had killed Edward it was hardly likely to have happened on the spur of the moment. Either could have arranged to meet him on some pretext late that Saturday night, or come to the cottage after he had returned home. The forensic experts couldn't pinpoint with any precision the day, let alone the time, of the murder and all the police had to go on was the fact that nobody had seen Edward alive after he left the pub with Tom. What about Corcoran or Musgrave? Corcoran had disappeared; clearly I had to locate him and find out if he had any information to offer. Unfortunately, if he had killed Edward, which I very much doubted, he was hardly going to advertise his present whereabouts.

Musgrave had to be considered a suspect after those phone calls and Edward's failure to deliver the right result in the Gold Cup. He had lost at least a quarter of a million pounds according to the *Sportsman* and that was on the course alone. If he had laid generous odds in his betting shops the deficit could be considerably greater. Edward's murder might well satisfy his instinct for revenge, yet I somehow doubted if he would have done the dirty work himself. According to recent newspaper reports, the going rate for a contract killer was five thousand pounds; that would certainly explain the professional nature of the crime. To a hardened East End villain, a human barbecue probably had the same clinical attraction as a concrete overcoat. It was only the blood stains on the bronze that had enabled the police to make a positive identification of Edward and nobody could have foreseen that bit of bad luck. I cursed myself. If I had only cleaned the bronze they could never have charged Tom and he'd be a free man instead of languishing in some grotty jail.

There was one person whom I had automatically discounted from my list of suspects: my father-in-law. Fathers don't kill sons, I reasoned, except no doubt in Greek mythology. I realised that Lord Pryde had a good motive: fear that his son's demands might increase now that he had become Lord Chief Justice, but I couldn't see why, if he had paid up for so long, he suddenly wouldn't be prepared to go on doing so.

I was still determined to go and face him. I didn't see why I should be told that I was unfit to bring up a child when he himself had stood by and condoned his own son's criminal activities. I also had a strong desire for revenge, to make him wriggle at the knowledge that I had inherited his guilty secret. Ever since our marriage, Lady Pryde had treated me like a second-class citizen; she had not let pass any opportunity to stress her family's social superiority. There was no doubt that Edward was better bred than me, yet even Northern Dancer has sired the occasional dud.

Not knowing where to begin, I decided to start at the end, at the scene of the crime. Before driving out to Melksham I went over to the cottage to collect the mail and generally give it a look over. I was interested to see if the police had disturbed or removed anything during their search. If they had, there was, alas, no longer any Mrs Parsons to clean up. She had felt it only decent to hand in her notice after the discovery of Edward's body.

To my astonishment the place was a complete shambles. Tables were upturned, books strewn all over the floor and the contents of the drawers had been hurled around the sitting and dining rooms. It was the same story upstairs. I couldn't believe the police could have behaved like this and immediately rang Inspector Wilkinson to complain. He was as surprised as I was.

'Mrs Pryde,' he said, this time putting on his most reassuring voice, 'I can guarantee that has nothing to do with us. Last week we undertook a careful and orderly search of your premises and in fact removed certain material, but only because we felt it to be relevant to our enquiries. I can assure you that my officers left the premises in the same good order that they found them. I know because I was there to supervise them. It looks like somebody else has paid you an unauthorised visit. Have you been staying there at all recently?'

I told him that Freddie and I were still living with friends.

'I'm afraid,' he went on, 'that this kind of thing does happen. We live in a sick society and there are a few nasty individuals around who take advantage of other people's misfortune to do a bit of petty thieving. Do you know if anything's missing?'

'Not that I've noticed so far.'

'I'll send a couple of men over straight away.'

'All right. Can you leave it for a short while? Let me just go through everything first and see what's gone.'

'If you insist, but please don't go putting your fingerprints everywhere, Mrs Pryde.'

Whoever had burgled the place had clearly not been a petty thief. The television and video were untouched, as was the silver cutlery, a family heirloom in the drawer of the sideboard. What had occurred was a systematic, although judging by the chaos, increasingly frenzied, search and there was nothing to indicate if it had been successful or not. Who, why and what, I wondered? I thought back to that Friday when Freddie discovered the diary and Edward's smug expression as he bragged about his investors. He had boasted of how he had kept a photocopy of the incriminating letter which his father had received from Lorenz. Perhaps that wasn't the only piece of evidence in his possession. With Edward dead, could it be that one of the investors had now come to reclaim the proof of his own indiscretion? I decided it was worth a fresh look around the cottage just in case the searcher had left empty-handed. There was no need to look in the obvious places, as the intruder had done that already.

I plonked myself down in Edward's favourite chair by the fire and surveyed the room. Behind the pictures or inside the photograph frames would be too simple. I also discounted the grandfather clock in the corner. The stuffed owl on the table by the window looked more promising. I was convinced it was winking at me. 'That's it!' I said aloud, congratulating myself on my powers of detection.

Edward had always hated that bird. I had picked it up one day in a junk shop for a fiver and brought it home in great triumph. He had taken one look and kindly said it reminded him of my mother. I rushed over and took it out of its glass box. There was no sign of the skin being broken, although I could well imagine the pleasure he would have taken in stuffing documents up its backside. I ran to the kitchen and took a knife from the drawer, now certain that I had discovered his cache. Asking my mother for forgiveness, I unceremoniously tore open the old bird's chest and back and stuck my hands inside, but all I got was stuffing, a sentiment echoed by the look of disdain in the owl's eyes. Feeling a complete idiot, I returned the mutilated creature to its former resting place.

As I did so, I caught sight of a photograph of Edward on the mantelpiece, taken when he was out shooting on his uncle's estate. The gun held proudly in his right hand was his most treasured possession. His father had brought him up on the saying, 'You should lend your wife before your gun', and that was exactly how Edward felt about it. He was endlessly cleaning and oiling it; I had once even caught him taking it to pieces. I remembered how angry he had been at the time. I ran upstairs to the spare room and looked under the wardrobe. The brown oblong case with his initials on it was still there. I pulled it out only to find that the lock had already been forced, although as far I could tell nothing had been removed. I looked down both barrels to no avail, and then studied the butt. Five minutes later I had removed the four screws which fixed the end-plate to the stock of the gun. I removed the plate and extracted its unorthodox contents. Replacing the screws, I returned the gun to its case and went downstairs with my discovery: a small bundle tied with a red ribbon. I slipped it off, my fingers trembling in anticipation. I was not disappointed.

There were four items: the first was a handwritten letter addressed to Gerald Pryde Q.C. from Peter Lorenz, in which he referred to an enclosure of a cheque for ten thousand pounds 'as per our agreement'; the second was a single sheet of scruffy paper, undated, containing a signed confession by Michael Corcoran that he had stolen the wages from Tom Radcliffe. No wonder Edward was so confident of his abiding loyalty. The third was a handwritten demand from George Musgrave for the settlement of one hundred thousand pounds' worth of losing wagers, each one carefully itemised on the rear. Presumably Edward thought he could use Musgrave's admission of illegal bookmaking as a bartering weapon. But the last enclosure was the most thrilling: it was a colour photograph with remarkable definition, considering its unusual subject matter. I couldn't resist a smile. Sir Arthur Drewe was dressed in his own racing silks and riding what looked like a very strong finish. The only problem was that his mount was a buxom brunette called Annabel Strong. She held a permit to train horses owned by herself and members of her family. I had no idea that Sir Arthur was her retained jockey.

I wondered how on earth Edward had obtained the photograph. All in all a very exciting find; my only disappointment was the absence of anything positive on Brennan. I suppose he would hardly have been foolish enough to commit the existence of a cash retainer to writing.

I waited for the police to arrive and then headed for

Melksham and the chalk pit. Motoring across the rolling Wiltshire Downs it was hard to believe that my journey had such a ghoulish purpose. The old chalk pit had been abandoned over twenty years previously and apart from the occasional courting couple or gang of hell's angels on their motor bikes, it was a lonely and desolate spot. When I had worked on the Newbury paper I had once written a piece on the pit as part of a series on our neglected countryside. My editor had described it as a load of sentimental bilge, full of clichés and tired metaphors. Now the pit had earned itself a place in history and would no doubt become a tourist attraction in the not too distant future.

I turned off the B216 and drove along a narrow single-track road. After three miles I parked the car on the side of the road and walked the fifty yards or so back to the old track which led up to the pit. It was clear from the tyre marks that there had been plenty of recent traffic. Today, however, it was deserted again. Ten minutes later I reached the top of the pit itself, and below me I could see an area about twenty feet square which had been roped off. It could be reached by the worn drive that the lorries once used to collect the chalk. I walked down and inspected the site where no doubt the car had been found. There were scorch marks on the ground, but apart from that there was nothing to indicate that it had been the scene of such a gruesome crime.

I strolled on and into the heart of the pit. I didn't

128

expect to find anything as the police had no doubt carried out a thorough search of the area for evidence. It was eerie and depressing and I tried to picture the scene on the night of the murder, Edward's body curled up in the boot as paraffin or petrol was poured over it and then the car set on fire. I wondered whether the murderer or murderers had stood by and watched the blaze or whether they had set off straight away in a waiting car. Out here, miles from anywhere, they had very little chance of being disturbed. A cold and ruthless murder, an act wholly beyond Tom Radcliffe.

I was beginning to feel nervous hanging around there, so I returned to my car and drove to Oxford in the hope of gaining an audience with my father-in-law. The courts were on vacation and I knew that he was likely to be in his study writing up judgements to be delivered at the beginning of the next legal term. I took the precaution en route of phoning up to see whether Lady Pryde was at home. If she had been I would have aborted my mission for the present. I had no desire to come face to face with that most formidable of battle axes; Doris, the housekeeper, didn't recognise my voice and said that Madam was away until late evening. I had hoped as much, remembering that Friday was usually her bridge afternoon in Abingdon.

Lord Pryde was positively displeased to see me. I could sense his legal mind evaluating whether he ought to refuse to talk to me and kick me out. In the end it was only the fact that Doris had let me in which embarrassed him into being civil and inviting me into his library. It was a magnificent room, lined with thousands of leather-bound books. At the far end sat a large mahogany desk piled with legal-looking documents. A fire was blazing and he beckoned me to sit down on one of the leather armchairs beside it. It reminded me of my last serious discussion with Edward.

Lord Pryde looked tired and drawn, although nowhere near as drained emotionally as one would expect from a man who just recently lost his only son. He went straight on the attack, a family characteristic.

'Victoria, it really is quite wrong of you to come here uninvited. If Eleanor had been here you would have caused her considerable distress, and that's the last thing I want at the moment. As you can imagine, Edward's death has come as a terrible blow . . . to us both,' he added, apparently as an afterthought. 'I must ask you in any event to be brief. It would be dishonest of me to pretend that you are welcome in this house, and if it's young Freddie you've come to talk about, then you're wasting your time. It's quite clear to us that his interests are best served by being brought up here.' He stood up and started pacing the room, giving me no chance to speak. 'I realise that we are no longer young, but the boy is a Pryde, and quite frankly your involvement with this Radcliffe man makes your continuing custody of the boy quite out of the question. Of course, we would have no objection to your seeing him now and again, say once a month during the school holidays, but it's quite impossible for him to remain with you.'

I wanted to scratch his narrow, arrogant eyes out, but his spectacles would have got in the way. I went on the verbal attack instead.

'How very generous of you,' I replied aggressively. 'As it happens, it's not Freddie I've come to talk about, not directly at least. I'll leave that fight to the lawyers, and it will be a fight, I warn you. No, I'm here to talk about this,' I said, triumphantly waving a piece of paper in front of him. 'The letter from a certain Mr Lorenz, which my late beloved husband treasured so much.'

His complacent air gave way to a vitriolic rage.

'Where the hell did you get that?' he demanded, walking over towards me.

'No you don't!' I replied, putting it back inside my handbag. 'Don't worry, Gerald, I'm not a black-mailer. Your secret is dead along with your son. I just want to ensure that justice is now done. You must tell the police what Edward really was, so that they start investigating all those other people who had a real reason for wanting him dead.'

'Don't be ridiculous! Do you seriously think that a man of my standing can afford to expose himself so that some two-penny-ha'penny racehorse trainer is acquitted of a murder he almost certainly committed in any event? Think of my position. I would have to

131

resign, lose everything I've worked all my life for. How would Eleanor feel? Isn't it enough that she's lost her son? No, Victoria. I've absolutely no intention of doing what you ask. Here, you're going to give me that letter right now!' He shoved me hard and grabbed the handbag. In a second he had opened it and removed the letter. He threw it straight onto the fire without even looking at it. As it burned he held me back from the fire with his right arm.

'There. Gone is your one and only piece of evidence.'

'How do you know I haven't made a copy?' I countered.

'I wouldn't care. Only originals are admissible in court. Now, leave this house and never ever return.'

I smiled condescendingly at him. 'As you will. Just one last thing. The next time you burn one of my mother's letters, I would prefer you to ask permission.' I didn't wait to see his reaction. Only his overweening arrogance would have let him think I was naive enough to bring actual evidence with me.

I returned to Ralph's house to find a message waiting for me to contact Amy Frost as a matter of urgency.

Freddie was running around the house with Ralph's dog. It was amazing how well he had taken the news of Edward's death. It was either a consequence of his age or more likely an indication that its true implications had not yet sunk in. When he saw me walk through the door he left the dog and came running up to me. I bent down and picked him up in my arms and we gave each other a big hug.

'What have you been up to today?' I said as I kissed him on his forehead. As he rushed through a seemingly endless list of things he had done, I pulled my head away and admired him. He was the spitting image of Edward, but had blond hair like my own. Once he finished telling me his various achievements, I put him down and told him to go on playing with the dog while I called Amy. I wondered if she had any news of Tom's committal hearing, which was due to take place in a couple of days' time. By now the prosecution statements would have been served and Tom given full notice of the case against him. Clever Amy had befriended the solicitor acting for Tom and with a bit of luck, she would have been tipped off as to its strengths and weaknesses.

I caught Amy just as she got in the door.

'Any news?' I asked anxiously.

'I'm afraid so and it's not all good. Hold on a minute while I take my coat off and make myself a little more comfortable.'

I couldn't believe that she could sound so calm.

'Shall I fire away?' she asked, a minute or so later. 'They've served the statements on Tom's solicitor and to be honest, although I haven't actually been shown them, they don't seem to make that happy reading.'

'What do you mean?' I already sounded anxious.

'As I told you, in the absence of a confession or an eye witness, the police case has to be based on circumstantial evidence. You know what I mean, once they prove the body is Edward's, all the clues have to point to Tom as the murderer.'

'But what clues?'

'Hold on a minute, I'm coming to that. Just let me get my notes out. Right. To begin with, the row in the pub was a very acrimonious affair and was overheard by half the saloon bar. Apparently Edward was asking Tom to leave you alone and Tom lost his temper and threatened all sorts of things if Edward didn't treat you better. I gather they very nearly came to blows and both were the worse for drink when they left, just before closing time.'

'But that doesn't prove anything. Tom doesn't mean it when he makes those kinds of threats.'

'You know that, Victoria, but the police don't. Can I continue?'

'I'm sorry.'

'It's all right. I do understand, but if you let me finish with the evidence we can dissect it afterwards. Next comes the forensic stuff. On the track leading to the chalk pit they've discovered four footprints which match the shoes Tom admits wearing the night he met Edward.'

'But he's got the same size feet as half the men in England.'

'I thought you were going to let me finish! And on those shoes they've found traces of chalk which match that found in the pit. Finally, hidden in a disused stable in his yard under a load of machinery they've found a petrol can which they believe was used to set fire to the car and Edward's body.'

'I just don't believe it. The chalk on the shoes is probably the same as you will find near those gallops Tom uses and the petrol can proves nothing. There must be a million discarded petrol cans on farms and in stables.'

'You're probably right but not all their owners have a motive for wanting Edward dead or, for that matter, have petrol stains on the clothing they were wearing the night the victim disappeared.'

'On his clothing! But how?'

'Tom says he must have done it when he filled his car up with petrol on the way to the pub.'

'It's very likely – he's a clumsy bugger.'

'It's just unfortunate I'm afraid. I'm sorry, Victoria, but you've got to accept that Edward's dead and Tom's going to be on trial for his murder in less than two months' time.'

I thanked her for her help and asked if she would attend the committal hearing to keep an eye on the proceedings. I would be elsewhere, at Tom's yard trying to locate the present whereabouts of Michael Corcoran and hoping that he might admit to the police that he was being blackmailed. I took out his letter of confession and clenched it tightly in my hand. Ironically, a spot of blackmail of my own was now called for.

Chapter 8

I arrived at Tom's yard at ten-thirty, when I reckoned
I would find Jamie Brown, the head lad, in the office
sorting out the race entries and declarations with
Tom's assistant trainer. When the governor falls ill
or, much more unusually, is languishing in prison on
a murder charge, it becomes the responsibility of the
assistant trainer and head lad to run the yard in his
absence and to try and keep the winners coming. Tom
had a large and on the whole fairly loyal bunch of
owners, although they were unlikely to want to let
their own financial interests suffer because of their
trainer's present difficulties. I had heard that several
horses had already been removed from the yard and
no doubt many more would follow if the flow of
winners dried up.

Unfortunately a virus had hit the yard at the end of
March and since Tom's arrest, a number of the
runners had struggled in towards the rear of the field
and returned home to their boxes with runny noses. It

was beginning to look as though even if, or rather when, Tom was acquitted, he was going to have plenty on his hands rebuilding his professional reputation.

I found Jamie alone in the office wading unhappily through a pile of entry forms. He was in his late forties, his wrinkled and weather-beaten face bearing testimony to a lifetime spent on the gallops. He loved horses and hated human beings, and his least favoured species was the lesser spotted female jockey. He made no attempt to stand up as I walked into the room and went on working as if I didn't exist. I tried the humble approach.

'Good morning, Mr Brown. I'm very sorry to disturb you, I really am, but it's very important. It's about Mr Radcliffe.' He still didn't move or look up, preferring to growl from behind the form book he was holding upright in his right hand.

'Haven't you caused enough trouble already, Miss? Do the police know that you're here, snooping around?'

'No, why should they? There's no law against it, unless you mean I'm not allowed to talk to you because of that statement you've given them.'

That succeeded in upsetting him. He shoved aside the entry forms, put down his book and glowered at me. 'Look here, all I told the police is what I heard in the yard that morning the day after the Gold Cup. I never thought I would get the governor into trouble, 'cos if I had I would've kept quiet. It was what *you* said I thought would interest them.'

'Mr Brown, I didn't kill my husband. Nor did Tom Radcliffe. But at the moment nobody seems to care about the truth. Do you know where I can contact Michael Corcoran?'

'Corcoran? Don't know and frankly don't care. I can't see how he could help you. He walked out of here without so much as a by your leave, after all we'd done for him.' Jamie Brown shook his head as if despairing of the whole of the human race.

'Did he tell anyone where he was going?'

Brown gave me a contemptuous look. 'You don't know so much about racing, do you? Stable lads come and go, it's not as if they were well paid. For all I know at this very moment he could be working for some other trainer who hasn't got round to registering him.'

'Come on, Mr Brown, have you really no idea? Surely he told some of the other lads where he was going or what his plans were?'

He shook his head. 'I don't interest myself in stable gossip. As far as I'm concerned he didn't turn up on Monday morning to do his two and that was his lot. I'm hard pressed enough as it is.'

'Would you mind if I had a chat with one or two of the lads to see if they know anything?'

'Yes I would. I don't want you going round asking questions, upsetting my staff. He'll turn up somewhere, they always do.' He returned to his entries, making it clear he regarded the interview as over. I could see I would make no further progress and wandered back into the yard in the hope of finding a lad or girl who might be able to help me. There was no one in sight so I decided to say hello to Mrs Drummond.

I nervously rang the bell to the house in anticipation of one her more frosty receptions. To my surprise, she welcomed me with open arms and invited me in for coffee. Knowing her affection for Tom, I decided to take her into my confidence and tell her about Edward's blackmailing and how Corcoran was one of his victims. Then and there she offered to phone his parents in Ireland to see if they had any news. After a little difficulty getting through, she eventually spoke to Corcoran's mother. Mrs Corcoran had not heard from her son for two months, but that in itself was not unusual. She explained that he wasn't much of a writer and every now and again would phone home, normally when one of his half dozen brothers or sisters had a birthday. She promised to let Mrs Drummond know as soon as she heard anything.

The call over, Mrs Drummond offered to pursue her own enquiries among the lads in the yard and we arranged that she would telephone either me or Amy at work in London as soon as she heard or discovered anything. Frankly I wasn't optimistic and was beginning to suspect that Corcoran had no wish to have his present whereabouts discovered.

Having drawn a blank, I headed to Kempton Park and the day's principal race meeting, to see if George

Musgrave was to be found taking bets on the rails. It was the first time for as long as I could remember that I had been to a racecourse without having a ride booked and it was a curious sensation wandering round the members' enclosure, rubbing shoulders with the punters and being just another spectator. Of course, jockeys are not allowed to bet, at least officially, and I certainly couldn't afford any approach I might make to Musgrave being misinterpreted.

Weekday meetings draw surprisingly large crowds and the six race card had no shortage of runners to keep them interested. It was an ideal setting for the bookies and I would have been surprised if Musgrave was not on hand to try and relieve the public of their readies. My instinct was right. I watched the first race from the stands, although for most of the eight fences my binoculars were trained on the sleek, immaculately groomed figure of my late husband's bookmaker. Positioned about six down on the rails, he was a tall, thin-faced man with a thick crop of brown hair, and his complexion bore the healthy remnants of a tan, no doubt from a recent cruise in the Caribbean. Appearing confident and assured in his well-cut dark blue cashmere coat he could easily have been mistaken for a stockbroker or merchant banker. The only give-away was the pair of tinted glasses he put on every now and again to look at the prices on the boards of the bookmakers standing in rows behind him. Beside him, also on the other side of the rails, stood his clerk, his head buried in a ledger recording

the day's bets. Too smooth by half, was my first
impression of Musgrave and I began to work out the
right way to approach him. I decided that the best
tactic would be to wait and see if he left his position to
go and have a drink or whatever and then to follow
him in the hope that a suitable opportunity would
arise.

In the meantime, I amused myself watching him in
action. The third race on the card was a handicap
hurdle and it was attracting a good deal of betting.
Eamon Brennan was on the 2–1 favourite and judging
from the action in the ring, and the odds on offer
from the bookies at the top of the rails, the horse was
a warm order at that price. Standing only two yards
away from Musgrave I heard him lay three separate
punters' bets of two and a half thousand to win five
thousand and he seemed prepared to take as much as
any of the other bookies wished to unload. Either he
had nerves of steel or he knew something they didn't.
To cap it all, only one minute before the off he started
offering 9–4 and was nearly submerged in the flood
of takers. Once the race was under way he perched
himself on the rail that divides the members from
Tattersalls enclosure and fixed his binoculars on
Brennan's mount.

You had to hand it to the Irishman, he really knew
how to ride – it takes a real artist to lose when the
world thinks you're trying like hell to win. Coming
with a well-timed run to join the leader going over the
last he managed for a moment to take the lead and a

roar went up from his backers. Just then his opponent rallied and to all those screaming encouragement in the stands Eamon was pulling out all the stops in an attempt to win, flourishing his whip like a man whose own mortgage depended on it. Of course it didn't, and his heroic efforts just failed in what was called as a photo finish but to the trained eye was going to amount to a short-head defeat. Musgrave put down his binoculars and winked at his clerk. A perfect result for the book and no doubt for Eamon a packet of readies in prospect substantially in excess of the winning percentage he had sacrificed.

George didn't take a lot of interest in the next race and made no attempt to offer competitive odds. He was content to take the occasional bet from his credit customers and once the runners were off, he left his position and walked briskly through the gate that led to the members' entrance and on towards the ground floor bar below the stands. I followed him and waited until he had placed his order, then walked up to the bar beside him and asked the girl serving for a gin and tonic. Musgrave appeared immune to my presence as he went on studying the Stock Market prices in his copy of the *Independent*. I tapped him on the shoulder and introduced myself:

'Mr Musgrave. Victoria Pryde. I don't think we've met but I believe we've spoken on the phone. You remember, the evening of the Gold Cup.'

If looks could kill, they could have sent there and then for the undertaker.

'I think you've made a mistake,' he replied, folding up his paper and downing his whisky. 'I make a point of not talking to jockeys. It can get you into trouble with the authorities and I have no intention of losing my licence. Now if you'll excuse me, Miss Pryde. I must go and look after my customers for the next race.'

I grabbed him by the arm, although he quickly and firmly removed my hand. I let him have it. 'That sounds very noble, Mr Musgrave. No doubt you told them that Brennan's horse wouldn't win in the last, that Fainthearted wouldn't be allowed to win at Worcester last time out and that I was meant to be on a non-trier at Cheltenham.'

His expression showed I had hit a raw nerve and for a brief moment I thought he was going to strike me. He quickly recovered his composure as the bar filled up with racegoers. He moved even closer to me so that our bodies were almost touching and he couldn't be overheard.

'You'd better watch what you go round saying or I'll have my lawyers onto you.'

He was making a real effort to control his temper and I had no intention of helping him. 'Really? Surely not your lawyers! No doubt you would also ask them to explain to you the consequences of taking bets off course and not paying tax on them. I think they call it fraud. If they want some proof on that score tell them not to hesitate to get in touch with me. It would be such a tragic end to your career as a bookmaker.'

He poked me menacingly in the ribs. 'You're a dead

person,' was all he said before striding out of the bar.

George Musgrave apparently decided not to bet on the final two races, judging by the empty space which suddenly appeared on the rails. I was left wondering what his next step would be while having no doubt about mine. I telephoned my mother in Wincanton and asked her to come and collect Freddie. It was time he took a holiday.

I drove on into London and that evening had dinner with Amy. It was a welcome relaxation from my own problems to catch up on the latest developments in her social life and hear about the men who were vying to win her favours. You somehow don't think of lawyers as having sex lives. By all accounts her admirers divided into two groups: barristers who took themselves extremely seriously and regarded it as an outrageous snub to their *amour propre* when she refused to go to bed with them and journalists who spent the evening disclosing their sources over bottles of champagne and were then too drunk to remember what happened next. I thoroughly enjoyed her company and admired her ability to shake off in her spare time the shackles of her serious and demanding professional life.

I left her flat just before midnight, after endless cups of black coffee, and began the long drive to Ralph's yard in the Cotswolds. Traffic was light, and an hour and half later I was heading away from Cirencester on the last twenty miles of the journey through the countryside. As I drove along I took stock of my investigations to date. Viewed dispassionately, they were long on effort and short on success. I was no wiser as to Corcoran's whereabouts and had succeeded in antagonising Lord Pryde (not altogether unintentionally) and extracting a death threat from George Musgrave. I hadn't yet mustered the courage to confront Sir Arthur Drewe with his extra-curricular activities. It was all very well going round planting mines, and even watching the explosions, but I was no nearer discovering who really had murdered Edward. All I could hope was that his assailant might try the same tactics on me and thereby expose himself. It was a risky and dangerous ploy on my part and that was why I had decided that the time was right to keep Freddie well out of it.

I had no idea how long I had been followed. At first I had assumed that the car about a quarter of a mile behind was just another late traveller returning home and I hadn't paid any further attention. I had been perfectly content to cruise along listening to a Tina Turner tape and pondering my next moves. I would probably not even have noticed the car if I hadn't overshot the turning to Stow on the Wold and had to reverse twenty yards to take it. My pursuer had been far enough behind not to make the same error, but I had no doubt that he was also taken by surprise by my late manoeuvre and his brakes screeched as he jammed them on to make the turning. From then on he kept his distance, accelerating and slowing down to match my own changes of pace. He was somehow always just that one bend behind and each time I thought I had shaken him off, the lights of his car would reappear in my mirror.

I told myself not to panic, that if I drove speedily yet carefully I would reach Ralph's without being caught. I would then hoot my horn as I came up the drive, waking everybody up, but at least scaring the tail away. My only problem was that there were still fifteen miles or so left to go, through winding countryside, and I was also in no doubt that I had the less powerful engine. Combe Hardy was about two miles ahead and I remembered that there was a pub there. It was well after closing time, although there might just be a chance that the landlord was still up. I decided that if there was a light on as I approached, I would take a late turn into the car park, run from the car screaming rape and bang on the door for help. I would probably be taken for a neurotic woman who was imagining things but that was better than being murdered or whatever other fate was being planned for me.

I thought of Freddie and Tom and whether I would ever see them again. I looked in the mirror. He was still there all right. I assumed he was on his own, although without street lighting and any cars coming in the opposite direction to illuminate the road behind, I couldn't be sure. I accelerated as we reached Combe Hardy, hoping to give the impression that I was going to drive straight through. I looked in desperation for a light, any light, in the pub ahead. Alas, like the rest of the village, it was in darkness. I kept my foot on the accelerator and sped on into the night and the long desolate stretch of road across the hills which led to the next village of Charlton Bywater. He now drew even closer, almost flirting with my rear bumper, his headlights blinding me with their glare. All I could do was to move over to the centre of the road to stop him overtaking.

My attention was so consumed with these antics that I nearly hit the oncoming car. Appearing at sixty miles an hour out of the darkness, it swerved to avoid me and then repeated the manoeuvre just in time to avoid colliding with my shadow. For one brief moment, as the car flashed past, its lights caught the face of my would-be assailant, yet all I could make out was the silhouette of the driver crouched low behind the wheel. For a second I lost my concentration and he seized his chance. Forcing his way past, he cut in sharply ahead of me. Instinctively, I swerved to avoid running into him, steering the car off the road and to my horror down the hill to my left. As I somersaulted I tucked my head into my chest as if I had fallen from a horse and was rolling over to avoid the other runners. I held my breath and waited for the end.

I hit the tree just as the engine cut out and came to rest upside down. I couldn't believe it: I was alive. Drops of blood trickled down my face and into my hair, but I didn't care. The important thing was I had survived. I tried my fingers. They all moved. I had forgotten about my legs. Without them I could never ride again. The front of the car had caved in on impact and the dashboard and steering wheel had been shoved forward to within a few inches of me. I wiggled my toes inside my shoes and kicked out with my legs. I thanked God I wasn't paralysed. My back ached but it wasn't so painful that I couldn't shift it slowly side to side. The stock-taking was going well.

I think it was the sound of a twig snapping that told me someone was out there. It had never occurred to me that he would come back. I wanted to scream for help, yet there was no point. I was in the middle of nowhere, in the dead of night, and trapped upside down in the front seat of a wrecked car. It would be the final irony if both Edward and I met our deaths in a motor car. I regretted not joining the RAC.

I could make out the sound of footsteps more clearly now, moving slowly and deliberately around the back of the car. He was certainly taking his time, no doubt waiting to see if I was still alive. I wondered whether he would go away if he thought I was dead. Or maybe he wanted to take no chances and be absolutely certain. A well-aimed blow to the forehead would almost certainly be put down to the crash. I could just see it in the papers: TRAGIC DEATH CAUSED BY JOCKEY'S CARELESS DRIVING. That other oncoming car would be able to say how fast I had been travelling and I would go down as just another statistic in the year's toll of fatal road accidents.

I looked around the car. Just below me on the floor – or was it the roof? – lay a bottle of cologne spray which I kept in the glove compartment. It must have fallen out as we came down the hill. I stretched out the fingers of my left hand and grabbed it. I was just in time before a torch shone through the window of the passenger seat. I kept my eyes closed and remained motionless. I could catch the filter of light as the torch was carried round to my side of the car. I held my breath. A hand rattled the handle but to no avail. The door had jammed tight. Now I was locked in and he was locked out. Not for long.

There was a short pause and then pieces of glass flew into my face as he smashed the window. I kept my eyes closed, praying and hoping that he would first examine me to see if I was dead. I could sense a hand feeling for the door handle beside me and then tugging at it and wrenching the door open. It was then I moved. Releasing the safety belt with my right hand I rolled out onto the grass, and at the same time squirted the spray upwards in the direction of the impenetrable face behind the torch. And then I ran as fast as my aching legs could take me. I didn't look round to see if I was being followed – I was once cautioned by the stewards for doing that at Towcester when I nearly got caught on the line – and headed I knew not where. Twenty minutes later, and utterly exhausted, I found myself in the outbuildings of a farm and, deciding that I must have shaken him off, collapsed exhausted on a bed of straw in the nearest barn.

The Friesian cow who came to take my breakfast order did not seem in the least perplexed by my presence and soon wandered away to continue with her own munching. I was anxious not to be asked any questions by the farmer who had unwittingly provided me with hospitality and made at once for the nearest village. After a two-mile walk, I found a telephone box and called Ralph. I hadn't been missed. When I had failed to show up to ride out the first lot, they had assumed I had stayed on overnight at Amy's and was motoring down first thing. I told Ralph what had happened and his first question was whether I had reported it to the police.

'Not yet,' I replied, 'and I'm not sure I will. They won't believe me and all that will happen is I'll be charged with driving without due care and attention.'

'We'll see about that. If someone really tried to kill you last night it's a serious matter and the police have to investigate.'

'Ralph, there's no if about it. Whoever was driving that car last night also killed Edward, I'm certain of it.'

'Hold on, Victoria. You're almost certainly still in a state of shock and shouldn't jump to conclusions. Wait there and I'll be over in, say, twenty-five minutes. Where did you say the car was again?'

'On its back in a field somewhere off the Combe Hardy and Charlton Bywater road. If you collect me first we can go and find it together. Please don't be long.' I told him where I was again, according to the sign in the telephone box, and then rang Amy. She at least had no trouble believing me.

'The police won't,' she warned, corroborating my own instinct. 'It stands to reason. Everyone who drives off the road blames it on some other lunatic.'

She was right. By the time Ralph had picked me up and we had located the car, the police were already on the scene. From the local bobby's very first question, when he asked how I could explain the skid marks up on the road, I knew that my account would be treated with ridicule. I saw no point in telling him about the final incident after the crash and confined myself to an account of how I had been followed and forced off the road by a driver I couldn't identify in a car whose number plates I never noticed and whose make remained a mystery to me. I gave Ralph a dirty look when he tried to interrupt. The bobby's last question left me in no doubt about the way his methodical mind was working.

'Had you had anything to drink last night with your meal, Madam?' I admitted that I had drunk about half a bottle of wine in the course of the evening. The knowing way the officer shook his head made me wonder whether I was going to be charged with driving under the influence as well as with sundry other road traffic offences.

Ralph drove me home and I was having a much needed bath when Mrs Drummond called. I rushed downstairs to take the call, convinced that my luck had changed and that Corcoran had turned up.

'He's in Ireland,' announced Mrs Drummond.

'You're a marvel,' I chortled. 'How did you find out?'

'I talked to a couple of the lads, who said that they were not surprised when he failed to return that weekend, as he had been talking about clearing off once he had sorted out a problem over here.'

I wondered whether that was a euphemism for disposing of my husband.

'And then by chance,' Mrs Drummond continued, 'I got a call last night from the man himself, asking to speak to Mr Radcliffe about his holiday money and unpaid wages. He obviously hadn't heard about the murder. He was pretty reluctant to talk when I said Mr Radcliffe was unavailable and all he'd tell me was that he was in County Limerick looking for work in a racing stable and wanted to be left alone. I could hardly hear him, he talked in such a quiet voice. I'm sorry, dear, he refused to be more specific or even give a forwarding address. There's always his mother, I suppose.'

I hid my disappointment, thanked Mrs Drummond profusely for her help and told her not to hesitate to contact me again if there was any more news. I was still determined to locate and talk to Corcoran, yet wondered what realistic chance I had of finding him in Southern Ireland. That was one place in the world where if you wanted to disappear no one held it in the least bit against you.

Chapter 9

I had bruised my back quite badly in the crash and
Ralph insisted on calling in his own doctor to examine
me. Having given my body the once over and made
the usual knowing noises, he declared that I had
sprained my spinal ligaments and ordered me to lie on
my back for the next three days. I started to protest
until Ralph reminded me, in a friendly yet firm way,
that I was his retained jockey and if I wanted to
remain that way he expected me to make every effort to
stay fit. I was, he said, entitled to do what I liked in my
spare time but so long as I wanted to go on riding the
horses in his yard he would give the commands when
it came to my fitness. And the first command was to
do what the doctor ordered.

I realised Ralph was right. I had no desire to give
up being a jockey and anyway it was the only way I
knew to make a decent living. Edward's estate had
only one asset, the cottage, and that had been left
to Freddie. I hardly expected to be remembered in his

will, whatever his legal obligations to me as his wife, but at least he had ensured that it stayed in the family.

Being bedridden didn't mean that I was helpless. There was always the telephone, and letters to write. My first call was to James Thackeray. I had thought of leaking the details of my crash to the racing press and trying to enlist their help in tracking my attacker, but on reflection thought better of it. Apart from the real risk of having my tale greeted with the same incredulity as the police had displayed, I wanted to attract as little publicity as possible to my extremely amateur sleuthing. I said nothing to James about what had happened and limited myself to asking him a couple more favours.

The first concerned Corcoran. I was still determined to locate him, and apart from travelling over to Ireland and physically combing the countryside, I decided the best approach was to make an appeal to his wallet or that of someone who now knew where he was. Accordingly I read over to James the following notice for inclusion in the next seven issues of the *Sportsman*:

MICHAEL CORCORAN
Formerly employed in Tom Radcliffe's yard at Wantage and now believed to be working or seeking employment in stables in Ireland. Would the above or anyone knowing of his whereabouts contact Amy Frost at Messrs Arthurs, solicitors,

Lincoln's Inn, London. Substantial reward payable. All replies treated in strictest confidence.

I didn't know what I meant by substantial, or for that matter where I was going to find the money to pay even a modest reward. I hoped I could deal with that particular problem as and when the occasion arose. James said he would make sure the notice would be given a prominent position in the classified section of the paper.

The second favour concerned Musgrave. When I encountered him at Kempton Park, I had accused him of being behind Brennan's efforts to stop me winning at Worcester. I was convinced that he had been responsible for Fainthearted drifting out in the betting – knowing I wouldn't win allowed him to offer generous odds – and once again I was hoping that James's contacts in the betting world would help me find out if I was right. He agreed on one condition.

'What's that?' I asked good-humouredly, expecting another request for an exclusive interview.

'I think it's time you let me in on this one, Victoria. My keen nose for scandal smells a juicy tale of corruption and skulduggery and I want to be in on it. What precisely is the low-down on Musgrave?'

I didn't bother to argue. Even if Musgrave had nothing to do with Edward's death, I was certain to obtain a more sympathetic hearing at the Jockey Club on my appeal if I could prove a direct link between Brennan's riding and the odds offered by a crooked bookmaker. I told James about my suspicions over the running of the Worcester race and how I was certain that Brennan and Musgrave were in each other's pockets. Brennan's performance at Kempton the day before had only confirmed my theory. James was cock-a-hoop at the prospect of a scandal.

'I like this a lot,' he announced as soon as I had finished. 'I can see it already splashed across the front page of the *Sportsman*:

"TOP JOCKEY AND BOOKIE IN BETS PROBE."

Yes, this could be very good indeed.'

'Hold on. Don't forget yours truly. I want you to make it clear that I was the innocent party at Worcester and that Ralph was utterly blameless. That's even more important than clearing me.'

'I won't let you down. I'll get cracking straight away, checking out all the races over the past six months when Brennan has been riding the likely favourite. Whenever it's drifted in the market and then been beaten, we'll find out if Musgrave was responsible for the odds going out.'

'It's not just horses ridden by Brennan, don't forget. At Worcester he was on one of the less fancied runners, and devoted his energies to stopping me winning on the favourite.'

'And Musgrave offered generous odds on your horse?'

'Got it in one.'

'That means rather more work to do. I suppose I'll have to look into every race in which Brennan has been riding to see if anything untoward happened. That's a pretty major task and it's going to take some time, I'm afraid.' James was sounding a little less ecstatic.

'You can do it,' I urged him. 'Why not start with yesterday's race at Kempton and work backwards? At least it's still fresh in everybody's mind.'

'I agree. I'll try and persuade the editor to order the videos of that race and yours at Worcester, although it won't be easy. He's so tight he makes Jack Benny seem generous.'

'Jack who?'

'Forget it. I'd better crack on with the work. Promise you'll keep in touch and I'll let you know as soon as I've got anything. Bye – and Victoria, take care.'

Having finished with James, I wrote to Sir Arthur Drewe. Penning a letter to the steward who has reported you to Portman Square takes a fair amount of courage and to give me inspiration I took out the incriminating photograph of the noble baronet from its hiding place in my wardrobe. It did the trick.

Dear Sir Arthur,

I have just cleared out my late husband's posses-sions and in doing so found a touching photograph of you giving the benefit of your racing knowledge to a lucky permit holder. I had forgotten how strik-ing your racing colours are and didn't realise that

you knew how to ride so well. I wondered whether you and your wife would like the original back for your album or if you would prefer I disposed of it in any manner I saw fit. No doubt the racing press would welcome its inclusion in their picture library for the day when you are appointed senior steward. Assuring you of my best intentions at all times,
   Victoria Pryde.

I addressed the envelope to Sir Arthur at his estate in Gloucestershire and gleefully stuck on a first class stamp. I would have given anything to see the old boy's face as he read that over breakfast.

There wasn't much else I could do with myself for the rest of the day, except catch up with the form books and, most importantly of all, telephone my mother and talk to Freddie. He always enjoyed staying with his grandmother and she for her part loved having him. I could tell from his cheerful voice that I wasn't missed and he was quite content to ride around the farm on the pony which my mother kept for that very purpose. I was extremely glad that he was no longer at Ralph's. Up until yesterday I had never given any serious thought to potential danger to myself, let alone to Freddie. Musgrave's threat had changed all that and last night's events had vindicated my decision to send the boy away. There now had to be a real risk that whoever wanted me dead would try again.

Arming myself against another attack was one of

my first priorities, but to be honest I had no idea where to begin. Eau de cologne had done the trick the other night although it was hardly likely to be as effective a second time. I considered buying a gun, but even if I managed to obtain one I was a rotten shot and would be more likely to injure myself than anybody else. A knife was a more practical possibility yet even then I wasn't confident of being dextrous enough to wield it properly. In the end I settled on the idea of a container with a suitably toxic substance that I could throw or spray into an attacker's face and I made a note to ask Amy for a suitable suggestion when we next talked. As a lawyer who had acted for all sorts of hardened criminals she was bound to know about that kind of thing. I spent the rest of the day and Saturday sleeping and recuperating and on Sunday felt well enough to drive over to my mother's house to see Freddie. As far as I know, nobody followed me there or back.

On Monday the doctor called again – personally I would have been just as happy with the vet – and after a lot of umming and aahing, punctuated by the occasional prodding of my back with his cold hands, he declared that nothing was broken and the bruising would soon go down. As far as he was concerned, I was fit to walk around the place and as from Friday could ride again. Ralph was delighted and made me promise to take things easy all week and return to race riding the following Monday. Reluctantly I agreed. I could do nothing until James Thackeray came up with the further information on Musgrave, or there was a positive response to the notice in the *Sportsman* about Corcoran. Amy had telephoned on Sunday and agreed to contact me as soon as she received any serious response. She didn't pretend to be hopeful. Monday's silence suggested she might be right.

Tuesday morning started badly with a letter from Tom. I had had no contact with him since his arrest, as his lawyers had advised him against communicating with me. As a likely, albeit reluctant, witness for the prosecution I was deemed one of the enemy. Happily it now seemed that he had decided to ignore his lawyer's advice and, recognising the handwriting on the envelope, I eagerly tore it open. The letter, headed Brixton Prison, made sad reading.

My dear Victoria,

How are you? You have been constantly in my thoughts since this whole ghastly business began. I like to tell myself that it is all a bad dream and that I will wake up in the morning in Wantage and leap out of bed to ride out. This cell is damp and cramped, and I'd swap it for a horse-box any day. Victoria, you know I didn't kill Edward. There were times when I wanted him dead but that's a far cry from actual murder. I've heard from my brief (that's what they call your barrister in here) that Jamie Brown told the police about our conversation that day after the Gold Cup and the police are going to call him as a witness at the trial. Poor old

Jamie! I'm sure he thought it would get you and not me into trouble. He never did like women jockeys! I understand the police are claiming that I drove Edward out to the pit – do you remember the time we had a picnic out there? – and then killed him and set fire to the car to destroy any evidence or any trace of the body. I can't remember what happened that night after we left the pub; all I know is I'm innocent. My solicitor tells me that you're trying to find out who really killed him. Please be careful. Freddie mustn't grow up an orphan. Yours with love, Tom.

Looking again at the envelope, I suspected that it might have been opened and resealed before reaching me. Thank God the letter didn't contain anything that might incriminate Tom, except possibly the reference to our picnic at the chalk pit. I remembered it well.

I couldn't be sure, looking back, whose idea it was; all I knew was that it had been a glorious summer's day and, I suppose, like any other illicit lovers, we had gone up there in search of privacy. We had made love on an old rug that Tom kept in the back of his car, covered in dog hairs. It was the first time I had ever done it in the open air. What I would give to be able to do it again with him. The sound of Ralph's voice telling me that Amy was on the phone put an end to any such further reflection. I rushed to the receiver in the hope that she had some news from Ireland.

'I think we've hit the bull's eye!' she said, gleefully.

'After three obscene calls and a man who tried to sell me a share in a racehorse, I eventually got a call this morning from the man himself.'

'How can you be sure it was him?'

'I did what you told me. I asked him the amount of wages that had been taken that day from Tom Radcliffe's yard. He sounded a bit shaken but still managed the correct answer – nineteen hundred and fifty pounds.'

'Great, that's our man all right. Will he talk to me?'

'Yes, but only on certain conditions.'

'Go on, tell me the worst.'

'He'll only meet you in Ireland; you mustn't tell the police beforehand and you've got to come on your own. And finally he wants five thousand pounds to admit publicly that he was being blackmailed by Edward.'

'Obviously this blackmail business is contagious. But five thousand pounds! Where will I find that kind of money? I've only got about five hundred in the bank and it's not as if the winners are coming in by the handful.'

'What about your percentage for winning the Gold Cup?'

'The bank's already been promised that. You see there's the additional bank loan on the cottage to keep up and clothes and food for Freddie.'

'Couldn't Ralph lend it to you?'

'I've asked enough of him already. I can't even raise any money against the cottage as it was in

Edward's name and now belongs to Freddie, in trust of course.'

'You could always ask your father-in-law, or Sir Arthur,' Amy chipped in.

'You mean, do my own spot of blackmailing?'

'I'm only joking – or I think I am. Even if you do somehow raise the money, how can you trust Corcoran? For all you know he could make you hand it over in some dark lonely spot and then do a runner. Result, unhappiness.'

'I know, the same thing had occurred to me. All this stuff about coming on my own and not telling the police is pretty damned suspicious.'

'First Edward and then you?' Amy asked rhetorically. 'It's unlikely. He wouldn't have talked to me about it if he had that in mind.'

'I suppose so, but he might see it as the only way to get at me. He's not very bright, you know.'

'Does that mean you no longer want to see him? He's phoning back at three o'clock for an answer and if it's on to make the necessary arrangements.'

'No, I'm definitely going ahead. I've no option, whatever the risks. What's the time now?' I had left my watch upstairs in my bedroom.

'Ten-thirty and I'm just wondering which client I'm going to charge the last hour out to!'

'I'm sorry, Amy. I really do appreciate what you're doing for me and I'll try to pay you back one day.'

'Don't worry, I wasn't being serious. Look, why don't I come with you? Corcoran doesn't know me from Adam, or rather Eve, and provided I keep at a safe distance I can keep tabs on what's happening and at least be near at hand if he tries anything.'

'I couldn't ask that of you. You've done enough already and as you yourself just said, this could be dangerous.'

'All the more reason for me to be there. You set about trying to raise the money and I'll try and beat Mr Corcoran down on his charges. I'll be in touch after he's called back this afternoon.'

'Thank you, you're a real friend.'

'Don't embarrass me. By the way, is Saturday all right for you to rendezvous?'

'Fine. I'm not riding again until Monday and we can fly there and back over the weekend. At my expense of course.'

'We'll argue about that later. Perhaps we could go to the races before meeting him. I've never been racing in Ireland before.'

'What a great idea. Hold on, I'll have a look and see where they're running. You never know, I might even try and find someone to give me a spare ride.'

I put the receiver down and walked across the hall to the kitchen, where a racing calendar was pinned up on the wall beside the Aga. Limerick and Fairyhouse had the honour. I returned to the phone and suggested that we tried Limerick and met Corcoran in the town afterwards. Amy sounded delighted.

'It's agreed. I'll tell Corcoran we'll meet him there after the races. For the kind of money he's demanding

I don't see why we can't lay down the odd condition.'

'Bravo, that's fighting talk. I'll wait to hear from you.'

I liked the idea of having a ride over there and on the basis of nothing ventured nothing gained, decided to call Willie O'Keefe, a trainer with stables in County Limerick. Willie had chatted me up over the years and had promised to give me a ride if I ever came over.

I obtained his number from directory enquiries and dialled it straight away. Willie was at home, but only just. He was on his way to the races where, he said, he had a sure thing running. He sounded delighted to hear from me and when I told him I was coming over for the weekend to Limerick he took the hint and asked if I wanted that spare ride he had always promised.

'I'd love to,' I said, 'if you've got anything entered.'

'For sure I have,' he replied in his rich Irish brogue. 'What an honour this is for the rider of the Gold Cup winner to be phoning me, a humble Irish trainer and asking for mounts.'

'Stop taking the mickey,' I replied. 'The honour's all mine.'

'I've just the thing. He's called Jimmy the One and he's entered in a two mile handicap chase. He's a stone cold certainty.'

I remembered that with Willie they always were. 'But haven't you already promised the ride?' I asked, not wanting to go round jocking somebody else off.

'No bother. It's only my nephew, Shaun, and the way he's riding at the moment even the horses are begging for the virus. I think it's a great idea and I look forward to seeing you in the weighing room before the first.'

I thanked him and spent the rest of the morning in Cirencester and then Cheltenham trying to pawn my wedding ring and a gold bracelet my grandmother had left me.

That afternoon Amy phoned me back with Corcoran's proposals. At four-thirty, I was to go to Mrs Moloney's tea rooms in Limerick, where I was to await further instructions. After ten minutes' tough negotiations Amy had been able to beat his financial demands down to four thousand pounds, two thousand up front on the day of the meeting and the remainder after he had made a statement to the police in England. It was agreed that he would travel back with us that weekend to avoid any risk of his having second thoughts and pocketing the money.

Amy herself was becoming a little sceptical.

'How do we know we can trust him? He's a self-confessed thief and for all we know may even have murdered your husband. Don't you think we should play safe and call the police in now and let them help us?'

'Are you being serious? I doubt whether the English police have any jurisdiction in Ireland, although you'll know that better than I do, and in any event

Wilkinson regards this whole blackmail business as something I've dreamt up to protect Tom. Can you see the Garda offering to tail me, or for that matter Corcoran being so naive as not to notice?'

'I thought you said he wasn't very bright.'

'I did, but that doesn't mean he's not cunning. No, we're going to have to do it this way and take the risk. If you don't want to come along I quite understand, I really do.'

'Of course I want to come. It was my idea, wasn't it? I'm not going to let you go and meet this man on your own under any circumstances. What's more, I'm coming armed.' That reminded me that I'd forgotten to ask Amy about my own protection.

'What? You're bringing a gun with you?'

'Don't be ridiculous. Where could I get a gun from? I'm bringing a bottle of ammonia which, I'm reliably informed, will temporarily blind any would-be assailant.'

'Can you do me a favour?'

'What's that?'

'Bring two bottles with you.'

She laughed. 'And how are you getting on raising the money?'

'Pretty badly. Fifteen hundred pounds so far, but I've decided I'm going to ask my mother for a loan.'

'Can she afford it?'

'Probably not, but when she realises how much hangs on all this she'll help and she knows I'll repay her as soon as I can.'

'As long as you're sure, otherwise I'll lend you the rest. Let's just hope it's going to be money well spent.'

By Friday I had two thousand pounds in my hands – a fat wad of fifty and twenty pound notes – and I felt an irresistible urge to keep on counting it. I had spent the morning schooling two novice chasers for Ralph and my back had come through without any twinges of pain. During the week I had made no attempt to pursue any of my other leads, having reached a temporary impasse as far as Musgrave was concerned and being too afraid to risk any further contact with Brennan. I had a sneaking suspicion that it had been the jockey who had run me off the road – I had no proof, just an instinct – and I had no desire to give him a second chance to hasten my departure from this world. To my surprise, I hadn't heard from Sir Arthur Drewe. I had somehow expected that he would contact me immediately on receiving my letter to find out what I was after, but it now appeared that he was prepared to play a waiting game and possibly even to call my bluff. What could I do then? To be honest, I didn't have the faintest idea.

The last person I expected to see that afternoon appeared just after five o'clock. Eleanor Pryde swept into Ralph's house as if she owned the place and asked if she could have five minutes alone with me in private. I was having a cup of tea with Ralph at the time, discussing future race plans, and I have never seen him so lost for words. Tall and refined, with a generous application of rouge on both cheeks, Eleanor conveyed an unmistakable air of authority: here was a woman who was used to giving orders and expected them to be obeyed. I agreed to her request, remarking, to Ralph's horror, that it was the first time in five years as my mother-in-law that she had ever voluntarily sought out my company for such a long period. Having been ushered unctuously by Ralph into his study – he even apologised for the mess it was in – Lady Pryde went straight into the attack. I had expected to be harangued about Freddie and asked how I could be so selfish as to want to bring him up. Not a bit of it. Her first act was to thrust out her right hand in front of me and demand: 'Where is it then?'

'Where is what?' I replied, trying to play the innocent.

'Don't be so stupid, you silly girl. Gerald has told me everything. He has been very foolish, very foolish indeed, but I have no intention of seeing everything he has achieved thrown away now.'

'There's no need for that to happen.'

'It's money you want, is it? Or are you trying to blackmail us into letting go of our little Freddie?'

I liked that! Suddenly my own son had become their property.

'I'm not looking for your money and you can leave Freddie out of this. He's staying with me. What I want is that old-fashioned thing called justice.'

'What a noble sentiment! What you really mean is

that you want your lover to escape spending the rest of his life behind bars, where he belongs. How could you behave like this, after what has happened to my poor son? Edward never hurt a soul in his life.' She gave out a strangled, and in my view theatrical, sob and started searching her handbag for a handkerchief.

'Your poor son?' I exclaimed in disbelief. I was beginning to wonder just what Gerald Pryde had told his wife. I went on the attack.

'Lady Pryde, your poor son, as you call him, was a blackmailer who regularly beat me up into the bargain.'

'How can you talk like that, after everything we and Edward did for you? I told him never to marry you, I warned him that you were a scheming little social climber who would drag him down, and how right I was. Give me the original of that letter, please.'

'I can't.'

'What do you mean, you can't? Where is it?'

I lied. 'In a safe place with instructions that if anything happens to me the letter is to be sent to the national press.'

'So *you* are the blackmailer?'

'No, Lady Pryde, just think of me as an instrument of justice. If your husband admits to the police that he was being blackmailed by his own son I undertake to destroy that letter.'

She stared at me with an expression of complete and utter contempt.

'My dear, you are quite mad. My Edward would

172

never have done such a thing. I warn you, you are playing a very dangerous game and if you persist with it someone is going to get hurt.' With that less than noble parting sentiment she turned and strode majestically out of the room and from the house into her waiting car.

Chapter 10

We were like a couple of giggly teenage girls playing truant from school. We checked in one after the other at Heathrow, without giving away we were travelling together and then sat in different sections of the departure lounge. Once on board the plane, having been allocated seats right next door to each other, we dropped the subterfuge and talked away nineteen to the dozen. I suspected that Amy was as nervous as I was, but we were both making a real effort to appear calm and even jolly. She had remembered my ammonia and I slipped it in my bag.

We had agreed that when we arrived at Shannon we would act as complete strangers just in case Corcoran had taken the precaution of coming to the airport to ensure I was keeping to my side of the bargain. We had rented separate cars and Amy was going to make her own way to the racecourse and then leave before I did to go to Mrs Moloney's tea rooms. That way, if Corcoran was waiting there himself or watching my every movement, no one would connect us. He had never met Amy and until the publication of the notice in the *Sportsman*, there was no likelihood of his having heard of her either. Finally, when I left the tea shop she was going to follow me at a respectable distance. It all sounded so simple!

I arrived at Limerick just after twelve-thirty and as far as I was aware, Amy was about ten minutes behind me on the road. From now on, as far as the world was concerned, I was on my own. Willie O'Keefe, his curly grey hair protruding beneath his tweed cap, was already in the weighing room, engrossed in conversation with an extremely rough-looking individual, who had the furtive air of a man who expected to be summoned before the stewards at any moment. Both his front teeth were missing and his right eye was the colour of a bloody mary. He did not look at all happy at whatever Willie was saying to him. To either side of them were groups of owners, trainers and jockeys swapping jokes and lyricising about their chances that afternoon. I waited for Willie to finish his conversation and then went up and patted him on the shoulder.

'Your jockey reporting for duty,' I said brightly.

He grinned with pleasure and doffed his cap. 'Now there's a real treat, and me a married man with eight children! You're looking mighty well under the circumstances and to think that in less than an hour you'll be booting home a winner.'

'Are you really that confident, Willie?' I asked, hoping that he was just hooking me up. On the way over I had studied Jimmy the One's form and it struck me that even carrying ten stone two on his back, he had at least six pounds to make up on the favourite.

'Confident? The money's already in the bank. Did you see that chap I was talking to just now?'

I nodded, wondering what the particularly villainous individual and Willie had in common.

'That's my nephew, Shaun. Ugly looking fellow isn't he? My sister's eldest boy. He's a bit disappointed that he's not got the ride today after his efforts last time out on the horse.'

'Why, what happened then?'

Willie dropped his voice to a confidential whisper and turned me away from the nearby group of trainers. 'Shaun rode a waiting race.'

'There's nothing wrong in that, is there?'

'Only that he was waiting for today's race. That's why Jimmy the One's half a stone better than his handicap rating, and is going to start at 6–1. With you on his back, my little darling, and no offence meant, the odds might well be longer.'

'And Shaun is very upset?'

'Don't worry about him. I just told him he can count himself in for a monkey at the starting price.'

I gulped. Five hundred pounds at 6–1 or better for not even riding in the race was not to be sniffed at. I shuddered to think what Willie himself was going to wager. Here I was coming over to Ireland for a fun ride, followed by some very serious and possibly dangerous business, and I now found myself in the middle of a betting coup. Keep calm, I told myself; remember you've ridden the winner of the Gold Cup. I just hoped Willie didn't notice my hands shaking.

'And the opposition, Willie? Do they have any triers amongst them?' I asked anxiously.

'Just a couple. There's going to be a lot of money for the favourite and the word is the connections are going for a right touch on the bottom weight, Hill of Tralee. They've even flown a jockey over from England for the job.'

I could feel the butterflies in my stomach. 'Who's that?'

'That devil, Eamon Brennan. But don't you worry, my darling, my fellow is fit as a fiddle and you sure showed Brennan how to ride a finish at Cheltenham. Oh yes,' he said, rubbing his hands gleefully, 'the money's in the bank.'

I couldn't believe my bad luck. I was desperate to avoid Brennan and here he was being presented with yet another opportunity to attack me. I made up my mind to leave the course as soon as the race was over.

There was still half an hour to go before the first race and therefore nearly fifty minutes before I needed to change for my ride in the second. Since I had never ridden at Limerick before, or even in Ireland for that matter, I decided it would be sensible to walk the course and take a look at the Limerick fences.

For the first two furlongs past the stands the course was perfectly straight and then two sharp right-handed bends led round to the far side where the ground began to undulate. You then went up a slight hill to the turn, from where the course runs down steeply before reaching the final fence, followed by a stiff climb up to the winning post. Considering the time of year, the going was on the soft side and I had even noticed one or two boggy patches on the far side, almost certainly explained by the close proximity of the Shannon Estuary. It wouldn't be an easy course to ride and if I was stuck on the rails behind a tired horse turning for home, the race would be over before I had time to take part. I was going to have to keep my wits about me and hope that Jimmy the One was as good as his trainer cracked him up to be.

I watched the first race, which was won by an outsider who led all the way, changed and weighed out. Willie was waiting for me in the paddock grinning from ear to ear.

'There he is,' he said, pointing to Jimmy the One being led round by a ginger-haired lad. 'What a picture. Remember he's got speed and stays all day, so do what you like, my darling.'

The horse certainly looked superb. He wasn't exactly thin, yet there wasn't an ounce of fat on him either. He followed his lad around with an air of the utmost confidence, as though he could take on anyone. I began to think this might be my lucky day after all. The bell rang for the jockeys to mount and Willie legged me into the saddle. He just smiled benevolently and wished me luck and I couldn't believe he was so relaxed and confident. He was acting as if Jimmy the One had at least two stone in hand and the only interesting question was who would come second.

Once on the course, we hacked alongside the iron railings in front of the old stand and then cantered back to the two mile start on the far side of the course. Five minutes later, having had my girths adjusted, we were called in by the starter and I lined up on the outside. If Jimmy the One was the business, that was the position I wanted to go round.

For the first couple of fences I just felt my way, sitting about eighth of the ten runners and finding out how Jimmy liked to jump. In fact he was as near perfect as I could have hoped for, measuring the take-off point for each fence to within the inch. I was beginning to enjoy myself, flying through the air at thirty miles per hour on the back of an animal who oozed confidence. Provided Brennan stayed out of my way, I was going to have an enjoyable race.

Everything went smoothly until we came to the regulation fence, or the ditch as we call it in England. Eamon had dropped back on his mount to race beside me on the inside and as we galloped towards the fence, matching strides like chariot horses, he deliberately bumped into me. This attempt to unbalance Jimmy and bring him to the ground failed miserably. Jimmy just changed legs and popped over as if nothing had happened. I now began to make up ground on the leaders and as we jumped the final fence on the far side there were only three horses ahead and I knew I could pick them off whenever I wanted. Feeling cocky, I decided that it was time to teach Brennan a little lesson.

As we rounded the far bend, I took a pull and let Brennan come almost upside me before cutting in sharply and jamming him against the plastic running rail. I could hear him shouting a stream of obscenities as his ankle bounced off the rough pieces of plastic where the rail was held by the uprights. I didn't bother to look round and instead coolly picked off the leaders going down the steep hill and pinged the last to win hard held.

The roar from the stand told me that Willie and his muckers had got their money on and for a few brief seconds I was the toast of Limerick. The cheers that greeted me in the winners' enclosure brought back memories of Cheltenham and Gold Cup day.

I weighed in and changed. Willie couldn't understand why I wanted to leave the course straight away and seemed surprised when I asked him to escort me to my car.

'The bookies won't lynch you, you know. They're a friendly bunch here, even if you have taken thirty thousand out of the ring!'

I smiled, seeing no need to tell him that it was Eamon Brennan whom I really feared.

'My darling,' Willie put his arm around me paternally as I unlocked the car door. 'You were magnificent. Are you sure you won't come to the stables tonight for the party? It'll be one hell of a hooly.'

'I wish I could, Willie, but I've already accepted an invitation from friends in Kilmallock.'

'Bring them along too.'

'They're teetotal.'

'No problem, we've all been vaccinated against it!'

'No, it's just not possible, but thanks all the same. And thanks again for the ride.'

'The gratitude's all mine,' he replied, throwing what looked like a wad of Irish punts onto the back seat, 'and if you ever want a job over here just give us a call. Shaun will understand.'

I'm sure he will if he gets that well paid every time I ride a winner, I thought to myself.

Five minutes later and with no sign of Brennan I was on the road to Limerick town and the first step on the way to my rendezvous with the elusive Corcoran. I killed an hour or so walking round the town and by the time I arrived at Mrs Moloney's tea rooms it was fairly crowded. I was shown to a small table in the corner and a pretty, dark-haired waitress took my order.

Over on the other side of the room I could see Amy hiding behind a copy of *The Irish Times*, doing her best to appear inconspicuous. I had been told to wait at the tea shop for further instructions and that was just what I proposed to do. I wondered whether they would be delivered over the phone or by written message. I looked inquiringly at the middle-aged woman behind the till, whom I took to be Mrs Moloney by the way she shouted commands at the waitresses and asked the customers if they had enjoyed their tea. She smiled back and turned away. My pot of tea and two pieces of toast arrived. Twenty minutes later, having finished both, I was beginning to feel like a prize lemon and tried desperately to catch Amy's eye. I was sure she could see me, although she steadfastly refused to give any acknowledgement of my presence. Perhaps she thought Corcoran might be watching us, but unless he was under one of the tables, he was nowhere to be seen.

What, I wondered, if the whole thing was a practical joke and we were out here on a wild goose chase? At least I hadn't parted with any money; in fact, as a result of the race, I was another thousand-odd pounds better off. I looked over again at Amy and saw Mrs Moloney talking to her. Amy was shaking her head and for a brief second she lifted up her hand as if to indicate in my direction, but then just stopped herself in time. Mrs Moloney was carrying a letter in her hand and now walked over towards me.

'You're not Victoria Pryde, by any chance, are you?' she asked.

I nodded.

'Well that's good, because I've just asked that young lady over there and I was beginning to worry that there'd been some mistake. I've a letter here for you which I was asked to hand over at five o'clock on the dot. A friend of yours, perhaps?' She winked knowingly as she handed it over.

I just smiled, took it from her and waited until she

was behind the till again before opening it. The instructions had been typed out: 'Leave here and drive out of Limerick in the direction of Tipperary. After half a mile, take a left turning signposted Kilconnell. Go through the village, and then take the third turning on the right signposted Tipperary. After two miles turn right at a crossroads and after another two miles you will come across a track on the left, leading to Milligan's Farm. Drive down the track, park in front of the farm and enter by the back door.'

I began to feel tense and uncomfortable. One thing Amy and I had omitted from our plans was how I was to pass on any further directions. She couldn't just walk out of the tearooms behind me, as Corcoran could be watching me for all we knew. My only course was to copy out the instructions and leave the original piece of paper behind where Amy was bound to find it. The waitress was hovering near my table waiting to clear up; by now there was only one other couple and Amy still having tea. In a voice loud enough for Amy to hear I asked the waitress where the lavatory was and then paid it a visit.

There was no obvious place to hide the letter other than in the cistern, which was black and peeling and could be reached only by standing on the seat. I climbed up, lifted the cover off and put the letter on the top of the ballcock. I just had to hope it wouldn't slip into the water. As I was about to open the door, it dawned on me that if I didn't pull the chain some-one – I didn't stop to think who – might regard it as suspicious. I therefore recovered the letter, pulled the chain and then replaced it again inside the cistern. It was obvious I would make a lousy secret agent.

I washed my hands and returned to the main room and paid my bill. Although I caught Amy glancing at me, I pretended not to notice her. I followed the directions without any problems, and twenty minutes later, after resisting a plaintive voice from within telling me to turn around, I arrived at the front of Milligan's farm.

The building was semi-derelict; at least two of the windows on the first floor were smashed and vandalised. The farmhouse had the dilapidated air of having been uninhabited for months if not years, and I prayed hard that Amy had used her imagination and found those directions. I reluctantly got out of the car, taking the bottle of ammonia in one hand and clutching my handbag with the two thousand pounds in the other. I had already hidden Willie's wad of fifty-pound notes inside my bra. I walked, or rather tiptoed, round the side of the house, avoiding the weeds and what looked like stinging nettles. The back door was closed. Before opening it, I peered through the least dirty of the panes of glass in the window immediately to its right. Over in the far corner I could see what appeared to be an old stove and on top of it a frying pan.

I turned the handle and pushed open the door. It creaked under the pressure and I stepped gingerly over the threshold and into what had once been the

kitchen. I paused and listened. Not a sound. 'Is anyone here?' I called out, the words fighting to stay in
my throat. Still that dreadful silence. I walked across
the kitchen and into the hall. By the front door were a
couple of circulars from which I learnt that a Mr
O'Malley had once lived there. I opened the nearest
door and found myself in what had been the sitting
room. In the hearth were the remnants of a log fire
and dozens of cigarette ends. Now for the stairs. I
took each step as slowly and deliberately as if it led to
the gallows and clung tightly to my bottle of ammonia. I was sweating terribly; my heart was pounding as
if at ramming speed. I was forcing myself to look in all
the rooms – I owed that much to Tom – and then I
was going to run down those stairs, out of the back
door and drive to Limerick as if the devil himself was
chasing me. Amy will be here by now, I told myself.
There's no way she wouldn't be within shouting distance, probably a few yards down the drive. I pressed
on. There were only four doors, thank goodness. The
first three rooms were empty. Just one left. I thought I
heard a noise.

'Michael, are you in there?' I asked out loud,
although it sounded more like a whisper. 'It's me,
Victoria.'

Again, silence. Courageously, or at least it felt that
way, I threw the door open and stood back. Empty. I
ran downstairs and grabbed the handle of the back
door. It was locked. As I opened my mouth to scream,
a gloved hand came over my face, and the ammonia

bottle was jolted from my clammy grip by a powerful blow to my wrist. My mind went dark as my legs gave way under me and I fell to the floor.

'Victoria! Victoria! Wake up, please wake up!'

It was Amy's voice. She was kneeling over me and although my eyes were closed, I could feel her breath on my face.

'Say something, anything, please.' She put her hands on my shoulders and started to shake me.

I opened my eyes and all around me was in darkness. I couldn't feel any pain, only a sense of bewilderment, loss and failure.

'What happened?' I asked, putting out my hand to touch the profile above me.

'Thank God you're all right.' She started sobbing. 'I'm so sorry.'

'Amy, please calm down.' I struggled to my feet, pulling her up with me in the process. 'What's the time for God's sake?'

'It's about eight o'clock.'

'What? Do you mean I've been here for over two hours?'

'I'm sorry, I'm so sorry.'

'Don't keep apologising, let's just get out of here and we can discuss everything in the car. Hold on, where's my handbag?' There was no electricity working in the kitchen and we both crawled round the floor feeling in vain with our hands for the handbag. 'It's no good,' I said after five minutes. 'It's gone and all the money with it. The bastard.'

We walked quickly to the cars, which were both parked in front of the house. I was lucky he hadn't stolen my hire car because I'd left the keys in the ignition. 'Come on,' I said. 'Let's drive in convoy to Tipperary and park under the brightest light in the main street and talk.'

I stopped near the police station, parked and went and sat in the passenger seat of Amy's car. The poor thing still looked as though she had seen a ghost.

'I'm so glad you're all right,' she said, holding my hand. 'I thought for a ghastly moment you had been murdered.' She started to sob again.

'That makes two of us,' I replied, trying to appear calm and rational. 'But here I am alive and well.'

'What happened in there?'

I told her everything right up to the moment when I must have passed out.

'Did you get a look at him?'

I shook my head. 'It was all over so quickly. He must have watched me go in the back door and waited for me in the kitchen. I feel such a fool.'

'Don't blame yourself. He sounded so genuine on the phone, all that stuff he told me about wanting to help his old boss out. Victoria, are you sure you're all right? I mean you – he didn't do anything to you?'

That thought hadn't occurred to me. 'I'm sure he didn't touch me.' It was then I remembered the wad of money from Willie O'Keefe which I had stuffed inside my bra. I asked Amy to excuse me for a second. She watched in astonishment as I slipped my hand down inside my jumper and started feeling about. It had gone.

'The bastard!'

'What's happened?'

'Some money I was given for riding that winner. I put it in my bra for safe keeping. It's gone.' I shuddered at the thought of Corcoran searching me while I lay on the ground.

'How about you?' I said, changing the subject. 'Didn't you find where I had hidden the directions?'

'Oh yes, that was easy. I knew that's why you said you were going to the loo so loudly. I waited five minutes before leaving the tea rooms, only when I came out into the car park the car had two flat tyres.'

'Sabotage?'

'That's what I thought, but Corcoran doesn't know me and remember I did get there well ahead of you. I mean, there was no reason to connect us. The man I eventually persuaded to repair them said it was almost certainly the work of local schoolboys who've nothing better to do with their Saturdays.'

I shook my head in disbelief at the mess we were in. Two thousand pounds of my mother's money down the drain and no further progress in locating Corcoran. Only a short time ago I was sympathetic to the Irishman for having suffered so long at Edward's hands, yet now I hated him. It was my turn to be penitent. 'I'm sorry, Amy, I should never have got you into this mess.'

'Don't you be sorry, I'm just as much to blame. It'll

teach us both to play detective. The real question is where do we go from here? Should we tell the Garda, do you think?'

'What's there to tell? How two girls have come out here to pay an ex stable lad two thousand pounds as a down payment for confessing that he was being blackmailed. They'll laugh us out of Ireland. No, we're going on the first plane back to England and when I'm there I'm going to . . .' I paused.

'You're going to what?'

'Expose that sod Musgrave and make one of my late husband's blackmail victims admit to the police just what was going on.'

'And which one do you have in mind?'

'Sir Arthur Drewe.'

'And how do you propose to drag him down to the police station?'

'By the balls, if necessary.'

Chapter 11

We spent the night in a hotel near Shannon airport and took the first plane in the morning back to London. We were both feeling pretty despondent and Amy's well-intentioned attempts to make me look on the bright side fell embarrassingly flat. The simple truth was that Tom's trial was less than eight weeks away and we were no nearer producing any evidence that might help him. Amy, doing her best to reassure me, made great play of the fact that the case against him was purely circumstantial, and that from now on, our energies might be better directed elsewhere, like trying to find a witness who had seen Tom in the car park after he and Edward had left the pub. That was fine in principle, but the trouble was knowing where to begin, assuming such a witness even existed. No such person had as yet come forward voluntarily. Tom himself had no recollection of what he did or where he went that night. And indeed, as Amy admitted, all the attempts by his own solicitors, including hiring a fleet of private detectives, had proved fruitless. Most people are in bed late at night and those who aren't don't necessarily want to advertise their movements. We were at an impasse.

I arrived back at the yard to find Ralph in a state of deep depression. A date had been fixed in six weeks' time for our hearing at the Jockey Club in London and even though he had done nothing wrong and his conscience was clear, the prospects of an acquittal were about twenty to one against. The disciplinary committee had wide powers, ranging from a fine, to suspension, to the withdrawall of a licence to train, and as far as Ralph was concerned, either of the last two would be extremely damaging. He was in the habit of running his horses on their merits and he certainly would not welcome any public adjudication to the contrary. No respectable owner wants to be associated with a crooked stable. I knew Ralph didn't blame me for what had happened at Worcester, yet equally I was under no illusion that he believed the incident wouldn't have been avoided if a male jockey had been riding instead of me. For my part, I really didn't see how in the circumstances anyone could have ridden any differently. Although I would think that, wouldn't I?

The next day we travelled up to Wolverhampton, where Ralph had two runners. The Midlands course is notorious for its penultimate fence, which claims innumerable victims, and I did well to finish on a novice chaser who seemed to think that the art of jumping was to go through the fence rather than over it. My second ride, in the long-distance hurdle, was a good deal more comfortable. Having ridden a patient waiting race, without any Eamon Brennan to box me in, I was able to come with a strong late run and win, going away by a couple of lengths.

There is simply nothing like the taste of victory and even though there was only a small crowd, I felt the usual sense of elation as I was led back to the winners' enclosure. There are always a few punters who have backed you and come along to voice their appreciation; at that moment I really welcomed it. Even Ralph had recaptured his usual bonhomie and the owners were full of praise and congratulations for the way I had ridden. They wanted me to join them for a celebratory bottle of champagne in the bar and Ralph encouraged me to come along as soon as I had weighed in and changed. Usually I would have jumped at the chance, as there is no greater fun than sharing moments of triumph, but on this occasion I wanted to go down by the rails and see if Musgrave was in action. I realised it was unlikely that he would venture out of London on a Monday to one of the smaller courses, yet you could never tell where greed might lead a man. If he was there, I wanted to go up and ask him why I hadn't heard from his solicitors since our last meeting at Kempton Park. Could he have something to hide, perhaps?

I was disappointed. There was only a handful of bookmakers betting on the rails and none of them looked as though they had done much business. A couple near the top, representatives of the biggest firms, were busy on the telephone, receiving the latest betting information from their employers' shops around the country and finding out what horses, if any, they had to bet on course to keep the starting price down. I stood and watched for a few minutes as the betting got under way for the fifth and penultimate race.

As I did so, it suddenly dawned on me that I was looking at a possible key to Musgrave's dishonesty. Every clerk keeps a written record of the bets his governor strikes and the sheets of paper they use have to be retained for inspection by the tax authorities. Musgrave, for all his dishonesty in not recording off-course bets, wouldn't dare take a similar chance with those made on course. If only I could obtain access to, and copy, his records, I would have conclusive evidence of each and every occasion when he had bet over the odds against a favourite winning, or had offered more extravagant prices than any other bookie. The difficulty was going to be finding out where Musgrave kept them. I was now going to have to add burglary to my qualifications.

Being realistic, I recognised that it would be no use gaining entry to Musgrave's premises and photographing every document in sight. I first had to establish from James Thackeray if he had come across any races where Musgrave and Brennan had been up to no good together.

I phoned Thackeray at work that evening and for once my luck was in. He announced gleefully that his researches were bearing fruit. He had already discovered six occasions over the last six months, excluding the races at Kempton and Worcester, where Musgrave had taken a different position from his fellow bookies and offered generous odds against fancied horses being ridden by Brennan. All six duly ran and were beaten. In addition, there was of course the Gold Cup when I was riding Cartwheel. On that occasion, Musgrave had taken bets from all and sundry and dropped at least a quarter of a million pounds as a result. Thackeray was no fool and he asked me on the phone whether I'd been aware that anything improper had been going on in the Cheltenham race. I hesitated before replying. On the one hand I wanted and needed James's help and that required my co-operating with him. On the other hand, to tell him that I knew Cartwheel was meant to lose implicated me in Musgrave's crookedness. I decided that it was time to come clean – well, almost clean – and tell him about Edward's involvement with Musgrave. I admitted that I had pulled two horses on Edward's orders earlier in the season and had done so only because I had had no option. It was James's turn now to hesitate. I could sense that he was torn between his instinct as a good journalist to expose the whole sordid story, and his loyalty to me as a friend and as the original source for his broader investigation.

'This isn't easy, Victoria,' was his first comment.

'I know that, James. It hasn't been that easy for me keeping it from you. I'm not asking forgiveness or pity for what I did; I know I've flagrantly broken the rules and cheated not just the owners of those two horses and dear old Ralph, but a whole lot of punters as well. That's why I couldn't go through with it on Cartwheel at Cheltenham. I was intending to stop riding for Ralph after that, as a kind of punishment to myself, but then Edward was murdered and I had no reason to cheat any more. That doesn't mean I killed him, by the way. I want to stay in racing and I don't want my son to grow up knowing that his mother was warned off the turf for being a cheat.'

'But there's mitigation; everyone will understand.'

'James, are you serious? Of course they won't. Nobody wants to believe that Edward was a grade A shit who forced his wife to pull horses. The police, and more importantly the Jockey Club, will think this is something I've dreamt up to excuse my own deplorable conduct. You aren't allowed to blame the dead because they can't answer back.'

'Are you suggesting that I cover this up, leave your involvement out of any story I write?'

'In a word, yes. You don't need to implicate me in order to expose Musgrave as a villain.'

'And what if he spills the beans and says you were in it right up to your racing goggles?'

'I'd deny it and call him a liar. That's where

Edward's enforced silence works to my advantage, don't you see? Musgrave can't prove I threw away the Fontwell and Worcester races unless I confess, and I did win at Cheltenham, don't forget. That was hardly the ride of a bookie's stooge. "Inspired" I think you called it at the time. Please, James, if not for my sake, then for Freddie's?' I could feel he was wavering.

'All right, provided you give me all the help I need to fix Musgrave.'

'It's a deal and I've an idea just where to begin. His betting sheets.'

'The field sheets? You mean the records of all the bets he's taken on course?'

'Whatever. He's obliged to keep them by the tax authorities, isn't he? If we can obtain copies of the recorded entries for the races you suspect were crooked, we'll be able to nail him.'

'It's a brilliant idea and about as feasible as photographing a flying pig. How do you suggest we get hold of these records? Give Musgrave a call and ask him for permission to come round and photocopy them?'

'Not exactly. Assuming he keeps them at his office, what's wrong in us breaking in one night and taking photographs?'

'Oh nothing at all. I mean, I used to blow safes in my spare time at university and . . .'

'Don't be so cruel. It was only a suggestion.'

'I'm sorry, I was just teasing. No, Victoria, I simply don't see how it's possible.'

'I've got a better idea. Bookies have to keep records so that the tax men can come and check they've paid up the proper duty on off-course betting, right?'

'Correct. Although they've abolished tax for on-course bets they still levy it for off-course. The Customs and Excise boys are in charge of it and can be quite difficult, so I'm told. One of their tricks is to place bets themselves in the shops and then make unannounced calls on the bookmakers concerned and see if the bets are accurately recorded.'

'I wonder if they ever back any winners? That's it then! Why don't we pose as a couple of Excise officers and call in and do a random check at Musgrave's head office one afternoon? Once alone with the books, we could photograph the relevant pages and bob's your uncle. How about that for a touch of genius?'

'It won't work. Even if he lets us in the office in the first place, Musgrave would insist on being present throughout.'

'Not if we choose a busy race day when he's at the races betting. How about this Friday, the day before the National? I haven't got a ride and he's bound to be at Aintree for all three days of the meeting.'

James was on the ropes this time. 'I wish you weren't so damned ingenious! It might just work. My problem is that I'm meant to be going up there to cover the meeting, too.'

'Play hookey, watch a couple of the races on the box and phone in your copy as if you were there.'

'Hold on a moment, you don't know my editor. The

last chap who did that is selling racecards at Uttoxeter.
I'll take the unusual step of telling him the truth.'

'The whole truth? Is that wise just yet?'

'Well, not the whole truth. I'll say I'm working on
one of the greatest racing scandals of the year and am
pledged to secrecy, and if I don't do it, our rival will.
There's nothing like the threat of competition. We all
live for exclusives.'

'Wonderful. We're agreed. You find out where
Musgrave's head office is in London and on Friday
we'll pay them a surprise visit.'

'Victoria, this worries me, you know.'

'Call yourself a punter?'

There was one other piece of information which I also
hoped to glean from Friday's visit. According to
Edward, Musgrave had never recorded the off-course
bets he had struck with him. That had been done to
avoid paying betting tax and was quite simply a fraud
on the Revenue. The only proof of those bets I had
in my possession was the written demand from
Musgrave, along with the other incriminating documents I had found in the butt of Edward's gun.

If, as I hoped, the records contained no mention of
any bets struck by Edward, I could establish that
Musgrave had been cheating and therefore had a
motive for wanting Edward dead; that Edward had
tried to make me pull Cartwheel in the Gold Cup in
part settlement of his gambling debts and when I had
failed to go along with the plan, Edward had paid

with his life. I had so far kept the secret of Edward's gambling debts from James, and decided that I would give him the final piece of the jigsaw only if and when our visit had been successful.

I couldn't wait for Friday to arrive, and apart from having a single ride at Plumpton on the Wednesday, kept a deliberately low profile. I knew that I still had to take some action about Sir Arthur Drewe and was torn between a showdown and finding a way to put indirect pressure on him. I no longer suspected him of murdering Edward – Musgrave and Corcoran were now far more likely candidates – but I did want him to admit to the police that he was being blackmailed. If the prosecution at the trial had to concede that the deceased had several major enemies, that could throw enough doubt in the jury's mind at least to secure an acquittal. At the moment all they would have was my word for it, backed up by apparently meaningless entries in a diary that I couldn't even produce. Amy had already warned me that there was every chance that if I tried to raise the question in court, the judge could well rule the evidence irrelevant and therefore inadmissible. Indeed, if the prosecution took the view I was a liability, they might not even call me as a witness!

I met James at a pub in Paddington, just round the corner from Musgrave's head office. Since our phone call, he had made a few discreet enquiries, in other words, bought someone a couple of rounds of drinks, and had found out that Musgrave's credit business was definitely run from the same address. There was therefore every chance of all the records being available for inspection. I resisted the temptation to have a stiff whisky, as it always made me go a little pink in the face and feel light-headed. Today more than ever I needed my wits about me if I was going to pass myself off successfully. I felt as nervous as I had done before the Gold Cup. James was pretending to be full of confidence, although I noticed he disappeared to the loo three times in the space of twenty minutes.

At two-thirty we synchronised our watches and marched over the road. In his white shirt, pale blue tie and dark suit, James looked every inch a Revenue man. I also felt the part in a cheap grey skirt and navy jacket which I had bought that morning in C & A. I was wearing my hair up and had further altered my appearance by putting on a pair of plain glass spectacles which James had bought for me from the antiques market in Covent Garden. The big question now was whether Musgrave's lackeys would be fooled.

To my surprise, they hardly registered a protest when we entered. The manager was politeness itself when we explained that we were from the Customs and Excise and were carrying out a spot check on their records on behalf of the district office. As a result, we needed to see all the books and credit ledgers for the last six months.

'You boys usually call beforehand to give us some notice. If I'd known you were coming, I'd have cleared the desk in the governor's office,' he remarked with seeming lack of interest.

'There it is,' said James. 'We've got a new governor, you see, and he's very keen on these random checks. I suspect it'll wear off when he finds out it doesn't produce any results. Where would you like us to work, then?'

He led us towards what I guessed would be Musgrave's office through a room about twenty feet square, in which at least six men were taking phone calls from clients placing bets on the day's greyhound and horse racing. The most up-to-date information and satellite screens were banked against the walls and judging by the activity, there was no shortage of clients trying to get their money on.

The manager, a morose slightly-built individual in his late fifties, saw that I was fascinated by the goings-on.

'Surprised we're so busy, I suppose?'

I grinned nervously.

'It's the Aintree meeting,' he continued. 'Tomorrow's the National and I can't pretend I'm looking forward to it. Like a mad house in here, it'll be.'

'The Grand National, you mean? How exciting, with all those big fences!' I exclaimed, feigning innocence. Once we were seated behind Musgrave's desk, James asked again for all the records and ledgers for the last six months' betting both on and off course.

The manager wearily asked if we wanted him to stay and James politely declined.

'I'll call you if I have any problems,' James added.

As soon as the door was closed, James produced from his pocket a list of the races which he thought had been fixed. The first entry confirmed our suspicions – a race at Chepstow in December, where Musgrave had taken over fifteen thousand pounds of bets on the favourite at prices starting at 6–4 and going out to 5–2. The more money he took, the longer the odds he offered. The same approach could be seen on five other occasions and when it came to the Gold Cup, James whistled in disbelief at the size and number of wagers Musgrave had taken. The only difference was that on this occasion the wrong horse, Cartwheel, had won, and James calculated his losses to be over three hundred and fifty thousand pounds. All the big bookmakers had used him to lay off the bets that they themselves had taken on the same horse at a shorter price and the result was that he had taken a hammering.

I stood guard in front of the door as James photographed all the incriminating entries. He was on the last one when there was a knock on the door and the manager asked if he could come in.

'Hold on,' James shouted as he hid his camera. I moved away to the side and opened the door.

'I'm sorry to disturb you, but I've just had Mr Musgrave on the line from Aintree. He's not best pleased that you've arrived without giving him notice and wants to take it up with Head Office after racing. He's asked me if you would leave your names and those of your superiors.'

I looked imploringly at James who, for the first time that I had known him, was lost for words. His lips were moving, yet no sound was coming out.

'Of course,' I said, taking the initiative. 'I'm sorry Mr Musgrave has taken exception but we're just doing our job. He's nothing to hide, I hope.'

The manager visibly paled. 'Oh no, nothing of the sort. It's just that . . .'

'Anyway my name is Dawn Lunn and my colleague here is Dick Lear. Our boss is Roddy Owen. Unless there's anything else, we've still got quite a lot to go through.'

The manager took the hint and left, whereupon James miraculously recovered his powers of speech.

'Dawn Lunn, Dick Lear, Roddy Owen; where the hell did you dream them up?'

'I'm sorry. There you were, sitting like a lemon and all I could think of were the names of racehorses who'd won the Gold Cup. Dawn Lunn came from Dawn Run and Dick Lear is a cannibalisation of The Dikler.'

'And Roddy Owen?'

'I thought you knew your racing. He won the Gold Cup in 1958.'

'Well you fooled old misery guts there, but I'm not so sure the joke will be lost on Musgrave . . .'

'Who cares? He might guess it was me, but he's no

idea about your involvement and by the time he finds out it'll be too late. Come on, finish off taking the photographs and then I want to look at something.'

Five minutes later, I was seated at the desk studying the credit ledger for off-course bets struck by clients whose surname began with a P. There was not a single reference to Edward Pryde, or any Pryde for that matter, yet I knew full well that he had lost more than a hundred thousand pounds to Musgrave in off-course bets. I asked James to double check for me and he agreed that Edward's name was missing.

'What's it all mean, Victoria?' he asked, when he had finished his scrutiny.

'I'll tell you later. It's time we were on our way.'

We bid the manager goodbye, made a speedy, albeit dignified, exit and hailed the first passing cab.

'The *Sportsman*'s offices in Fleet Street,' said James to the driver and, feeling extremely pleased with ourselves, we headed off to present the editor with our coup.

Chapter 12

I had never been into a newspaper's offices before and my image of them was based entirely on what I had seen in the movies and on the television. In fact, the real thing wasn't that far different except that I didn't spot anyone running around frantically shouting 'Hold the front page' and the atmosphere generally appeared a good deal more relaxed than I had expected. The editorial department of the *Sportsman* was situated on the third floor and consisted of a long open-plan room with offices housing senior staff on the right-hand side. James's desk was over in the far corner and apart from the odd knowing wink and glib comment as we walked over to it, our arrival attracted little attention. Tomorrow was, of course, the National and that was one of the major events in the calendar for any racing paper. There were the usual selections to be made and special features to be put together on the personalities, both human and equine, that made it such a memorable day for racing. James, of course, was hoping to change all that and persuade the editor that the cosy copy which traditionally dominated that day's paper should be surrendered to his sensational exposé of Musgrave and Brennan.

On the way over in the taxi, he had warned me that it would be an uphill struggle. His first task on arriving was to send the roll of film he had taken at Musgrave's office downstairs to the laboratory to be developed. He then sat me down at his desk, fetched a cup of black coffee in a paper cup (they had run out of milk), threw me a couple of racing magazines and disappeared into the editor's office. This was a bit more like it, I thought, the cut and thrust of investigative journalism. He was gone a good half hour before he returned, looking dishevelled and angry. I could tell he had been arguing and I feared the worst.

'Sometimes I wonder,' he said, throwing his notes on the desk, 'whether this is a serious newspaper or merely a *Boy's Own* for horse lovers. You'd think he'd jump at a story like this.'

'He?'

'Carlton Williams, the editor.'

'Do you mean he's not going to print it?' I asked, not trying to hide my astonishment. It had never occurred to me that they might not publish it.

'It's not that bad. I think I've persuaded him that it's a better front page lead than PIN MONEY TO BE THE HOUSEWIFE'S FRIEND.' (Pin Money was the ante-post favourite for the race.) 'He's now phoning the lawyers to see what they think and knowing that bunch they'll be seeing problems here there and everywhere. I can hear it already: "How can you prove this, Mr Thackeray? How do you know Victoria Pryde is telling the truth? How did you obtain entry to Musgrave's offices? What! By posing as government officers? Did you know that you were committing a criminal offence? Have you put these allegations to Mr Musgrave and Mr Brennan?" '

'Will they kill it?'

'Probably not. Old Carlton actually hates lawyers – I think his brother-in-law is a solicitor – and at the end of the day he prefers to act on instinct. Just feels he has to go through the ritual of consultation to keep the proprietor happy. Shit, look at the time! Do you mind if I start writing the copy and then we can go through it together? I think we ought to have a photograph of you to adorn it and I'll just call up the picture library to get one of Brennan and Musgrave as well, if we're lucky.'

An hour later, after a lot of cussing and swearing and discarding of paper, James ripped the final sheet triumphantly from his typewriter and handed the completed copy over to me for approval. He certainly hadn't pulled any punches and on seeing it in cold print I could understand why the lawyers might be anxious.

'It's very good,' I said. 'Do you think you'll get away with it?'

'It's not just very good, it's brilliant. This, Victoria, is the racing scandal of the year and tomorrow is the perfect day to lead with it. Can you imagine what a sensation it will create? Ah, here comes that film back.'

A young gum-chewing messenger dropped a brown envelope on James's desk. It was full of the photographs taken at Musgrave's offices. They had come out beautifully and all the relevant entries from his ledgers and field sheets were clearly legible. James studied them intently for ten minutes or so.

'Good, aren't they? Wonderful things, these miniature cameras. I think we'll use the entries for the Worcester race – that should help you before the disciplinary committee – the ones at Chepstow in December when I reckon he made at least twenty thousand pounds, thanks to Brennan, and finally Cartwheel's race at Cheltenham. It's getting a bit late if this is going to be tomorrow's lead. Oh damn! I've just seen the lawyers arrive. You can always spot them by the sadistic gleam in their eyes – as if they were going to judge a thumb-screwing contest. Excuse me while I go and stand up for myself.'

I had run out of form books and newspapers to read by the time James returned. The broad grin on his face spoke for itself.

'Do you want the good news or the bad news?'

'The good news.'

'The good news is that it's tomorrow's lead; the bad news is that the lawyers have vetoed the references to Edward's murder and his link with Musgrave.'

'But why?'

'Contempt of court, love. With the trial coming up we mustn't publish anything which might create a substantial risk of real prejudice – those were the words the chap used.'

'I don't understand. Surely it couldn't do that?'

'I agree with you, but the barrister in there said that we can't go round making out your husband was a bad egg and so on, as it might lead the jury to say he deserved his fate and acquit Tom Radcliffe on sympathy grounds or because someone else might have done it.'

'They both sound like excellent reasons to me! So Edward won't be mentioned?'

'Not by name, I'm afraid. I'm sorry, Victoria. I did my best, I promise.'

'I thought you said the editor hated lawyers and always ignored their advice.'

'Normally he does, but when they told him he could be imprisoned for contempt, his resistance withered. Can't blame him really.'

'What about the pen being mightier than the sword?'

'Depends on who's holding the sword.'

'I follow.' I was trying to appear reasonable, although deep down I was bitterly disappointed. I desperately wanted Musgrave to have his comeuppance and had hoped that in the process I might have helped Tom.

'Cheer up,' said James, 'it's not all bad. Let me just put the finishing touches to the story, give it to the sub and then I'll take you out for a bite at the Italian round the corner. It'll come off the presses just after midnight and we can see then just how well they've laid it out.'

Three hours later, we had been joined by Amy and the three of us were standing in the machine room waiting for the first copy to come off the presses. As soon as it arrived, James let out a whoop of delight.

'That should fix them!' he cried. 'What price Musgrave and Brennan being warned off now?'

He handed me a copy to read and I had to admit that the editorial boys had done a good job when it came to presentation.

'JOCKEY AND BOOKIE IN CORRUPTION PROBE' screamed the banner headline above black and white mug shots of Brennan and Musgrave.

EXCLUSIVE.

Today the *Sportsman* breaks its time-honoured tradition of devoting its front page to the world's greatest steeplechase. We make no apology, because in order to survive, and for great races like the National to have any standing, racing must be honest and above malpractice. When a corrupt jockey and a crooked bookmaker conspire together to ensure that horses do not run on their merits, it is the duty of any newspaper that loves racing to expose such iniquity. Such is the case of Eamon Brennan, the well-known Irish jockey, and George Musgrave, owner of the chain of betting shops that bears his name and well-known layer on the rails. Our investigations, led by James Thackeray, have revealed an improper and unsavoury association between Musgrave and Brennan, which has enabled the bookmaker to offer generous odds on horses that had absolutely no chance of winning. Why? Because Brennan would ensure they didn't. Not content with their substantial and immoral earnings, the pair sought to involve other jockeys in their dirty work. Victoria Pryde, leading female rider and retained by the Ralph Elgar stable, was put under pressure to throw away the Gold Cup on Cartwheel. She refused, costing Musgrave over three hundred thousand pounds in losing bets. Victoria's punishment was to become the victim of as nasty a piece of improper riding as has been seen for many years on our courses. Deliberately boxed in on Fainthearted by Brennan in a hurdle race at Worcester, she managed only to finish a gallant third. For Musgrave there was the additional pleasure of cleaning up on the so-called generous odds he had offered to all and sundry on the horse, for Victoria only the boos of the crowd and the ignominy of being sent to Portman Square by the local stewards for not riding Fainthearted on his merits. This is one unhappy occasion when Sir Arthur Drewe and his fellow stewards appear to have been looking the other way.

We set out below copies of the entries in Musgrave's betting records for three separate races – the Union Jack Hurdle at Chepstow, the Cheltenham Gold Cup and the Topley Hurdle at Worcester. On each occasion, Musgrave offered better odds on a well-fancied horse than any other bookmaker, continuing to push the price out irrespective of the enormous amounts of money he had already taken. At Chepstow, where Brennan was riding the favourite (he eventually finished fourth), Musgrave made twenty thousand pounds out of on-course bets alone. At Cheltenham, he stood to make at least fifty thousand pounds but Victoria Pryde's courage lost him a fortune. At Worcester, he again offered long odds against the early favourite, Fainthearted, and collected more than fifteen thousand pounds when the horse could only just scrape into the frame. The *Sportsman* has details of six other races where a similar pattern has emerged. We have sent the results of our investigation to the Jockey Club and demand that the rulers of racing take the appropriate action to keep racing clean.

Beside the article was a flattering picture of myself in racing silks captioned 'Heroic'.

'Well,' said James, 'what do you think?'

I kissed him on both cheeks. 'It's marvellous. What do you think Musgrave will do? Sue the paper for libel or something?'

'I doubt it, not when he finds out, if he hasn't already, that we've got copies of all those betting sheets. My guess is that he may well soon be helping the police in their enquiries, along with your friend Brennan. You'd do best to keep a low profile for a bit, Victoria.'

'I agree,' said Amy. 'Why not stay with me for the weekend and we can watch the National on TV. There's bound to be a load of journalists trying to contact you and at the moment it wouldn't be sensible to talk to anyone other than the police and, I suppose, the Jockey Club.'

I saw the logic of their advice. I decided to phone Ralph to warn him about what was happening. It was well past his bedtime, but I guessed he wouldn't be too displeased to hear what was being published. After all, it would have a significant bearing on our hearing before the Jockey Club. Or at least, I hoped so.

We spent Saturday at Amy's flat watching Pin Money duly justify his position as favourite in the National and that night I went to bed early, intending to travel down in the morning to Wincanton to spend the day with Freddie. Amy and I were having breakfast when James arrived. He didn't look as if he had been to bed all night, being unshaven and generally rumpled. He gratefully accepted Amy's offer of a cup of coffee and then told us he had a treat in store.

'On Sunday,' said Amy dismissively, 'there's only one treat and that's lying in bed all day surrounded by the newspapers and the colour supplements.'

'Normally I would agree with you,' he countered, 'but today is special. I have just received a call from Mr George Musgrave, no less, asking me to go round to his office to hear his side of the story. Says he's prepared to blow the gaff on everything and name names, including that of a well-known steward.'

'Drewe?' I asked excitedly.

'He wouldn't say. All he wanted was a guarantee that I would print his version in tomorrow's paper.'

'And will you?' asked Amy.

'I'm not the editor. All I said was, I thought there was a very good chance of it appearing. I can't actually see how we can turn it down, because someone else will do it otherwise. I've agreed to be around there in Paddington in twenty minutes and wondered whether you fancy coming along.'

'What, both of us?' I asked. 'What about my low profile?'

'Yes, both of you. It's only fair you come, Victoria, since all this is your doing in the first place and I wondered whether you, Amy, might do the necessary legal bits if he's prepared to swear an affidavit.'

'I'd love to, but you can't swear them on a Sunday.'

'Typical. At least you could witness his signature on a piece of paper: that would impress the editor.'

'I'd be honoured. Only do you think it's safe?'

'Who knows? I can't seriously imagine Musgrave attacking us, can you? He's got enough problems already and . . .'

'If he killed Edward, why should he hesitate now?' I interrupted anxiously.

'Because it's all become too public. For all we know, Victoria, he may confess to Edward's murder and then Tom is in the clear. Had you thought about that?'

I hadn't, and to be honest I very much doubted that Musgrave saw James as an alternative to twenty minutes with a priest and a dozen Hail Marys. Nonetheless, I still wanted to go with him, if only to have the pleasure of seeing the bookmaker squirm and to find out who else was involved in his wrongdoing. I just felt certain it was Drewe.

The door to Musgrave's offices in Paddington was locked. Ringing the bell and a good deal of banging and shouting produced no reaction from within.

'I just don't understand it,' said James. 'He was most insistent that I was here at ten-thirty and it's now a quarter to eleven.'

'Maybe he's been held up,' suggested Amy. 'Did he say where he was coming from?'

'No, but I somehow got the impression he was phoning from here. Let's wait another ten minutes or so just in case he turns up. I hope he hasn't had a change of heart.'

'Where were you when he phoned?' I asked, out of curiosity.

'At home. I hadn't been in for very long.'

'I believe you. You look like you've been out on an all-night bender. How did he find your number?'

'I didn't think to ask. I suppose he must have phoned the paper last night, or found it in the phone book. There aren't many James Thackerays listed.'

'Do you think there's a back entrance?' asked Amy, who was clearly getting tired of hanging around.

'I doubt it,' said James. 'Do you want to go and have a look while I stay here with Victoria?'

Amy nodded and walked down the street for about twenty yards and then disappeared down an alleyway. She returned a couple of minutes later and signalled us to follow her. The small alley was in fact a cul de sac, used probably for delivering to the buildings on either side. Half way down on the left was a door marked 'George Musgrave. No entry'. Amy turned the handle and the door swung open.

'Simple, when you know how,' she said, beaming.

We climbed up a narrow flight of steps and at the top opened the door that led into a corridor. We walked along it for a few yards until we came to another door, which in turn led into the big square room through which James and I had passed during our recent visit en route to Musgrave's own office. It was strangely, almost disturbingly, quiet without the sound of the phones ringing and the commentary from the racecourse service. The televisions were off and there was not a sound or sight of human life.

'Mr Musgrave, are you there?' James shouted out. Unless he was hiding under a desk it was a waste of breath.

'How about his own office?' I asked, feeling extremely uneasy and trying to put a quick end to this particular adventure.

'Where is it?' asked Amy, who appeared far more

relaxed than James – or me for that matter. It may have been the effect of his hangover but I noticed a distinct lack of the self-assurance he had shown at the start of our visit to these premises.

'Over there,' I replied, pointing to the other corner of the room.

Amy led the way through the desks and for some reason stopped in front of the door and knocked. 'Are you there, Mr Musgrave?' she asked boldly.

There was no reply and looking towards me for approval, she turned the handle and pushed the door open.

People used to queue to watch hangings, yet the sight of George Musgrave dangling from the ceiling made me want to throw up. He had used his tie as a noose and attached it to the old ventilator above his desk. I was surprised that it had taken his weight. Judging by the chair lying on the floor, he must have climbed up on the desk, using the chair as a step, and then kicked it away from under himself. While James leaned out of the window catching some fresh air and making a series of unattractive retching noises, Amy and I just stood and stared in disbelief at the limp and pendulous corpse, its face congested and purple.

'He's killed himself,' said Amy, with that lawyer's gift for stating the obvious. 'We'd better call the police. Come on, James, pull yourself together and dial 999.'

'Do you think we should cut him down?' I asked. 'It looks so undignified.'

'I think we should leave that to the police,' answered Amy. 'You never know, they might want to check it for fingerprints and things.'

'Fingerprints? You don't think . . .?'

'No, of course not. It's just it never pays to interfere. Leave it to the professionals. Come on, James, are you going to call them or shall I?'

The intrepid journalist came reluctantly over from the window, looking distinctly green and under the weather. He dialled the number and asked for both the police and an ambulance, an act which inexplicably had an immediate restorative effect on his demeanour. Suddenly shock and revulsion gave way to the investigative instinct and he produced his notebook from the inside pocket of his coat.

'Right, let's make a note of these details before the Old Bill arrives. Height, five foot eleven, say, although it's difficult to be precise from this angle; shoes best quality leather soles.'

'James, that's a bit insensitive!' I said.

'Sorry, it's just the view. Dark grey flannel suit, nicely cut, brown hair, neck disjointed and eyes bulging. What colour would you say they were, Victoria?'

'Do you have no sense of decency or respect?' I replied.

He shook his head. 'It depends on the circumstances. Musgrave was a crook; he's been caught. He's taken the easy way out. He wanted me round here so I could have the dubious privilege of being the first on the scene. No doubt he wanted to make me feel guilty. As I'm here, I might as well make the most of it. It'll make great copy in tomorrow's paper.'

I couldn't be bothered to argue. 'I think they're bluey green.'

'Do you think the records are still here?' James asked, looking round the office.

'Unless he's burnt or removed them. I hope he hasn't, as they're what I need to prove the link with Edward.'

'I don't think you should try and find them now,' said Amy. 'The police will be here in a minute and we're going to have a bit of explaining to do as it is, without being caught snooping around amongst the dead man's papers.'

James didn't try to argue and we decided to wait in the big room next door for the police to arrive. As we left the office, James turned round and went to glance through the papers on the desk. It was a curious and macabre spectacle – the animated, inquisitive figure of James, and dangling above him the lifeless body of Musgrave.

We duly gave our statements to the police and watched the ambulance men remove the bookmaker, covered by a white sheet, on a stretcher. As they carried him out I felt neither sadness nor relief, only an uneasy feeling that one more avenue of escape for Tom had now been closed.

Chapter 13

I left Amy at her flat and drove down to Wincanton, badly shaken by Musgrave's death. I was conscious that I had been neglecting Freddie over the past weeks and no doubt if the Prydes or their lawyers were to discover he was staying with my mother, it would be paraded in court as a further example of my inadequacy as a parent.

Freddie was delighted to see me and I spent the rest of the day with my little boy, catching up on his news and doing my best to kick a football in the garden. I had kept him away from school since his father died and was determined that as soon as Tom's trial was over, he should return. If the law permitted it, I would sell the cottage, which was now owned by him, and buy another home in the Cotswolds or somewhere like that. Starting life afresh was going to be a daunting prospect and I hoped that at some stage Tom might be able to help me enjoy it and fill the role of a father to my son.

I stayed the night and left at the crack of dawn to return to Ralph's yard to find the governor in none too good a mood. The phone had been ringing non-stop with journalists wanting to find out just how much I knew of Musgrave's activities and trying to suggest a possible link between the bookmaker's suicide and Edward's murder.

Not surprisingly, perhaps, Ralph himself had a lot of questions to ask, beginning with why I hadn't told him about the pressure put on me to throw the Gold Cup and whether that was the only occasion when I had been asked to pull one of his horses. While he recognised that Musgrave's exposure would help our case in front of the Jockey Club, he scarcely wanted to retain a jockey who might be bent. I decided that the best thing to do was to come clean and tell him the whole story, starting with the very first race at Worcester when, on Edward's instructions, I had pulled Fainthearted. He listened intently for nigh on half an hour, during which I recounted the threats and assaults to which Edward had subjected me. Finally I explained why I had changed my mind about the Gold Cup. From his impassive expression it was impossible to tell whether he had any sympathy or not, and as I spoke I had to accept that my racing career might be on the point of collapse. When I had finished, assuring him as I did that I really had tried to win on Fainthearted on that second occasion at Worcester, he rose from his armchair without saying a word and went over to the drinks cabinet and poured two large whiskies. He thrust one into my hand. I thought to myself, this is it, the big heave-ho. I couldn't blame him really. I had cheated him and then enjoyed his hospitality when my own fortunes had taken a turn for the worse. Breach of trust was what they called it in the courts.

To my astonishment, Ralph cheerily raised his glass and simply said, 'Well, here's to us and the future.'

I was momentarily too shocked to react and then, clinking my glass against his, all I could say was 'Thank you,' before throwing my arms around him. He reciprocated by giving me a paternal hug and pat on the back and promptly changed the subject to his favourite topic, the horses in the yard.

'I've decided to run Admiralty Registrar on Tuesday at Sandown. I thought you'd be pleased.'

That last comment was Ralph's idea of a joke. He had bought the horse out of a field on a farm in Tipperary three years ago and this was his first season as a novice chaser. Admiralty Registrar undoubtedly had ability, only it wasn't allied to the slightest respect for the fences he had to jump. He had run four times, winning on the second occasion with me up and carting me twice and the champion jockey once. His owners were fanatical enthusiasts of National Hunt racing and wouldn't have a word said against their 'little chap' (all sixteen hands of him!), who in fact would have been more aptly described as a juvenile delinquent. Sandown was their favourite course and since they paid the bills they were entitled to call the tune as to which track he raced on. Tuesday's race now had every chance of being a painful experience.

Admiralty Registrar's owners were brimming with enthusiasm in the paddock, and going down to the start, their 'little chap' was as docile as I could remember him. Maybe all those weeks of schooling were at last going to pay dividends. For the first mile and a half he jumped like the proverbial stag and as we rounded the right-handed bend to gallop down the far side of the course, I started to believe we even had a chance of winning. He met the first of the three quick railway fences spot on and I patted him on the neck by way of encouragement. It obviously went to his head.

Six strides from the second, I knew we were all wrong. I had either to take a pull on the reins and make him shorten his stride or give him a kick in the belly and hope that he found the energy to quicken his pace and put in a big jump. If I chose the first, bang went our chance of winning, so I opted for the second. It was a mistake. Admiralty Registrar was willing in mind but his weary body couldn't respond to his brain's command. Too late, he tried to save himself coming down right in the middle of the fence. We both turned a complete somersault and as we hit the ground, as if in tandem, I felt a shattering pain in my left hip and thigh. I tried instinctively to roll across to the sanctuary of the nearby rail, yet the mere attempt made me scream in agony. All I could do was lie on my buckled left leg with my right leg outstretched and throw my hands around my head in a protective reflex. I was vaguely aware of following horses racing past but the excruciating pain in my thigh monopolised my senses until there was a searing crack somewhere in my right leg.

A few minutes or so later – it seemed like an eternity – I was lifted into the course ambulance. I know they were doing their best, but it seemed to find every bump and rut as it proceeded at a stately pace across the centre of the course. The crew had strapped my legs in an inflatable splint and given me a pain-killing injection, yet every slight disturbance to the wagon's suspension was transmitted directly to the grating bones in my legs. The St John's ambulance man tried to comfort me but I just felt sick and out of it.

Arriving at the hospital, I was shipped onto a trolley and by comparison with the earlier drive the journey down the corridors was a glide. Even being pulled across and onto a hand X-ray couch was not too distracting, although the fear of having my poor bones reground made me tremble and feel close to tears. Then came the questions, the interminable questions:

Yes, I've had an anaesthetic before . . . broken collar bone, twice, and arm once. No, no serious illnesses but I'm Rhesus negative, discovered during pregnancy. Next of kin? I hesitated on that one, having been about to say Edward. I gave my mother's address. Yes, I'm sure I've had nothing to eat or drink since 11 am. Do I have to sign my name?

They then cut away my riding boots and I begged

the nurse not to try and take them off. She responded by giving me another injection in my backside and within an instant I felt myself slipping away. How delicious it was not to be in pain any more; suddenly I didn't mind my mouth being so dry.

Soon we were off again, gliding down another corridor and into a smoothly plastered room where for some reason they were playing piped music. Yes, I thought I recognised the tune: 'Let it be.' A man in blue pyjamas with a green mask around his neck appeared by my side, smiling reassuringly: 'Just a little prick in the back of your hand,' he murmured as I looked up at him in complete submission.

'Come on Victoria,' he said, 'give me a cough.'

I woke several times and asked Amy whether I was going to have an operation. Finally I emerged from my slumber and surveyed my surroundings. I was on my own in a badly painted room and everywhere around me were vases full of flowers and baskets of fruit covered in cellophane. The sight of a drip pumping somebody else's blood into my left forearm frightened and startled me. My god, I wonder if they've checked it for Aids? Hadn't anyone told them I had banked some of my own blood in a London clinic in case I ever had an accident? My legs. Gingerly lifting my head from the pillow, I tried to take in the scene and the full extent of the damage to my body. My left thigh was enormous and discoloured with a long white dressing applied to the side. My right leg was encased in white plaster of Paris from the foot to above the knee. Why did I feel so tired? I fell back onto the pillow and drifted into sleep again.

'Mr Maddox is here to see you,' announced the neatly pressed sister. Mr Maddox, a powerfully built bearded man of about forty, introduced himself as the bone surgeon responsible for the battlefield that had now replaced my previously shapely lower limbs. He had a certain rugged charm, but I had done my share of swooning in the back of the racecourse ambulance.

'That was a pretty nasty fall, ma'am.' The southern American drawl took me by surprise. I had thought the transatlantic brain drain was one way.

'I'm fine,' I muttered, knowing full well I was anything but.

Maddox responded with an understanding wink and started to explain the nature of my injuries. The impact of my fall had been so great that my left femur had snapped in the middle and the consequent muscle spasm had caused the two pieces to cross over in the well-known pirate flag design. The swelling of my thigh was due to several pints of my blood being pumped into the surrounding muscles and that was why somebody else's was now being used to top me up.

'I'm afraid, if that wasn't enough, you had even more bad luck when one of the horses following on behind you stamped on your right shin as he was passing. We've managed to reduce that fracture and get good alignment so it's just a question of time for the tibia to knit together with the plaster of Paris holding things in position. All clear?'

'Painfully so. Thank you.'

'The femur was hard work and I've screwed in a metal plate to keep the healing bone in proper alignment.' He took an obvious satisfaction in his work and at least I could feel confident I was in safe hands.

'How long before I can walk again?' I was too terrified to ask the question I most wanted answered.

'Well, that will depend on a number of factors. We'll take a couple of X-rays in the next day or so to check that the positions are satisfactory, which I'm sure they will be. You're young, so the bones should reunite quickly.'

'How long then?'

'Hold on, little lady, don't rush things. You have to accept this is going to be a long and frustrating recovery. The first target is to get you out of bed and then gradually walking on crutches. If you ask the bones to take any weight or strain they won't mend and you'll end up a cripple – which wouldn't be in anybody's interest, would it? Is there anything else?'

I thought that was plenty to be going on with. I thanked him and he left me to my own thoughts.

I tried to forget everything by sleeping, but even that was difficult. My body had been given over to medical light-engineering and all that entailed. My right foot had begun to itch under the plaster, my left leg throbbed and I felt thoroughly seedy. I still had that confounded drip in my left forearm although the nurse did at least tell me she thought it would come down tomorrow. That would be Thursday. Every time I attempted to find a comfortable position or moved a lower extremity, the ensuing sharp pain woke me from my slumber and brought me back to the depressing reality of my side room.

Around about midday, or at least I thought it was, I received my first visitor. If you had offered odds on who it would be, I would have expected at least 66–1 *against* this particular individual. Without bothering to inquire after my condition, he came and stood beside me at the head of the bed and launched into a tirade of abuse and threats.

I had never regarded Arthur Drewe as a very endearing or prepossessing character and as he raged on, I was fascinated by the way his left eye twitched in harmony with his increasing frustration. I had no intention of giving up the photograph and told him so in words of four letters.

'How dare you talk to me like that!' he stormed. 'You leave me no alternative but to report you to the police as a blackmailer.'

'Go on, go ahead. Nothing would give me more pleasure.'

I noticed him eyeing the plaster that encased my right leg and I sensed that he was debating whether to try a more physical line of persuasion. I pressed the buzzer beside my bed, and within seconds a nurse had appeared.

'Could you give me something for a headache,

please?' I asked her. 'My uncle was just leaving.' I smiled my broadest smile at Sir Arthur, and presented my cheek for him to kiss. 'So sweet of you to come.'

Caught between rage and embarrassment, he leant forward and under the benign gaze of the nurse gave me a hasty peck, the hair of his moustache tickling me in the process.

'You'll regret this,' he muttered.

'Give my love to auntie,' I said loudly as he turned to leave, 'and to Annabel of course.'

He hardly wanted reminding of his favourite permit holder.

Drewe was followed a while later by Ralph and Amy. They understood that I was too weak and tired to make much conversation. I chose not to mention Drewe's visit in front of Ralph but asked him whether Admiralty Registrar was all right, as my last recollection of the horse was of following me only a few inches away through the air.

'He's fine,' Ralph answered. 'He was legless and winded for a little while but soon recovered and now he's as right as rain. The owners want to run him again this Saturday.'

'Tell them I'm willing if the doc gives me the all clear!' And with that parting comment and a mumbled apology I closed my eyes and surrendered to sleep.

I awoke with a start and sat bolt upright in bed. The resulting pain in my left thigh reminded me in no uncertain terms where I was and why I was there. The room was in darkness and I wondered what time it was. I was sweating all over and my forehead was clammy, as if I'd been having a nightmare. Strangely for me, I couldn't remember a single detail of my dream; normally such experiences linger with me for hours.

My left arm was beginning to burn and sting from the drip, which already felt like a permanent part of me. For some inexplicable reason I was afraid. But perhaps it wasn't really surprising after the attacks over the past weeks and the accident on Tuesday. I tried in vain to adjust my eyes to the blackness that enveloped me like smog. I reached for the small box on the table beside my bed which contained the buzzer for calling the night nurse. I knew it was unfair but I just wanted to see a friendly face and have a reassuring chat. My outstretched right hand could feel the contours of a glass and the cover of a magazine that Amy had brought me, but that was all. I must have knocked the box onto the floor during my nightmare and now I was in no state to bend down and pick it up. At least I had stopped sweating and I was beginning to feel more relaxed.

I rolled over and tried to work myself into a more comfortable position in which to sleep. I dropped myself firmly onto my right shoulder and after wriggling my head against the pillow, began reliving my victory in the Gold Cup. I had reached the second-last fence from home when I thought I heard a rustling sound in the far corner of the room, where they had stacked the flowers and fruit. I listened

carefully for another noise or movement. The back of
my neck was beginning to prickle and I chided myself
for behaving like a child. I held my breath for what
seemed like a good thirty seconds. Not a sound, not
a murmur . . . I shifted my weight yet again and
returned to the race. Cartwheel pinged the last two
fences and we galloped up that gruelling final hill to
the winning post. As we passed the line, I lifted my left
arm, drip and all, to give the old fellow a pat on the
shoulder, just as I'd done all those weeks ago. Out of
the darkness a hand shot forward, forcing my forearm down onto the mattress, and a coarse cloth
engulfed my face, stifling my screams. I thought I felt
the drip moving as I twisted and struggled to draw
breath, before fading and falling headlong into a
bottomless pit.

I awoke in a hysterical state, screaming. I opened my
eyes expecting to see the face of my intruder and was
puzzled and relieved to see the gentle smiling face of a
nurse.

'Who are you?' I asked, almost in a whisper.

'I'm Agnes, your night nurse,' she replied with a
definite Italian accent.

'Where's he gone? Did you catch him?'

'Who?' asked Agnes, calm and comforting.

'The man who came in here just now and attacked
me.'

'There was no man. You've just been having a bad
dream. You've been through a lot lately, poor thing.'

I wasn't going to stand for that. 'I'm sorry, but there really was a man. I wasn't dreaming. He grabbed my arm and did something to the drip. Look,' I said, holding up my arm for her to see. 'The bandage is loose.'

'The safety pin must have come off while you were asleep, that's all. Let me tidy it up for you.' Agnes took the bandage off and then wrapped it round my arm, fastening it again with a safety pin.

'You go back to sleep and I'll ask Dr Fox to see about taking the drip down first thing in the morning.'

She doesn't believe me, it's obvious, I thought to myself. Nobody's going to believe me. I kept on repeating it to myself until I fell asleep and dreamt I was on trial for my own murder.

Dr Fox did not inspire quite the same degree of confidence as Mr Maddox. It might just have been his youthful looks, or the blond curly hair that made him look as if he'd be more at ease on a plinth in Ancient Greece than in a hospital in Surrey. I would have bet any money he was a ladies' man who liked to start the day with a nurse for breakfast, preferably sunny side up.

'Good morning, Mrs Pryde. I hear you had rather a disturbed night.'

'That's an understatement. A man came into my room and attacked me.'

He didn't reply and concentrated his attention

instead on the clip board he had just picked up from the foot of my bed.

'Some of those pain killers you're taking are very powerful, you know,' he said, flicking over the pages of the chart and deliberately avoiding my eye. 'Are you drinking all right now?'

'Yes, I am, but I did *not* imagine what happened last night. It's my legs that were hurt in the fall you know, not my head.'

'You're going through a very difficult time, Mrs Pryde, I do understand. I'll tell staff nurse to come and take your drip down and I'll have a word with Mr Maddox about your drugs.' He flashed me a nervous smile and shot out of the room.

Ten minutes later the staff nurse arrived to take the pipe work out of my vein.

'Can I have a look at that?' I asked politely, as she was turning to go with a half empty bag of saline and drip set.

She hesitated, her face betraying considerable doubt about the wisdom of allowing me such an inspection. Fox's diagnosis had clearly taken hold in the nurses' room.

'I suppose so,' she said, handing it over to me slowly, as if it was a loaded shotgun and I had just been declared unfit to have a firearms licence. I studied the plastic tube intently, gently bending it between finger and thumb. A few inches from the end, tiny beads of the clear saline leaked through a microscopic hole into the wall of the tubing. I held it up triumphantly for the nurse to see.

'Who's mad now?' I asked, defiantly.

I insisted on holding onto the drip and showing it to Amy when she arrived. She listened in horror as I told her about my night visitor, and went on to fill her in about Drewe's threats the previous day.

'You don't think it could have been him, do you?' she asked, when I had finished.

I shook my head. 'It's the usual story: I just didn't get a proper look at him. This is the third time I've been attacked and I'm becoming more and more terrified. Look at me: I'm helpless. But if it *wasn't* Drewe, how the hell did whoever it was know where to find me?'

'That was easy. The news of your fall was all over the papers yesterday and the *Sportsman* made it their front page lead. You're a hot property, you know, because of all this Musgrave business.'

'Am I? I'm not doing Tom any good that way. It's very kind of you to come and see me again. At times like this you really know who your friends are.'

She smiled. 'Has Freddie been told?'

'All he knows is that mummy's had a little riding accident and has to spend a few days in hospital. In fact it could be more like weeks. They won't give me a date when I can walk again and I expect I'll have to give evidence from a wheelchair or standing on crutches. Never mind. Back to business. What are we going to do with this drip? I want to have the hole looked at and if possible the contents analysed. Could you fix that? Somebody tried to kill me last night and I'm not going to blame it on the National Health Service.'

Amy laughed. 'At least you seem to be keeping your

sense of humour. Do you think they'll let me take it away with me?'

'Almost certainly not, so we won't ask them. By the time they discover it's gone it'll be too late. Do you know someone who can examine it?'

'There's a forensic chap, lovely old boy, we use in criminal cases. It'll cost a bit, I'm afraid.'

Corcoran's antics had left me strapped for cash, but I had no other option now left open to me.

'Okay. I'll find it somehow. Can he do it quickly?'

'I'll send it round this afternoon and ask him to do it at once as a personal favour. It should work. What about you? Will you be all right on your own here?'

'I'll have to be, and anyway, I don't see him making a return visit. If I kick up enough fuss they may even step up the number of checks by the night nurse.'

'Good. I'm sorry I've got to get back to the grind. I'll crack on with this and come and see you after work tomorrow.' She carefully wrapped the drip in a tissue from my bedside table and slipped it into her handbag. 'Is there anything else you need?'

'I wouldn't mind some mint chocolates actually! Since I won't be riding for a few months I might as well enjoy myself.'

'That's the spirit,' she said, squeezing my left leg affectionately. They could hear the scream in the nurses' room down the corridor.

Chapter 14

I had hoped for a peaceful day on the Friday, but it was not to be. The sight of Amy and James bursting into my room, just after breakfast, told me something was up. It was Musgrave. The police had visited James the night before to discuss the results of the pathology report on the bookmaker's body. Tests showed that he had already been dead for at least nine hours when we found him. None of us was in a position to argue with that piece of forensic evidence, although if that was the case, just who had telephoned James at nine o'clock in the morning pretending to be Musgrave, and why? The police were suspicious without giving anything away and James wasn't at all clear from their line of questioning whether they accepted his version of events or whether they were hinting at more serious goings on. They wanted to make an appointment to come and see me as well.

'You don't think they're building up to another

murder case, do you?' I asked, wanting to pull the sheets up over my head.

James contrived to look extremely serious. 'That's exactly what occurred to us. Don't worry, I don't think *we're* going to be fingered, but if they're right and somebody did close Musgrave's account prematurely, the next question has to be who and then why?'

'Would you recognise the voice of the chap who talked to you on the phone?' asked Amy.

James shook his head. 'It was rather nondescript. I suppose, looking back, he could have had a handker-chief over the receiver to take away any distinctive features. To be honest, I was still half sozzled and in fact nearly didn't even get to the phone in time. I'd never spoken to Musgrave before so I just naturally assumed it *was* him.'

'Don't worry,' I said. 'Nobody can blame you for being taken in. This is all becoming pretty sinister. You don't think it could be Drewe trying to shut up everybody who has something on him?'

'I don't follow,' said James. 'What's Drewe got to do with all this? I'm fed up with all this talking in riddles. Is this another thing you've been holding back from me, Victoria?'

I looked to Amy for guidance and she duly obliged.

'Go on, you'd better put him out of his misery.'

'Okay, then. It's like this. In addition to his gam-bling exploits, my husband was, I'm afraid, a shame-less blackmailer and Sir Arthur Drewe, along with one or two other people whose names needn't concern you, was one of his victims.'

'How exciting! Why didn't you tell me this before? Do those names include Musgrave and Brennan?'

'I'm afraid so. Musgrave was also my husband's off-course bookmaker to whom he was in debt for about a hundred thousand pounds. Those bets were unofficial – you know, unrecorded, to avoid betting tax – and the only proof I've got is a written demand from Musgrave to Edward to pay up or else.'

James's eyes nearly popped out of his head. 'And I thought I was a bad gambler.'

'Can I continue? I also have in my possession an incriminating photograph of Sir Arthur in flagrante delicto with a lady permit holder. I suspect, from something Edward told me before he was murdered, that Sir Arthur was amenable to helping out in the stewards' room when it was necessary to have a result, shall we say, rearranged?'

'You mean if the wrong horse had won – let's say a horse that Edward or Musgrave didn't want to win – then Sir Arthur would do his best to get the placings reversed?'

'You've got it.'

'So Sir Arthur would have a very good reason for wanting to shut Musgrave up if the bookmaker knew about all this.'

'Exactly.'

'And you too, if he thought you knew?'

'He already knows I have the photograph.'

'How?'

'I wrote and told him.'

'You did what?'

'I thought I could pressurise him into telling the police that Edward was a blackmailer and that they might wake up to the fact that several people other than Tom had a motive for wanting him dead.'

'And have you had any results?'

'One very unpleasant scene here when he tried to bully me into giving it back.'

'Can I see the photograph? I mean, for professional reasons only, of course.'

'I haven't got it here, it's at Ralph's.'

'Christ, is that safe? Don't you think Amy and I ought to take care of it until you're out of here?'

I thought for a moment and reckoned he was probably right. I asked him to leave me alone with Amy for a minute and told her where I had hidden the photograph and the other documents. She agreed to bring them to me in the hospital over the weekend. We recalled James, who was obviously aggrieved at not being included in the secret.

'It's for your own good,' I told him. 'That photograph might give you the wrong ideas and for the present we need your full and undivided attention.'

'Thanks a bunch. While I was outside, and just to prove I wasn't listening at the key hole, I had an idea. If Sir Arthur did kill Musgrave, why bother to phone up posing as the bookmaker and tell me all that stuff about naming names and so on? Without that call

Musgrave's body wouldn't have been discovered until Monday morning and his death would almost certainly have gone down as suicide.'

It was a good point until Amy shot it down. 'Unless, of course, it was a game of bluff, or is it double bluff? In which case, it's working quite well. My main worry at the moment is about you, Victoria. Somebody out there wants you dead and I don't reckon you're very safe here.'

'There's not much we can do, is there, with me in this condition? I can hardly make a run for it.'

'I appreciate that,' said Amy, 'but how about issuing a statement that you've been moved to a London hospital for further treatment and not giving the name.'

'Very clever,' I said, 'but it'll only work if the staff here don't give the game away and at the moment they already regard me as a raving lunatic. I'll have a go and ask Mr Maddox.'

'I'll see it's in the *Sportsman* tomorrow,' said James, who was becoming restless and looking at his watch. 'If you'll excuse me I'd better be on my way. I'm meant to be at Stratford for the first race and I agreed to give one of the jocks a lift up. I'll call later to see if you're okay and in the meantime I'll make a few discreet inquiries about Sir Arthur's movements last Saturday night and Sunday morning.'

'And include the night Edward disappeared as well as the night before last while you're at it!' I shouted after him.

'Are you sure you're all right?' Amy asked, once we were alone. She took my hand.

I tried to reassure her and myself. 'I've felt better and I don't much like being a sitting target here. It's a great idea, though, to say I've moved hospitals. Good thinking, friend.'

'All part of the legal training. There's one other thing I didn't want to mention in front of James. I've had a preliminary report back from my old boy at forensic.'

'And?'

'You were right. He's found traces of insulin in the drip and they have no right to be there.'

'Does that explain why I passed out so quickly?'

'And also why you're still alive. Apparently, when introduced into a vein insulin knocks you out by instantly dropping your blood sugar level. It's then broken down very quickly into the bloodstream and as long as the dose isn't too massive or prolonged, the body rights itself very quickly. Whoever injected it into your system thought he had fixed you for good, only he undercalculated the dose.'

'And does it leave any traces in the body? I mean, if I *had* died, wouldn't they have discovered why?'

'Almost certainly not. The perfect crime. You see, insulin is a natural substance and so a trace is always present in the bloodstream. Anyway, I doubt whether anyone would have thought of testing for it. Let's face it, it was only because you found that tiny hole in the drip that we had it analysed.'

'Insulin is what diabetics use, isn't it?'

'That's right, to reduce the high sugar count in their bloodstream. Do you know anyone with diabetes?'

'There's only one person I know who injects himself with the stuff.'

'Someone who might have a motive for wanting you out of the way?'

'If his wife is to be believed. My father-in-law. Gerald Pryde.'

After Amy had left I asked to see Mr Maddox. I had taken a liking to the surgeon's relaxed and understanding manner and felt that if anybody at the hospital was going to be helpful, it would be him. He popped in after lunch and I told him about what had happened the night before last. It was clear from his demeanour that he had already heard the official version of events, which put everything down to the drugs I was taking. I couldn't show him the drip and the puncture mark, as it was still with Amy's forensic scientist, but I told him about the analysis and how it had revealed clear traces of insulin. His initial disbelief faded when he realised I was deadly serious and had pointed out that nobody, not even the laid-back Dr Fox, could claim that Amy and the forensic scientist were also on painkillers and fantasising as a result. He wanted to investigate the background straight away and find out whether anyone had noticed a man in the vicinity of my room during the night. I told him he was wasting his time as Agnes the night sister clearly hadn't observed anyone and that therefore my sole concern at the moment was to prevent a further attack. I then informed him of our plan to let the world think I had moved hospitals and asked whether he could issue an instruction to the staff to the effect that my whereabouts were under no circumstances to be revealed.

'It's a very unusual request,' he replied after a few moments' reflection, 'even for such a charming lady in distress as yourself. Why haven't you told the police about this?'

'Quite honestly, because I don't think they'd believe me. I'd rather not go into the whys and wherefores. I just want to be safe for the time being and this seems as good a way as any to achieve it.'

'Not knowing what's behind all this makes my decision all the more difficult. All right though, just this once. I'll tell the nursing staff that it's imperative you are not disturbed and that for special medical reasons, which I am not at liberty to disclose, I do not want your continued presence here to be made public. Of course, that must apply to everybody, including your friends.'

'You mean, no visitors?'

'Just that. And anyway, if you really are under threat – and I accept your fears may be well-founded – what is there to stop your would-be assailant simply following one of your friends here?'

I had to agree. That possibility hadn't even occurred to me. 'Can I keep in touch with them by phone?'

'I don't see why not, but you'd probably be better

using one of those portable ones. My instinct would be to take the hospital phone out of here and then there's no chance of a call being accidentally put through to you.'

'I suppose you're right. It's going to be very boring on my own. How long before I can get out of here?'

'Two or three more weeks, with a bit of luck, and then there's a lot of work to be done with the physiotherapist. I wish I could give you better news.'

'One last question.' I had to find out. 'Will I be able to ride again?'

'It's a matter of time and luck. But if you asked me for the odds I'd say it's about two to one in your favour.'

That was better than I could have hoped for. 'Thank you. I can think of one bookmaker who won't be laying them.'

As soon as Mr Maddox had left I telephoned Amy to tell her what had been decided. I was going to miss her company over the weeks ahead and wanted to ask her to bring down a portable telephone on her final visit that evening. I was very conscious of the debt I owed for her support and friendship and resolved to show it in a positive way as soon as the present ordeal was over. She was on the other line and I left a message with her secretary to call me back. I had hardly put the phone down when it rang again.

'Victoria, it's me.'

'That's quick. I just wanted to tell you what Mr Maddox has agreed about this moving business.' I proceeded to fill her in on my conversation with him.

'That all sounds very sensible,' she said, when I had finished. 'I've got some news for you. When you called just now I was on the phone to Tom's solicitor. There's been a sensational development in the case. Corcoran has reappeared on the scene and has offered to give evidence for Tom at the trial!'

'Do you mean he's back in England?'

'Not exactly. All I've been told by Tom's solicitor, who insists on playing his cards close to his chest, is that Corcoran has been in touch with them and made this offer. Exactly what evidence he's prepared to give the solicitor wouldn't tell me over the phone and I've an appointment to see him at three-thirty this afternoon. Apparently, there's something they think you might be able to help with and that's why they contacted me.'

'Have you any idea what they might have in mind? You know I'd do anything to help Tom.'

'Hardly appropriate talk from a witness for the prosecution! At the moment I'm no wiser than you. We'll just have to wait and see.'

'But what about his performance in Ireland, and my two thousand pounds? Can you trust the man?'

'I was going to ask specifically about that when we meet. At the moment we've nothing to gain by speculating. Be patient. I realise it's difficult, but you can expect me with the full story at about seven o'clock. I'll also bring a portable phone. In the meantime, take care.'

I said goodbye and spent the rest of the afternoon wondering what had prompted Corcoran's change of heart. The thought of more money, probably.

As it happened, Amy wasn't my only visitor that evening. Ralph popped in just after six-thirty with a side of smoked salmon and a bottle of champagne, which we proceeded to devour with shameless relish. My governor was full of good spirits and intent on finding out when he could expect me back in the saddle. As he sat beside me on the bed, I could see why he'd been such a ladies' man over the years. I repeated Maddox's forecast and he reiterated that my job would be waiting for me. From my point of view, the one bit of luck was that the National Hunt season was coming to an end and I could spend the summer months ahead recuperating.

'I've one piece of news for you,' he said, when we were on our second helping of salmon and third glass of champagne. 'I've had a look at the patrol film of the Sandown race.'

'And don't tell me it was my fault Admiralty Registrar fell.'

'No, my dear, no one could allege that. It's just you'll never guess who was riding that following horse, which trampled all over you.'

'Initials E. B., by any chance?'

'One and the same. Made no attempt to avoid you, almost as if he did it deliberately. The man's a common criminal and I hope they drum him out of racing.'

'With a bit of luck they will. Have you heard any more about the enquiry at Portman Square?'

'The investigation people at the Jockey Club were on to me about it this morning. They want to take sworn statements from both of us and they've hinted that if the allegations in the *Sportsman* can be sub-stantiated, it's almost certain they will drop the case against us.'

'They darn well ought to. That'll please old Drewe.'

'He's been out of the country for the past few days, according to the man I spoke to this morning.'

'Where?'

'Over at his place in Ireland.'

'I'd forgotten about that.' I now remembered that James had included a brief reference to it in his potted biography. That seemed to give him a good alibi for the night of my attack.

'Did he say exactly how long he's been there?'

Ralph shook his head. 'Do you want me to find out?'

'No, it's not important. How's everything at the yard?'

'Fine, I've put most of them away now, for the summer, but I'll run a couple at Devon and Exeter next week provided the going doesn't get too firm. I don't expect too much though. I'll pop in again on Sunday if that's all right.'

I told him that I wasn't allowed any further visits for a short while and that as a favour to me he was to tell anyone who asked that I had been moved to another hospital.

Ralph nodded. 'Not more detective work, I hope?'

'Not really. I'm sorry, Ralph, I'm just concentrating on staying alive and this is one further precaution.'

He didn't try to probe any further and before he left to return to the Cotswolds I warned him to expect a visit from Amy to collect one or two things from my room.

The ever reliable solicitor arrived on the dot of seven, carrying mints, magazines and some exotic French perfume, and wasted no time in telling me about her meeting with Tom's lawyer.

'It was all very dramatic. Yesterday afternoon, Tom's lawyer received this telephone call from a man introducing himself as Michael Corcoran, one of Tom's former lads. He said that he had some information which might be useful to Tom's case. When the solicitor asked to meet him to take a statement, he became cagey and said that he feared for his life and wasn't prepared to come out of hiding until the day he's needed to give evidence at the trial.'

'Is that good enough?'

'There's nothing wrong with it, only that it's extremely risky calling a witness without having a proof, a signed statement, first.'

'So what's happened?'

'Corcoran wouldn't budge on meeting the lawyer

but at least agreed to give a detailed statement over the phone and said he'd sign it if necessary before he goes into the witness box. Tom's solicitor wouldn't give me a copy, but was prepared to read it to me in his office.'

'And so?'

'It's pretty hot stuff. Corcoran admitted that Edward had been blackmailing him for years over the theft of the wages from Tom's office. He also claims – and this is the good bit – that on the evening Edward disappeared, he, Corcoran, had followed him to the pub where he met Tom and they had that famous argument.'

'Why did he follow him?'

'Because he wanted to make him return his confession note.'

'But why on earth would Edward hand it over after all this time? Once he'd done that he couldn't blackmail him any more.'

'I agree. Tom's solicitor asked him just that and Corcoran's answer was that he reckoned he had paid enough and the time had come when he wanted to start life anew back in Ireland. He thought he could talk Edward into it. Anyway, Corcoran says that after Tom and Edward came out of the pub, he saw them get into their separate cars. Edward drove off before he could have a word with him and Tom started to leave, appeared to think better of it, parked his car in the furthest corner and proceeded to pass out. I suppose he must simply have had too much to drink.'

'But that *proves* Tom couldn't have killed Edward.'

'There's better to come. Corcoran wasn't the only person following Edward that night. As he drove out of the car park, Corcoran saw another car follow him.'

'Did he recognise the driver?'

'So he claims. Who do you think?'

'Go on, surprise me.'

'Eamon Brennan. Corcoran was apprenticed with him for a short while in Ireland. What's more, he's convinced Brennan also spotted him. The next morning Corcoran took a boat to Ireland without collecting his kit from the yard and since the discovery of Edward's body he's been in fear of his life.'

'And he'll say all this in court?'

'He says he will. I warned the solicitor about our little experience in Ireland and he said he had already heard about that from Corcoran. The Irishman says he's bitterly ashamed about what happened, only he desperately wanted to get hold of the confession note and that's why he searched you, hoping you had brought it with you. He never meant to hurt you. The money was just too tempting.'

'Do you believe him?'

'From Tom's point of view, what really matters is whether the jury does. It certainly ought to place a doubt in the jury's mind and that's enough for acquittal. There's one thing the solicitor wants from us. That note. They'll have to produce it in court to corroborate Corcoran's testimony and want to keep it in a safe place till then. I said I thought you'd have no objection.'

'You're right. Ralph's expecting you to come and collect some stuff from my room. When you've got it all, hand Corcoran's confession over to Tom's solicitor and the rest you'd better lock away in your safe at work. At least that way it'll survive any further attacks on me.'

'I agree. What do you intend to do with it after the trial?'

'As soon as Tom is acquitted I'll burn it, having first invited Lord Pryde and Arthur Drewe to the bonfire party, of course!'

Chapter 15

I had been waiting for over four days to give evidence and kept wondering what could be taking so long in Court No 1. The prosecution had opened its case on Monday with a speech to the jury, in which it outlined the evidence to be called against Tom and put forward a motive for murder. I couldn't believe they had that much to incriminate Tom. As it was a criminal trial, I was obliged, like all the other witnesses, to wait outside until I was called. I just had to sit, fidget and let my imagination run riot. It wasn't easy. I could have read the newspaper reports of the first three days' hearing to keep myself informed but deliberately refrained from doing so. Amy had warned me that at this stage it was only the prosecution case that was being published and it would almost certainly paint a very dark picture of Tom's position, thus needlessly upsetting me. Somehow I had to keep cool and brace myself not to lose control when I gave evidence. If I started protesting Tom's innocence, it was likely to be counter-productive. It wasn't going to be easy and even though I could now move around on crutches, I still felt like a caged tiger, who knew he was going to be shot at dawn.

Jamie Brown had appeared in the witnesses' waiting room for the first time that morning and after only ten minutes, had been taken into court. I assumed that I had to be next. I was wearing a dark blue suit, no jewellery and hardly any make-up. I wanted to appear neither as the grieving widow nor the fast piece. I just hoped the judge would be kind to me, although from what Amy had told me about him, it was unlikely.

The Honourable Mr Justice Snipe was apparently one of the most feared and abrasive judges who had ever planted their ample rumps on the bench. Young barristers weakened at the knees at the mere mention of his name and even experienced senior counsel took refuge in the whisky bottle after a day in front of him. Once his mind was made up, no advocacy, however persuasive, or evidence, however compelling, could make him budge. One leap into the dark was followed by another even bigger one.

The morning passed painfully slowly and as the bright sunlight outside played through the window of what had become my 'cell', I despaired at the unreality of what was happening. Not far way in this same building a jury of twelve strangers was deciding whether Tom should be denied his freedom for the next twenty years. Shortly after two o'clock, I was summoned. A policeman popped his head round the door and asked me if I was ready. I reached for my crutches and hobbled slowly over to him, down a flight of stairs with his assistance and through two sets of swing doors into a crowded court. All eyes except those of the judge turned on me. Across the other side of the court sat the jury, six in each row, facing the witness box. Ahead of me, perched on high, and towering over his court, was the red-robed figure of Snipe. He was busy making notes and seemed indifferent to my arrival. As an usher led me towards the witness box I glanced over at Tom, seated in the enormous wooden dock with a policeman on either side of him. He smiled at me and grasped the rails which enclosed him.

I could hardly believe the change in his appearance. The warm, healthy glow had gone from his cheeks and, together with a dramatic loss of weight, had conspired to make him look years older. A short and ruthlessly executed hair-cut had robbed his face of its caring and friendly disposition and replaced it with a gaunt and surly air. It was as if he had been reduced from an approachable and understanding officer to a belligerent private.

After taking the oath, I was allowed to sit down and as I did so I noticed a middle-aged woman juror mutter something out of the corner of her mouth to the young man on her right. He nodded knowingly and I could sense that my reputation, whatever it now was, had preceded me. I turned nervously towards the judge, expecting him to say something, to give the signal to begin.

The Honourable Mr Justice Snipe was not, at least in appearance, anything like I had imagined. The stern face under the white horsehair wig was pinched and ascetic, with tortoise-shell glasses perching uncomfortably on the bridge of a hawk-like nose. Tufts of hair protruded from his cheeks, a fashion that I thought had disappeared with the Victorians. He remained buried in his notebook. Then I heard my name being called from the other side of the court. A barrister in a silk gown had risen to his feet and was addressing me. I assumed that this must be the counsel for the prosecution, Redvers Scott, who, according to Amy in her pre-trial briefing, was possessed of a devastating turn of phrase and a merciless manner in cross-examination. He was a highly paid and much sought-after advocate, who was brought in to act for the Crown whenever it was faced with a murder case dependent upon circumstantial evidence or with sensitive undertones. I assumed that the identity of this particular deceased meant this trial fell into both categories. Having led me through the formalities of my name and address and the chronological details of my marriage, he turned to my relationship with Tom.

It was only then that I noticed what was lying on the table in front of him. I had always kept Tom's letters tied together with a red ribbon and now Scott's left hand was gently playing with the bow as he questioned me. My heart sank. They had been missing when I searched the chimney of the cottage and here they were, two months later, in the Old Bailey. It just didn't make sense.

'Mrs Pryde,' he asked in his soft yet resonant voice, 'would you please tell His Lordship and the jury how and when you first met the accused?'

'Tom, Mr Radcliffe, was kind enough to let me ride a number of horses in his yard. I was an amateur then, of course.'

'And when was this?'

'I suppose the first occasion was about three years ago.'

'And did you see each other regularly?'

'Only when I was riding for him. Our relationship at that stage was purely platonic.' I knew that seemed a strange word to use but I was already anticipating his line of questioning. I told myself to calm down.

'And when did it cease to be "platonic"?'

'About eighteen months ago. I think we had both tried to fight against it for some time.'

'How would you describe your relationship with the deceased at that stage?'

'Edward? We were still living together and I had no desire to be parted from my young son.'

'Try and be more precise,' snapped Snipe. 'Ask Mrs Pryde the question again, Mr Scott.' There was no doubt whose side the judge was going to take.

'Let's put it another way, Mrs Pryde. Did you still love your husband?'

I hesitated. 'No.'

'Was the accused aware of this?'

'Yes. I told him my marriage was unhappy, yet equally he accepted that I had to stay with Edward for the sake of my son.'

'Did intercourse take place between you and the accused?'

What a ghastly, impersonal way of putting it. 'Yes, we made love together.'

Snipe's snort was loud enough to be heard by the jury, as he no doubt intended.

'Where did this occur?'

'If we were away racing together we sometimes made love in a hotel room and on other occasions in the back of the car or, if the weather was warm, in the open air, in the country.' Discussing our love-life like this in front of a crowded court made it sound so cheap and unsavoury. I could see the journalists scribbling away furiously in their note books.

'Do you know the disused chalk pit near Melksham?'

'Yes.'

'How often have you been there?'

That was a difficult one. I didn't want to mention the picnic with Tom; on the other hand, if they had intercepted and read that letter he sent me from prison, there was no point being caught out in a lie. I decided to tell the truth.

'Twice. Once with my husband and son, and once with Tom.'

'When did you visit it with the accused?'

'In, I think, May of last year.'

'And whose idea was that?'

'Mine. He'd never heard about it before.'

'How often did you see the accused during your relationship?'

'Not regularly, it just wasn't possible. I'd just turned professional and was trying to establish myself and then of course I had to do my best for my son.'

'But you still found time to sleep with this young man?' boomed a voice from the bench. It was clear that I could trust Snipe to know when and how to put the boot in. I didn't know how, or even whether, I was meant to answer that kind of judicial comment and decided reluctantly to hold my tongue. No doubt Lord Pryde's lawyers were in court taking all this down for the custody proceedings. The uncaring selfish adulteress was not a very flattering image.

'And during this time did the accused write to you?'

'Yes, at least once a week.'

'How did these letters reach you?'

'I used to collect them from a hiding place in the woods above his stables.' However I had answered that one I was on a loser. If they had been sent to my house I would have been called brazen and by telling the truth I appeared duplicitous and secretive.

'Would you look at this bundle please, Mrs Pryde?' He handed the bundle of letters to the usher who marched ceremoniously and self-importantly across the court towards me as if he was carrying the crown jewels. 'Can they be numbered exhibit seven, My

Lord?' asked counsel. A grunt from the bench presumably meant they could.

'Are these the letters you received from the accused?' There was a slight change in inflection in his voice, a quickening of the pace.

'May I look at them?' I asked. In fact there was no need for identification, but I wanted a few seconds to compose myself.

'Finished? Would you please take the first letter in the bundle? Do you have it?'

'Yes.' My hands were shaking as I put the others down on the ledge in front of me.

'Is that dated 16th November and does it begin "My precious darling"?'

'Yes.' It might sound like sentimental bilge in the cold and heartless atmosphere of a court room but at the time I used to live for Tom's letters, and the warm show of genuine affection they contained.

'Would you turn to the third page and read out loud the second paragraph?'

In my anxiety, I dropped one of the pages and only after a good deal of reshuffling did I find the passage.

'Do get on with it, Mrs Pryde,' barked Snipe, looking at his watch and tut-tutting. I began reading in a faltering voice:

' "Why won't you give him up? You say you're afraid of what he might do, but why should you go on indefinitely allowing that bully to stand in the way of our love and your own happiness?" '

The counsel stopped me there. 'By the word

"he", does the accused mean your husband Edward?'

'Of course,' I snapped back, and immediately regretted doing so.

'And do the sentiments expressed in that passage fairly represent the accused's attitude at the time?'

'Yes, but you must understand that Tom would never hurt a fly. I don't deny he wanted me to leave Edward but . . .'

'Would you please take the next letter in the bundle, I think it's dated 22nd December.'

'Just before Christmas Day,' remarked Snipe, pointing out the unchristian timing of my adultery.

Grange continued. 'Do you remember receiving that letter from the accused?'

I nodded.

'Please answer, Mrs Pryde, as otherwise your response will not be recorded.'

'Yes, I remember.'

'Was that left at your usual point of collection?'

I had prayed he wouldn't ask that question. 'No, he left it inside a magazine in the women jockeys' changing room at Fontwell race course.'

'What magazine?'

'*Playgirl*, but it was just a joke,' I muttered weakly. A titter of moral reprobation went round the court.

'Would you kindly turn to the last paragraph at the foot of the second page and read it out to My Lord and the jury. And a little louder this time, please.'

I found it straight away and tried to throw my voice so the whole court could hear me. Neither Tom nor I had anything to be ashamed of and now was the time to stop being so defensive.

' "I cannot go on like this much longer. I love you, Victoria, and want to spend the rest of my life with you. Unless you are prepared to leave Edward . . ." ' I stopped at the foot of the page. 'Shall I continue on to the next page?'

'Please do, Mrs Pryde.'

I read on, ' ". . . I will see to it that he gets the end he deserves." ' I stopped reading. 'But this isn't the next page, there's a page missing, My Lord.' I turned imploringly towards Snipe but My Lord was not impressed.

'Are you suggesting,' he growled, 'that this letter has been tampered with?'

'Yes, I am. I know these letters almost off by heart. Tom never threatened to harm, let alone kill, Edward. It's absurd. What he's referring to here is an old steeple-chaser he once used to train. The horse was being neglected by his present owners and Tom was planning to buy him and give him a decent retirement in one of the paddocks behind his yard. I tell you, there's a page missing.' I could see Tom nodding vigorously in the dock. My raised voice resounded ominously round the court room and I had the awful feeling that my explanations were being met by a silence of disbelief and contempt.

The counsel for the prosecution simply ignored my outburst and continued with his questioning: 'Did there come a time when your relationship with the accused ceased?'

'Yes. At the beginning of this year we talked it over many times and finally agreed that it had to end. I had no intention of leaving Edward if it meant giving up custody of my son. Tom accepted that.'

'So when was the last occasion you saw the accused before your husband's death?'

'The day after the Gold Cup, 18th March, a Friday. I went over in the morning to his yard to school some horses.'

'Did you discuss your husband on that occasion?'

I had wondered when this would come up. No doubt Jamie Brown had already given evidence about it that morning.

'Yes, but only briefly. Tom was upset because he knew Edward had attacked me the night before. He made some remark about giving him a thrashing, he didn't mean it.'

'Thank you, Mrs Pryde, I've no more questions. Will you just stay there, please?'

Immediately another counsel, sitting at the other end of the row, rose to his feet. I assumed he must be acting for Tom.

'Mrs Pryde, it is true, is it not, that Mr Radcliffe readily accepted that your relationship had to end?'

'Yes, I think we both realised it couldn't go on, and he took the initiative in bringing it to an end.'

'And Mr Radcliffe recognised and accepted that out of love for your son you were determined to stay with your husband?'

'That's right. We often discussed it and Tom never suggested that I was wrong in putting Freddie, my son, first.'

'Shortly before your husband's death, did you discover something unpleasant about him?'

'Yes. He was a blackmailer.' That took the court by surprise and I could see the heads of the public in the gallery and the press corps jolt forwards in anticipation of what was to come. Counsel for the prosecution however had other ideas. He was on his feet quicker than a greyhound out of the trap.

'My Lord, I must object. I cannot possibly see the relevance of this line of questioning. It's not the deceased's character which is on trial here.'

'I agree with you, Mr Scott,' answered Snipe, who wasted no time in turning on Tom's counsel. 'Mr Fenton, what on earth has this to do with your client's case?'

Fenton, thank God, wasn't of the school that quaked before Snipe's feet. 'If Your Lordship will be so good as to be patient, the relevance of this line of questioning will soon emerge.'

Patience, as far as Snipe was concerned, was a game for ageing spinsters. He snarled with exasperation and his jaw moved as if he was about to savage poor Fenton. Then for some reason it stopped as if he had thought better of it. 'Very well,' he grumbled. 'Continue for the moment, but be careful.'

'I'm much obliged,' said Fenton, dutifully bowing in feigned respect.

'And how did you discover this, Mrs Pryde?' was Fenton's next question.

'He told me himself, after the Gold Cup. I, or rather Freddie, had discovered a diary hidden in my husband's wardrobe and I challenged him about the entries. He boasted to me that the initials on a number of the pages were those of his victims and the figure against each set was the monthly sum the particular victim had to pay for his secret to remain just that.'

'Did he identify those victims?'

This time counsel for the prosecution flew the trap: 'My Lord, this just won't do. Is my learned friend seriously suggesting that this witness should tell the court about the contents of a diary no one has ever seen and in the process expose to the public gaze and obloquy a number of individuals who have no right of defence or reply?'

Snipe was with him all the way and now Fenton had become the hare. 'Mr Fenton, I sincerely hope you were not inviting this witness to name names. You are well aware that these courts frequently grant anonymity to the victims of blackmail and indeed in this case we have only the word of this witness that such blackmail ever took place. Tragically, her husband is in no position to defend himself against such an allegation.'

Two of the jury nodded in approval, and I could tell from the way he was swaying back and forward that Fenton was no longer relishing his present position.

'I hope to avoid any unnecessary naming My Lord.

I will restrict myself to one individual, who it is intended to call to give evidence on behalf of the defendant.'

I couldn't control myself any longer: 'But that's unfair. That list of names includes the very people who would have a motive for . . .'

'Silence!' boomed Snipe, glowering at me through his spectacles.

I carried on defiantly: '. . . killing my husband, such as . . .'

'I said silence!'

I looked over at Tom with a sigh, and realised by his demeanour that I was doing more harm than good. I stopped talking and waited for Snipe to lay into me. I wasn't disappointed.

'If that happens again, I will have no hesitation in committing you to prison for contempt of court. Mr Fenton, continue and don't forget, one name only.'

'Have you seen this note before?' He handed up via the usher the piece of paper on which Corcoran had written out his confession.

'Yes, I found it amongst my late husband's possessions.'

'Would you tell the court whose signature appears upon it?'

'Yes, a Mr Michael Corcoran.'

'And who is he?'

'A stable lad who used to work until fairly recently for Mr Radcliffe.'

'Would you please read that note out loud to the court.'

I did as I had been asked.

'Do you know how your late husband came into possession of that note?'

'He told me he obtained it from Corcoran by a trick and since then had been blackmailing him with it.'

'I've no more questions of this witness, My Lord.' Fenton sat down and I picked up my crutches to stand up and leave. No more questions.

'May I look at that note, Mrs Pryde?' The counsel for the prosecution was again on his feet.

I handed it to the usher, who in turn delivered it to counsel. He read it and then said, 'Perhaps the jury would also like to see it, My Lord.'

'After I have,' snapped Snipe.

It passed up and down the two rows to the accompaniment of a great deal of muttering. I was now to be re-examined: 'You told My Lord and the jury that you found this piece of paper amongst your husband's possessions?' asked the prosecuting counsel.

'That's right.'

'Was that after his death?'

'Yes.'

'Why didn't you hand it over immediately to the police?'

'Because I knew they didn't believe me when I said my husband was a blackmailer.'

'So you gave it instead to the accused's legal advisers?'

'Yes. They asked me for it and I willingly handed it over.'

'You appreciate that you are under oath, Mrs Pryde?'

'I am very aware of that fact, sir.'

'You know Mr Corcoran in his capacity as a lad in the accused's yard at Wantage?'

'Yes.'

'How do you know that it is his signature on this note?'

'Because it is his name there.'

'Have you ever seen his signature other than on this document?'

'No.'

'So anybody could have signed it with his name?'

'No, you're wrong. Corcoran did. I know he did.'

'Then no doubt he will come to this court and tell us so himself.' And with those words he sat down.

I felt impotent and helpless. I walked slowly across the court, found a place on a bench near the back and wondered what on earth would happen next.

My interrogator rose again to his feet: 'That, ladies and gentlemen,' he announced dramatically, 'completes the case for the prosecution.'

Chapter 16

After a brief opening speech by his counsel, Tom was now called to give evidence. His chances of an acquittal depended on the impression he made in the witness box and to an even greater degree on the testimony of Michael Corcoran. Despite the ordeal he must have been going through over the past two months, he walked purposefully from the dock. His voice was strong and clearly audible as he took the oath and I even detected a hint of defiance as he looked out onto the court.

His counsel began taking him through his evidence and for the next hour he spoke about his early days as a trainer, the initial struggle to succeed and attract owners and finally the fun and responsibility of running a successful yard. The picture emerged, at least as far as I was concerned, sitting at the back of the court, of a thoroughly decent, modest and agreeable young man. Then, candidly and without a hint of embarrassment, he told of how he fell in love with me

271

and freely admitted that he had implored me to leave Edward. Questioned about the letters he had written, he categorically denied ever having threatened to end Edward's life, or indeed that he had ever even considered doing so. He confirmed exactly what I had told the court about the missing page in the letter of 22nd December.

'Would you please tell His Lordship about the last occasion when you saw Mr Pryde alive,' asked his counsel.

Tom looked the jury straight in the eye and began to recount what happened on that Saturday evening: 'After seeing the state Victoria was in on the Friday, I decided to give Pryde a piece of my mind. I wasn't prepared to sit back and see Victoria's life ruined, whatever I had promised. I telephoned Edward Pryde and asked him to meet me at nine-thirty on the Saturday at the pub. As far as I was concerned, the affair was over, although I can't deny that I wished it wasn't. I'd never liked Edward and considering the kind of things he had done to his wife, I reckoned I'd have great difficulty in keeping my temper with him. But I thought it was worth a try to reason with him for Victoria's sake.

'I arrived a little late, say at a quarter to ten, and he was already in the corner of the saloon bar. For the first half an hour or so he was fairly sociable and talked about the horses in the yard and Victoria's success in the Gold Cup. I suspected he was playing the fool with me and as I returned from a visit to the loo I determined to stop beating about the bush. But before I could get a word in, and in front of a number of people in the pub, he started abusing me and telling me he knew all about my affair with his wife. I tried to calm him down, but with little success, and I'm afraid I gradually lost my temper with him. I felt he had set out to provoke me and I duly rose to the bait. A couple of times I got up to leave but on both occasions he grabbed hold of my sleeve and pulled me back. He said that if I didn't hear him out he would give Victoria a thrashing she would never forget.

'That was the last straw as far as I was concerned, and I told him that if he ever laid hands on her again, I'd make him pay for it. I was pretty well worked up by now and I'm not surprised I was overheard in the bar. When the landlord called for last orders, Edward asked for one more drink and I went and bought it for him, just to have a minute's break from his tirade. He took his time drinking it and by the time we reached the car park, we were the last to leave. I remember getting into my car, but after that, nothing, until I woke up still in the car park at six o'clock in the morning. I was lying across the passenger seat and had the most ghastly headache. I must have passed out, although I could only have had about three pints to drink. It must have been the combined effect of the alcohol and some pills I had taken to get rid of a bad headache earlier in the evening. That's all I can remember.'

'Can you explain how your footprints were found at Melksham pit?'

'I cannot. I have only been to the chalk pit once and that was last summer, with Victoria Pryde, as she told you when she gave her evidence. I can only assume that the footprints which were found date from that occasion, or that they belong to someone else who takes the same size shoes as me; I doubt if a size 9 is that uncommon.'

'Did you kill Edward Pryde?'

Tom turned to face the judge and then swivelled to the jury again. 'No, I did not. I have never so much as touched a hair on his head and that is the truth.'

The impassive faces of the jury gave no hint of whether they believed him.

Snipe sensed that this was a critical moment in the case and with his impeccable sense of timing suggested that the court should rise until the following morning when cross-examination would begin.

I took a taxi from the Old Bailey to Amy's offices in Lincoln's Inn. Feeling depressed and frightened, I couldn't pretend my own evidence had gone well. I had been caught out by the production of those letters and I knew that nobody had believed me when I'd said a crucial page was missing. I couldn't understand where or how the prosecution could have found them. Perhaps when the police searched the cottage they had come across them in one of Edward's hiding places. It didn't really matter now, as the damage had been done. Tom had been a really good witness, I felt, only it was impossible not to feel that the burden of proof had been reversed. It had fallen upon him to prove his innocence, not on the prosecution to establish his guilt beyond all reasonable doubt. They had presented the jury with motive and opportunity. Get out of that one, Radcliffe, I could hear them now saying. I only hoped Amy would have some news on Corcoran to cheer me up. Too busy to come to court, she had promised to liaise with Tom's solicitor during the afternoon to find out whether the former stable lad had made contact and signed his statement.

I was shown into her room as she was putting down the phone.

'How did it go?' she asked eagerly. I told her about the letters and my fears that I had, if anything, damaged Tom's case.

'You mustn't blame yourself,' she said, trying her best to reassure me. 'Remember, you were called as a witness for the prosecution, albeit a reluctant one, so all you could do was tell the truth about your relationship with Tom. Judges and lawyers have a way of making everything sound sordid and improper. Anyone would think they never had a dirty thought. I can tell you a few who I reckon never have a clean one!'

I managed a feeble laugh. 'Any news on Corcoran?'

'That's just what I was on the phone about when you came in. Good news at last, there. He's in London, staying at a hotel, somewhere behind Victoria station. Booked in this morning and signed the statement which Tom's solicitors sent round early this afternoon. Apparently he thinks he's being followed

275

and they've arranged a taxi to pick him up there in the morning and take him to court. Does that make you feel better?'

'Considerably!'

'Good. Now they've got the statement, they've given notice to the other side of their intention to call him, as he counts as an alibi witness. You're meant to give them due notice, so they can investigate it and if necessary call evidence to rebut it. You can rest assured old Snipe will get shirty and lay into Tom's lawyers about their disregard for the proper procedure and so on.'

It was obvious that the next day I was going to need all my strength just being a spectator at the hearing and I willingly accepted Amy's invitation to spend another night at her flat. I went to bed early only to dream of Snipe donning a black cap and smiling as he sent Tom to the gallows. The final touch of the macabre was that Edward was standing beside him dressed up as a priest.

I arrived at Court No 1 at ten-fifteen and paced up and down outside. I was too nervous to sit still, despite my crutches. I could see Tom's counsel in anxious discussion with two men I thought must be his solicitors. One of them, a middle-aged man wearing a striped shirt with a white collar, kept on looking at his watch and shaking his head. They were clearly worried about something and the absence of any sign of Corcoran made me guess what. I couldn't believe that, having made the effort to come over here and sign his statement, he wouldn't now appear. Amy arrived as I was about to hobble over and ask if something was wrong. I pointed out to her the group and she marched over and had a word with the man in the striped shirt. After a brief discussion she returned.

'It's very worrying, I'm afraid. There was no sign of Corcoran when the taxi went to pick him up this morning at nine o'clock. An assistant from Tom's lawyers had gone along to check all was well, but according to the manager of the hotel, his bed hadn't been slept in all night. All that was in his room was a suitcase with a shirt and some underwear. It seems he went out yesterday at some time in the afternoon and hasn't returned. It's only a small hotel with people coming and going the whole time – I suspect during the day as well as the night – so of course nobody remembers precisely when he went out.'

I couldn't believe what I was hearing. Not Corcoran as well. 'You don't think, Amy, that . . .'

'I know what you're thinking. I suppose it's possible. Brennan?'

'It would make sense. How could we have been so stupid as to have left Corcoran on his own there?'

'Hold on! It's not our fault. Tom's solicitors wouldn't even tell me where he was staying until today. We're lucky to have been kept as informed as we have been. Some solicitors would have told us to push off in no uncertain terms. Come on, we'd better go into court, they start at ten-thirty. We'll just have to pray he shows up by the time Tom's cross-examination finishes.'

At least Tom had no idea of the drama being played out in the corridor beyond the courtroom doors. He appeared relaxed and collected as Scott rose to cross-examine him.

The counsel spent the first hour sparring with Tom, who kept his head and answered politely yet firmly as Scott explored his background and life style. The niceties over, he went on the attack.

'Mr Radcliffe, are you in the habit of going to bed with other men's wives?'

Poor Tom rose to the bait: 'I resent that question. I most certainly am not.'

'But you obviously regard another man's wife as fair game?'

'No, I don't. I tried not to fall in love with Victoria for that very reason.'

'Yet you knew when you met her that she was married?'

'Of course.'

'And in fact her husband had been one of the very first owners to have a horse in your yard?'

'That's right, but that was four years before our relationship began.'

Scott didn't seem to take any notice of the answers, leaping into his next question. 'In fact, without the support of the deceased, your career as a trainer might never have got under way?'

I could see Tom considering his reply carefully. If he said no, he would appear ungrateful. If he answered in the affirmative, he would appear even more ungrateful and treacherous. 'He was one of a handful of people who had faith in me and at the time I was very grateful for his support.'

I wished he had added how, for the next four years, Edward had tried to do him immense damage by bad-mouthing him to anyone on the racecourse who would bother to listen.

'When you realised the nature and depth of your feelings for Mrs Pryde, did you still continue to offer her rides as a jockey on your horses?'

'I did.'

'There are not many women jockeys riding profes-sionally, are there?'

'Two or three.'

'Am I right in thinking that they enjoy considerably less success than their male counterparts?'

'You are. On the whole, they are less strong and less effective in riding a finish.'

'And Mrs Pryde is an exception?'

'Yes, I think she is. She has excellent tactical judgement and what she lacks in a finish, she more than makes up for by the way she sets a horse right before a fence.'

'Did you deliberately offer Mrs Pryde rides at courses which would necessitate her being away from home for the whole day, not returning often until late evening?'

'What are you suggesting?'

'It's my prerogative to ask the questions, Mr Radcliffe, but since you ask I'll put my suggestion to you. I suggest that the reason you continued to put up Mrs Pryde on your horses was not because of her riding ability but to create opportunities for you both to cheat on the deceased.'

'That's a monstrous suggestion. I choose the best jockey available on each occasion. I owe that duty to my owners. I never gave Victoria a ride other than on the grounds of ability.' There was an incongruous giggle from someone in the gallery.

'You were very much in love with her, weren't you?'

'Yes, but eventually I had to accept that in the circumstances it was impossible, and had to end.'

'Would you please look at the letter dated 22nd December, exhibit seven, My Lord. Do you see the final paragraph on page two and the opening sentence of the next page?'

'I do. I've already told this court that there is a page missing and what you have here completely distorts what I was writing about. I never threatened to end Edward Pryde's life.'

'Would you agree with me that if there is no missing page those words read very much like a threat to do just that?'

Tom turned to the judge. 'Must I answer that, My Lord?'

For the first time in the trial, Snipe was sympathetic: 'No, you don't have to. You're being asked your opinion and this court is concerned solely with facts.'

Scott produced one of the most obsequious smiles

I've ever seen and returned to the attack. 'Did you ever seriously think that Edward Pryde would give his wife a divorce?'

'No, not really. It was well known that he thoroughly disliked me and I knew from Victoria that he relied upon her heavily for financial support.'

'Nonetheless, you often asked Mrs Pryde to leave him?'

'That's not really surprising, is it? I hated the way he used to treat her and I genuinely thought that she would be better off without him.'

'And when you realised she wouldn't leave him, you killed him?'

'That's ridiculous. I never touched him, I tell you.'

'You accept that you argued with him that evening in the pub?'

'I lost my temper with him. He was taunting me about Victoria.'

'And you threatened him with violence?'

'That was only in the heat of the moment. If a man threatens to beat up the girl you love, even if she's his wife, you can't very well stand by and let him go ahead and do it. At least I couldn't.'

'Are you in the habit of passing out after a couple of drinks?'

'No, it's never happened before. I can only assume it was the combination of the alcohol and the tablets I had taken for my headache.'

'You were familiar with Melksham Pit, of course?'

'I had been there once before with Victoria.'

'What do you mean by once before? You accept, then, that you went there again?'

'It was a slip of the tongue. I've only ever been there once.'

'How can you explain the petrol stains which were found on the suit you were wearing that night?'

'I must have splashed myself when I filled my car up with petrol earlier in the evening. I'm a little clumsy and impatient and probably took the nozzle out of the tank before I'd finished filling. It's easily done with these self-service things.'

'And the presence of your footprints on the path leading to the pit, how do you account for that?'

'Possibly they were there from last year or just happened to match somebody else's.'

Scott signalled to the usher to hand up a pair of brown brogues to Tom in the witness box. They had a label attached to them and up till then had sat on a table in front of the court, along with what I had assumed to be the other exhibits. Among them was the bronze statue with which Freddie had struck his father; it had been used to establish Edward's identity as the body in the boot. It had a polythene bag around it and no doubt it had been produced and examined earlier in the trial in the course of the forensic evidence.

'These are the shoes you were wearing that night?' asked Scott, with what I detected was a hint of sarcasm in his voice.

'They are. They're probably like a hundred thousand others in the country.'

'But you're the only owner of such a pair who had a motive for wanting Edward Pryde dead, aren't you?'

'I had no such motive.'

'You wanted to marry his wife, didn't you?'

'Yes, but I've told you, I realised and accepted it was impossible.'

'You knew that so long as he was alive there was no chance of Mrs Pryde giving up her son and leaving him?'

'I knew that and had come to accept it. In this world you have to accept there are some things you can't have and in my case Victoria was one of them.'

'You regarded her, then, as a possession?'

'Of course I didn't. She is the most wonderful person I've ever met.'

'So you would do anything to have her for your own?'

'Not anything. I would never have murdered her husband.'

'How can you explain the empty petrol can which the police found hidden in a disused box in your yard?'

'It wasn't hidden, at least not by me. There are probably endless pieces of machinery and things pushed out of sight in any large stable. I can certainly assure you that I had nothing to do with it.'

'That's not true, is it, Mr Radcliffe? I put it to you that after you left that pub you asked the deceased to give you a lift, that you forced him to drive his car to the chalk pit where you murdered him and set fire to the car in order to destroy the body.'

'I did none of those things.'

'That you returned to your own car and fabricated this tale about passing out.'

'I did not make it up. I did pass out.'

'That you murdered Edward Pryde in order that his wife would be free to marry you. To satisfy your own desires you were quite happy to rob a young boy of his father.'

'That's completely and utterly untrue. It was because of Freddie that I accepted Victoria's decision to stay with Edward. I am innocent of this charge against me.'

Counsel for the prosecution sat down and Tom's counsel tried his best to re-establish his client's credibility during re-examination. It was no easy task. It wasn't that he hadn't told the truth, it was just that he was in the invidious position of trying to prove a negative against a substantial weight of damaging circumstantial evidence. What was needed now was for Corcoran to come into the witness box and corroborate his story that he really did pass out in the car park of that pub. I didn't care whether Corcoran then went on to say that he had seen Brennan follow Edward in his car. I wanted revenge on the Irishman, but that could wait.

As Tom left the witness box and returned to the dock, I watched the jury for their reaction. It was incredible how their expressions gave so little away. I suppose they felt the eyes of the court were upon them and at least they had to give the impression of taking their duty seriously. I wondered whether they were really capable of analysing the issues, or knowing that their duty was to be certain of guilt before they reached a verdict to convict. Of course, they could only act on the evidence they had heard and seen for themselves. They knew nothing of Corcoran or of Musgrave's suspicious death or the link between my husband and Brennan. Who knows what feelings and emotions ran through their minds as they listened to the evidence? Had one of the male jurors himself been cuckolded and therefore hated any adulterer? Or had one of the women been cheated by her husband? It was a rare person who was able to leave his or her own prejudices and moral values behind as they stepped into a courtroom and passed judgement on a fellow man. I still hadn't given up hope. There was at least one woman who had appeared sympathetic as Tom had given his evidence.

Up ahead of me, Tom's counsel was now anxiously talking to his solicitor sitting in the row in front of him. Corcoran had obviously not appeared. The counsel rose to his feet and asked Snipe if the court would be minded to grant a short adjournment. Snipe was plainly not in such a charitable mood. He pointed out in acerbic terms that he had only allowed cross-examination on the entries in Edward's diary on the strict understanding that the individual in question, Corcoran, would be called by the defence. He saw no reason, if the witness was available, why he should not now be brought into court. Tom's counsel could offer no explanation for his absence. His application was refused by Snipe with unashamed enthusiasm. He then ordered that the usher should call out for Corcoran in case he was in the vicinity of the court. There was no response.

On that disastrous note the case for the defendant came to an abrupt end. The triumph envisaged by calling Corcoran had now turned into unmitigated disaster.

Chapter 17

That afternoon, the respective counsels made their closing speeches to the jury. Scott, on behalf of the prosecution, began by analysing the evidence coldly and clinically without displaying the slightest trace of emotion or passion. He delivered his speech without once appearing to look at a note and you could sense that he was gradually persuading the jury that whichever way they approached it, all the evidence pointed inexorably in one direction: the guilt of the accused, and therefore his just conviction for murder.

The jury now with him, Scott began to quicken the pace, cynically and rhetorically destroying Tom's defence. There was, he pointed out, ample motive and opportunity. Just as hell knows no fury like a woman scorned, who was to know what terrible deeds might be committed by an otherwise sensible and upright man driven by jealousy or despair? He poured scorn on Tom's attempts to answer the evidence against him. Asked about his whereabouts on the night

Edward Pryde had disappeared, Tom answered that he was asleep, having passed out in the dark corner of the car park of a public house. How convenient! Pressed about the discovery of his footprints at the scene of the crime, he claimed feebly they must belong to someone else. Questioned about the petrol on his clothes, he explained it away as the result of an accident that same evening when filling up his car. Finally, when challenged about the incriminating contents of one of his letters to his lover, he is driven to claiming that there is a page missing.

By contrast, Scott argued, the attempt by the defendant to blacken the deceased's good name had deservedly failed. There was no sign of the mysterious Mr Corcoran who was going to tell the court what an evil blackmailer Edward Pryde was, and no doubt thereby seek to implant in the minds of the jury the notion that the world was a better place without him and that many people other than the defendant had a motive for wanting him dead. At the end of the day, urged Scott, it was simply a case of balancing facts, damning when considered in their entirety, against the word and demeanour of the accused in the witness box. There could be only one conclusion.

Tom's counsel, Fenton, earned his fee that afternoon. Reminding the jury throughout of their duty to convict only if they were certain beyond reasonable doubt, he proceeded to expose the truly circumstantial nature of the prosecution case. There was, he reminded the jury, no witness who had seen Tom follow Edward from the pub, no witness, even, who had seen them together after they had left the saloon bar just past closing time. It might well be that Tom had the opportunity to kill Edward Pryde, but so did hundreds if not thousands of other people. It was argued fiercely on behalf of the Crown that the accused alone had the necessary motive. What was that motive when analysed? An apparent desire to remove the obstacle between himself and marriage to Victoria Pryde. Was that, Fenton asked, really likely? His client had freely and frankly admitted everything from the outset, when questioned by the police about his affair with Victoria. He had told the court how he had accepted that so long as Edward refused to give Victoria a divorce, their love was impossible. It was Edward who had become aggressive and made a scene. If the prosecution case were seriously suggesting this was murder, Tom must have gone to that pub with a preconceived plan for disposing of his so-called enemy. And if that was so, why would he have been so clumsy as to have spilt petrol on his clothing when committing the murder? Or if he did spill the petrol, why didn't he then destroy the suit he was wearing? Instead, he freely handed it over to the police when they began their investigation. Would he really have been so naive as to have left that petrol can in a box at his own stable when he could have thrown it away in the undergrowth, or into a river where it would almost certainly never have been discovered?

His client, he invited the jury to conclude, was a

decent and honourable man who unfortunately had become involved with a married woman. That was not a crime in our society. He had accepted that the affair had no future and as far as he was concerned, that was an end to the matter. As for the incriminating letters, they were nothing of the sort. He invited the jury when they retired to read through the whole bundle and see for themselves that they contained the sentiments of a decent man who was sincerely in love. Why should the accused and Victoria Pryde not be telling the truth when they had both said that a crucial page was missing? After all, they were the only two people who really knew, and no explanation had been offered by the prosecution as to just exactly how those letters had come into the police's possession. Who was to say that a page had not become detached or gone missing by accident? It would be unrealistic and a cruel injustice to convict a man and condemn him to a life sentence where such a doubt existed.

It was, he continued, the duty of the jury to take into account the unblemished character of Tom Radcliffe, a man with no previous convictions and against whom nothing could be said to suggest he had a tendency to violence. Their decision had to be based, not on emotion or prejudice or morality, but on a detached and reasoned assessment of the evidence. That could lead to only one result: a verdict of not guilty.

I was certainly moved and I thought several members of the jury were too. It was now up to Snipe to sum up fairly and that task was adjourned until the following day.

No one who heard the Honourable Mr Justice Snipe would have been under any illusion as to what he considered the proper verdict. Of course, he was careful not to give any obvious indication of bias or make any statement blatantly prejudicial to Tom, but he was clever enough to review the evidence in a way which could lead any reasonable person to only one conclusion. By setting out in some detail the background to the murder – the development of our relationship, the secret and furtive sexual encounters, the gradual realisation by Tom that he could never marry me so long as Edward was alive – he planted the seed of motive firmly in the jury's mind. From there it easily and swiftly grew into opportunity. So much, he said, hinged on the accused's explanation of how he spent the night of the disappearance. Was he telling the truth when he said he must have passed out in his car after leaving the pub, or was that a highly convenient explanation fabricated to cover up for what he had really being doing? It was, of course, a matter solely for the jury as the arbiters of fact, but did they not think it a trifle curious that two or three pints of beer should have had such an effect on the accused? And so Snipe went on turning the screw a little more with each comment. Finally at three o'clock he sent the jury out to reach their verdict.

It was like waiting for the result of a stewards'

enquiry, only this time the outcome would be far more serious. When the jury returned, they all sat down and then the Foreman was asked to rise. An insignificant little man of about forty-five, balding and with glasses, rose hesitantly to his feet.

'Members of the jury, are you agreed on your verdict?' asked the Associate, solemnly.

'We are,' answered the Foreman.

'Do you find the defendant guilty, or not guilty?'

'Guilty,' came the firm, almost defiant response.

For a brief moment I felt nothing as the realisation of what I'd just heard sank in. I looked across the court at Tom and as our eyes met I burst into tears. He was white with shock and looked totally bewildered. I suddenly felt very sick and faint and struggled to keep control of myself as Snipe began to speak. He wasn't content just to commit Tom to imprisonment with a recommendation that he serve at least twenty years; he insisted on adding a few well-chosen sanctimonious words of reprobation:

'Tom Radcliffe, you have been found guilty, and rightly so in my view, of the murder of Edward Pryde. You have by your gross and callous act deprived a fine man of the rest of his natural life, and a young boy of the joy of knowing his father. This grotesque act of violence was born out of your betrayal of the Christian values which our society holds dear. Having coveted and seduced the wife of another man, you then proceeded to take his life when you could not have your own way and marry her. May God forgive you.'

As the police officers symbolically closed in on him in the dock, Tom twisted round and shook his head at me in disbelief. My first instinct was to get up and rush towards him, to tell him not to abandon hope. Alert as ever, Amy restrained me while Tom kept trying to say something across the court.

'What is it?' I asked Amy, unable to understand or read his lips.

She put her arm around me. 'Simply that he loves you.'

As I left the court in tears, a pack of journalists descended on me, asking for my comments. All I could say was that I still believed in Tom's innocence and that I would spare no expense or time in trying to bring the true culprit or culprits to justice.

Amy drove me back that evening to Ralph's yard. Neither of us could believe what had happened and only the references to the verdict on the radio news brought home the cold inescapable truth. We both realised that we would not help Tom by sitting at home and wailing; some form of battle plan was needed. Tom's lawyers were going to lodge an appeal and that would probably not be heard for three to four months. In the meantime, we were going to alert the police to Corcoran's disappearance and try and persuade Inspector Wilkinson that there was a possible link between it and Edward's death. Judging by past performance, there wasn't much room for optimism. No doubt Inspector Wilkinson was busy congratulating himself on a job well done and further enquiries would only delay his letter of commendation from the Lord Chief Justice.

Ralph had gone away for a week's holiday and his house was deserted. Amy was reluctant to let me stay in my cottage on my own, but I insisted. Now that Tom had been convicted, maybe my life was no longer in danger, and anyway I couldn't have round the clock protection. I had to try and live normally from now on. I intended to spend the summer holidays with my mother and then, at the end of August, when I had completely recovered from my injuries, return to Lambourn and put the cottage on the market. Amy refused to drive off until she had checked that there was nobody in the house. She opened all the doors to the bedrooms and looked inside and pronounced me safe.

By eleven o'clock I was ready to go to bed. I laboriously climbed the stairs and went along to my bedroom. The door was open and I closed it behind me before walking over to the chest of drawers beside my bed to take out a clean nightdress. I undressed and turned to go to the bathroom. It was then I saw it. Pinned by a knife against the back of the door was Edward's yellow racing jacket, the knife's blade smeared with blood. I was more angry than frightened and walked over and removed the knife. Stuck to the tip of the blade was a cutting from the *Sportsman* – the declaration of Edward's death – only this time the letter S had been added in black ink to the word MR. The message was inescapable. I had no intention of hanging around. Clasping the knife firmly, I ran down the stairs, as fast as my injured leg would let me, to the car I had borrowed from my mother after the crash. I was in no real condition to drive because of my leg but nothing would have prevented me from leaving at that moment. I somehow managed to negotiate the roads to Wincanton, though with less than my usual skill, and keeping a constant watch in the rear mirror. As soon as I arrived at my mother's house, I collapsed into her arms.

The damage I'd done my right leg by driving meant that I was confined to bed for the next three weeks and at least that gave me a welcome opportunity to see my son, and a sense of security against whoever out there was stalking me. I valued every moment of Freddie's company; with Edward's parents threatening to take him away, I felt that I was under notice of execution. Any thought I may have had that Tom's conviction would mark the end of the attacks on my life had now been dispelled, and I determined to get myself some concrete protection. There was a maniac at large and I was very much on his hit list.

I used the period of my confinement to regain my strength and determination. Tom was allowed to receive letters in prison and I wrote to him regularly, urging him not to give up hope. Unfortunately, I didn't have much concrete news to offer him.

Despite all her efforts, Amy had made no headway

in finding out what had happened to Corcoran. The staff at the hotel were unable to be specific about when he had last been seen and the police were unenthusiastic to the point of lethargy in their attempts to trace his movements. As far as they were concerned, the file on the Edward Pryde case was firmly closed. Corcoran, it seemed, had disappeared back into the shadows from which he had so briefly emerged, taking with him Tom's best chance of an acquittal.

It was Amy's idea that we should go and confront Brennan. Attack, she reasoned, was the best form of defence, and as my solicitor she could always volunteer to show him Corcoran's statement and ask him to comment on it. The worst he could do was kick us out of his house. After my experiences on the race track, I didn't share her confidence in his good nature, and finally reconciled myself to getting hold of some sort of firearm, however illegal. It proved easier than I expected. A quiet word with James Thackeray and one of his numerous 'contacts' produced a small revolver – no questions asked. James had been sufficiently shaken by my story of the blood-stained knife to overcome any qualms about aiding and abetting my attempt to protect myself. We didn't tell Amy.

I managed to find out that the Irishman had recently moved to a village just outside Newbury and was living there with his girlfriend. There was very little National Hunt racing on and he was spending his mornings schooling horses for one or two local trainers. We decided to call in unannounced early one Tuesday evening.

To say Brennan was displeased to see us was an understatement. He tried to slam the door in our faces, but I managed to wedge my walking stick inside and with great reluctance he agreed to let us come in. It is a curious sensation, facing a man whom you suspect to be a murderer. But the gun in my handbag was very reassuring. Brennan, belligerent as ever, went straight on the attack himself:

'What the hell do you mean, coming to my home uninvited?' His girlfriend now appeared from the kitchen and she was treated to a mouthful of abuse as the jockey waved her away.

'We won't be long,' said Amy. 'We want you to read this, please.' She thrust Corcoran's statement into his hands. The Irishman took it reluctantly and turned his back on us as he read it. It seemed to take him forever. When he had finished he walked into the kitchen and returned, smirking and clutching a newspaper cutting.

'So your Mr Corcoran says he saw me that evening at the pub and I was following your late husband?'

'That's right. What were you doing that night then, Brennan?'

He laughed. 'Have a look at this, my darlings.' He shoved the cutting at me. It was a photograph of Brennan and a number of other jockeys in dinner jackets, captioned 'Top jockeys celebrate at Racing Club dinner in aid of charity'.

'Do you see the date?'

It was the night that Edward had disappeared.

'Nothing personal, but if you ask me, this fellow Corcoran has taken you for a bigger ride than any horse has ever done, and that's saying something.'

As we returned to the car, Amy put her arm around me. 'I think the time has come when we really have to put this into the hands of professionals. Neither of us has the time to try and track down Corcoran and you really have to pick up the pieces of your life; you owe that much to Freddie. What do you think?'

Reluctantly, I agreed. Tom's lawyers were prepared to make unlimited funds available to track down Corcoran. But until he had been found there was no likelihood of any appeal succeeding. Even then, that didn't mean my safety would be assured. Hadn't I been declared dead, just like Edward?

Chapter 18

I had planned to return to Lambourn some time in the middle of July. The doctors had given me the all clear to start riding again and I had been getting myself fit by running but I wanted to have at least a couple of weeks' riding work on some flat horses so that I would be a hundred per cent fit for the start of the season at the beginning of August.

The news on the Corcoran front was bitterly disappointing. Private detectives had been unable to locate any trace of him whatsoever either in England or in Ireland. He had literally disappeared into thin air. In my last letter to Tom I had not been able to think of any good news to give him. All of the horses had now left his yard and, except for the head lad, all of the staff had gone as well. Tom had decided not to let Jamie Brown go until he was certain that there was no chance of his release, but as time went on, the chances of that happening seemed to become ever more remote. The only consolation as far as I was concerned was that during the past six weeks not one attempt had been made on my life. Something must have happened; something that I didn't know about to make whoever wanted me dead change his or her mind. I still kept the gun, though, just in case.

After the trial my name had faded from the newspapers, but since I still had to earn my living as a jockey, James had kindly suggested that the *Sportsman* do a small piece about my return to Lambourn.

'It would just let people know you're still alive,' he had said.

We were due to move back in on the Monday, and on the Saturday before, the *Sportsman* duly carried a photograph of Freddie and me outside the cottage, captioned 'Pryde returns after Fall'.

That night I had Amy and James to dinner to thank them for all their efforts on Tom's behalf and to discuss what steps we could now take to help him. His appeal had been fixed for the end of November and as a grim reminder of his predicament, Amy had brought with her the bronze statuette that had played such a fateful part in his conviction. The police had handed it back to her as my solicitor and it even still had its exhibit number attached to the jockey's arm. I was reluctant to have it on view in the house and put it in the cupboard under the staircase.

Not surprisingly, the talk about Tom cast a shadow on the evening, although Amy was determined to cheer me up. She was going to spend the night with her parents and devote Sunday to preparing for a trial at

Winchester Crown Court on the Monday. Her client was accused of bigamy and was alleged to have three separate families in different parts of the country. James asked whether the maximum penalty for this offence was three mothers-in-law and Amy made us roar with laughter as she read out selected extracts from her client's statement to the police, one of a number of documents in the file she had brought down from London with her and which she refused to leave outside in the car. According to Amy, her client wanted to plead guilty and on no account was his counsel to ask the court for leniency. The prospect of a long jail sentence was, he considered, infinitely preferable to facing his three spouses.

It was well after midnight when they left and I locked the front door after them. For a woman and child alone, the security in the house was hopelessly inadequate and I resolved to change the lock and have a couple of bolts fitted. As I tidied up, I came across the file that Amy had brought with her: she had obviously forgotten it after finishing off James's bottle of champagne. Feeling inquisitive I sat down and perused the contents for the next half hour. I could well understand, after reading his wives' statements, why the client was so anxious to go inside.

I went up to bed feeling a good deal more relaxed than I had for some time and I popped into Freddie's room to see if he was fast asleep and give him one last good night kiss. As I stroked his hair and looked down on his angelic little face, I realised that for his sake alone there was much to live for. I went next door, undressed and slipped into bed. It was an odd and unnerving experience being back there for the first time since Edward's murder and I could hardly believe that it was the first night I had ever slept without him in this house. I hugged the pillow and pretended it was Tom. Then, less romantically, I checked that my gun was safely tucked underneath.

The sensation of fingers running through my hair jolted me from my dreams. The tickle, in the darkness, of what felt like the cold, sharp blade of a knife against my throat stopped me from screaming. I didn't dare move or open my mouth. Freddie was next door and at all costs I had to keep his presence in the house a secret. My visitor had climbed into bed beside me and I was revolted and terrified by the thought that he might have been there for the past hour or so. At least he was fully clothed. Sensing I was awake, he took my left hand and ran it slowly over his face, beginning with his unshaven chin, then along his cheeks and finally around his nose.

I gasped. I'd recognise my husband anywhere.

'Isn't this a nice surprise?' he said. 'Back in bed together, just like old times.'

'But I thought . . .'

'I know what you thought and everybody else thought the same. There's no need to talk in a whisper. I know Freddie's asleep next door.'

I was no longer sure that Edward wouldn't harm his

302

own son. I certainly didn't want the boy to wake up and come in and see his father, because he would then be an eye-witness to the truth and a dangerous one at that.

'But whose body was it in the car?'

He laughed. 'Wouldn't you like to know?'

I nodded. If I could keep him talking, maybe I could get hold of the gun. I slid my hand gently under the pillow, fingers outstretched in search of the cold metal.

'Is this what you're looking for?' Edward sniggered and suddenly leaned over to turn on the bedside lamp; he kept the knife close against my neck.

'People who hide guns under their pillows need to be light sleepers.'

I saw the gun on the table, hopelessly out of reach, and my heart began to pound. Edward's eyes were locked on mine, and only inches away, but his expression was a million miles off – on another planet. I noticed a bubble of saliva creeping out of the corner of his mouth.

'Tell me how you did it.'

The question seemed to focus his attention. He got out of bed and started pacing round the room.

'The idea came to me after the fight downstairs when Freddie hit me with that bronze. When I came round and you had gone, I suddenly realised that here was a chance to disappear permanently. That would solve my little problem with Musgrave. There can be great advantages, you know, to being declared dead. You can even commit murder without anyone ever suspecting you.

'That Friday afternoon, your lover boy phoned up and asked me to meet him at the pub the following evening. Here was a marvellous chance to kill two birds with one stone. Isn't it a shame they've abolished capital punishment? I had known about your affair for ages. In fact, I had even followed you to Melksham Pit and watched you make love on that rug together. I must say that you certainly put more enthusiasm into it with him than you ever did with me. I hated you both for that. Anyway, that evening I telephoned Corcoran, who seemed the ideal victim, and asked him to meet me the following afternoon to discuss the return of his confession note. He had been pestering me about it for months. I met him in a car I had hired that morning in London and drove him out to Melksham Pit. He thought I was going to return the note. Instead, I pulled out a knife and plunged it into his heart, leaving a small pool of blood on the spot to give the police something to work on. You should have seen his face! Died instantly. I then struck him on the back of the head with the bronze statue, which I'd already cleaned and washed free of my own blood that morning. I dumped his body in the boot and left the car down the road from the pit. I duly met lover boy in the pub and provoked the scene overheard by so many other people. What they didn't see, though, was the barbiturate I slipped into his beer while he was in the loo. By the time he had reached his car, he was absolutely legless. I waited for the car park to clear, parked his car in the darkest corner, having first removed his shoes and poured a few drops of petrol on his trousers. Then I laid him down across the front seat. Nobody could see him; anyone seeing the car would think it was empty. I then drove out to Melksham. In the early hours of the morning, working, I thought appropriately, under the gleam of a full moon, I transferred Corcoran from the boot of the hire car into the boot of the Jag. I then drove the Jag up to the pit, dowsed the back seat and the body in petrol, threw a match into the car and watched it burn.'

'Weren't you worried that he would be identified?'

'There's no need to whisper. I'm afraid I'm not going to let Freddie grow up an orphan. Shall I continue? I'd put on Tom's shoes to watch the blaze, reckoning if the police were to find any footprints they might as well be his. When it was over, I drove back in the hire car to the pub, replaced Tom's shoes and then on to Lambourn. I put the bronze, with Corcoran's blood on it instead of mine, on the mantelpiece, and drove up to London. Once there, I left the car at the rental place – it was six-thirty, so nobody saw me – and took the train to Fishguard. That night I arrived in Ireland with a job well done. All my problems were over. Everyone would conclude it was my body in the boot of the car. I had taken the precaution of smashing Corcoran's teeth just in case they tried to look up the dental records. I reckoned that if they used that new process I'd read about in the papers, they would rely on the blood on the bronze and the pool of dried blood by the car I'd so kindly left them, just to make sure. Always willing to help the police, you know me. So they had a perfect match, of course, and then needed to look no further. The icing on the cake came when they arrested old lover boy, just as I'd planned.'

'Then if Corcoran was dead, who was it who lured me to Ireland?'

'Yours truly, of course. When I saw your notice in the *Sportsman* I thought I could have a bit of fun and get hold of some cash at the same time. You remember I only ever talked to that dreadful friend of yours, Amy Frost. I saw you both arrive at the airport and after you had left the tea house I slashed the tyres on her car to stop her following you. I was rather pleased with myself over that.'

It was all so obvious, but I kept asking questions, instinctively playing for time.

'And the time I was followed in the car?'

'Me again. As I was officially dead, I had no difficulty in coming back to England provided I kept away from the obvious places. I followed you to Kempton that day and then to London while you had dinner with Amy. I enjoyed the journey down to the Cotswolds and had thought I might even finish you off that night. You did very well to escape.'

'And the hospital?'

'That really did please me, although I underestimated the amount of insulin needed. I'd seen my father inject himself for years and when they were both out of the house, I let myself in with my key and borrowed some of the stuff. You should have died that night, too. Still, that would have denied me the pleasure of this evening's performance.'

I realised that he was mad, quite mad. I had to keep him talking. 'And it was you who put the notice in the *Sportsman* and phoned Tom's solicitors pretending to be Corcoran?'

'Yes, another enjoyable part of this affair. They had never heard the Irishman's voice and believed my passable imitation of an Irish accent. I was in two minds as to whether I dared risk coming to London again and booking into the hotel in Victoria, but then I said, why the hell not? No one at the hotel would recognise me and I could sign the statement implicating Brennan and clearing Tom, and then do a runner. Forging Corcoran's signature was easy as I had kept a copy of his note. I loved the idea of building up all your hopes of an acquittal, only to see them dashed again.'

'And the letters?'

'My final master stroke. I had discovered where you used to hide those letters early on. I used to quite enjoy reading them when you were out racing. Romantic bastard, that lover of yours. I moved them from the chimney and left them in the desk drawer where the police were bound to find them. Removing that page was a nice idea too, wasn't it?'

'And Musgrave; did you do him in, too?'

'I did. You should have seen his face when I walked into his office late on Saturday night. Your exposé in the *Sportsman* had put him into a panic and he was busy destroying his ledger and sheets. I forced him at knife point onto the desk, made him put his own tie around his neck as a noose. You know, I don't think he ever thought I was actually going to hang him – I'll never forget the look of horror on his face when I kicked the chair away!'

As he chuckled to himself, I could swear I heard a car pull up outside, and then a door slam. I could just make out the sound of footsteps in the road outside. It had to be Amy, coming back for her file. Edward had moved back to the bed and was too engrossed in caressing my hair to notice. My heartbeat began to quicken even more as I realised that Freddie and I might have a chance. I listened for a sound from downstairs, a knock on the door, a ring on the bell. None came. Only footsteps again in the road, and this time the slam of the car door was followed by an engine starting. I wanted to shout out, but I knew it was hopeless. It was all over.

'How about letting me have it for one last time, for old time's sake?' Edward asked, sending a cold shiver down my spine. He didn't wait for an answer, and I watched him fumbling with his trousers. For the first time he put the knife down and he rolled on top of me. I closed my eyes and prayed. I just heard the tiny movement of the door as it was pushed open. I kissed him long and hard to ensure his undivided attention. Freddie must have woken up and I desperately waved my right arm at him to make him go away, all the while

308

keeping Edward's attention on me as best as I could bear.

The force of the first blow on Edward's head drove his tongue deep into my mouth. The second and third rendered him limp and motionless. I opened my eyes and through my tears I looked up to see my saviour. Amy was clutching the bronze.

This time the blood on it was indisputably Edward's. Regaining her composure she rolled him off me on to what used to be his side of the bed.

'He's stopped breathing,' I whispered, still trying not to wake Freddie. Amy bent over him and listened to his heartbeat. 'He may have been declared dead, but Edward Pryde is still very much alive.'

At that moment, Freddie appeared in the doorway, and I ran to him and picked him up and put him back to bed.

'Who was that man on the bed, mummy? He looked like daddy.'

'You just go back to sleep and I'll tell you all about it in the morning.'

Amy sat with my gun pointed at Edward, while I went downstairs and telephoned Inspector Wilkinson.

Edward was just regaining consciousness as the Inspector and two of his men arrived to take him away. I could hear him swearing and cursing, but kept well out of the way. I didn't ever want to see him again.

As they went out of the front door, Inspector Wilkinson stayed behind and came to find me in the kitchen. Two seconds later Amy joined us and I told them exactly what Edward had said. When I'd finished, Inspector Wilkinson apologised for doubting my story, but I was too relieved to be worrying about grudges. I was more concerned to let Tom know what had happened. I looked at my watch.

'Inspector, I know it's after two in the morning, but do you think there's any chance of ringing the prison and letting Mr Radcliffe know about this?'

The Inspector agreed to see that it would be done straight away and said that he would come back in the morning to take statements.

'Amy, I haven't thanked you yet for saving my life.'

'Don't mention it. That's what solicitors are for,' she grinned.

There was no way that Amy and I would be able to go back to sleep now, so we opened a bottle of Scotch and stayed downstairs talking and making plans until dawn broke. It wasn't until Amy mentioned what the newspapers would have to say that I thought about James at the *Sportsman*, and the promise I had made to him. At seven o'clock I telephoned him and told him that if he wanted the exclusive interview that he'd been after, he had better be down at the cottage by eight-thirty to get it, because by nine o'clock I'd be going off to see Tom and tell him the full story to his face.

Epilogue

And so it transpired that Freddie and I owed our lives, and Tom his freedom, to Amy's bigamist. Realising that she had forgotten her file, she had turned back to retrieve it, and had been surprised to find the front door of the cottage open. Seeing a man's jacket draped across one of the armchairs had made her suspect that something was wrong. She heard voices upstairs so had pretended to leave, and then parked her car around the corner. Although petrified with terror, she returned to the cottage, fetched the bronze from the cupboard where she had seen me put it, and tiptoed up the stairs. The rest, thank God, is history.

Edward recovered consciousness completely in hospital and was charged by a bemused Inspector Wilkinson with the murder of Michael Corcoran and George Musgrave and the attempted murder of myself. Once again, I was to be a witness for the prosecution, only this time the role held no fears and I intended to play my part in seeing that justice would be done.

Less easy was breaking the news to Freddie that his father was still alive. For the time being, I decided to shelter him from the truth by telling him that Edward had not died in a car accident abroad as we had first thought; but his injuries would keep him away for some time. At least I would be able to give him all the love and attention he needed. Edward's reappearance had prompted a speedy withdrawal by his parents of their wardship application.

Tom was given an official pardon and we celebrated his release from prison by going together to the races. By coincidence it was at Worcester and I was riding a novice hurdler for Ralph. There was a fair amount of barging coming round the final bend, ending up with Eamon Brennan going unceremoniously through the rails, and lo and behold, I found myself in front of the stewards. For once, Sir Arthur was charm itself and went out of his way to exonerate me despite the evidence of the head-on film.

Ralph, Tom and James, who was covering the meeting for the *Sportsman* as part of a feature on Tom's return to training, couldn't believe I'd escaped without a fine, or at the very least a caution.

'Come on,' said Tom, putting his arm affectionately around me, 'what's the secret?'

'Feminine intuition and understanding. Just before the race, I did Sir Arthur a favour. I returned his favourite holiday snap. What he doesn't know is whether I've retained a copy or not.'

'And have you?' they asked in unison.

'Now that would be telling!'

JOHN FRANCOME

OUTSIDER

'Francome writes an odds-on racing cert' *Daily Express*

'Spirited stuff' *OK magazine*

'Pacy racing and racy pacing – John Francome has found his stride as a solo novelist' *Horse and Hound*

Already a leading jockey in his home country, Jake Felton comes to England to further his career and avoid confrontation with New York's racing mafia. But his plans to combine the life of an English squire with that of a top-flight jockey look like coming to a sticky end when he falls victim to a series of accidents that begin to seem all too deliberate.

Aided and abetted by typical English rose Camilla Fielding, Jake discovers that he's been targeted by a ruthless and professional killer. And now he urgently needs to find out why . . .

With an intricate and thrilling plot and all the drama and excitement of Derby Day, *Outsider* shows John Francome at the top of his form in this new novel of danger and skulduggery on the race track.

'A thoroughly convincing and entertaining tale' *Daily Mail*

'The racing feel is authentic and it's a pacy, entertaining read' *The Times*

FICTION / CRIME 0 7472 4375 1

A selection of compelling novels by John Francome

ROUGH RIDE	£4.99 ☐
STONE COLD	£4.99 ☐
STUD POKER	£4.99 ☐
BLOODSTOCK (with James McGregor)	£4.99 ☐
DECLARED DEAD (with James McGregor)	£4.99 ☐
EAVESDROPPER (with James McGregor)	£4.99 ☐
RIDING HIGH (with James McGregor)	£4.99 ☐

All Headline books are available at your local bookshop or newsagent, or can be ordered direct from the publisher. Just tick the titles you want and fill in the form below. Prices and availability subject to change without notice.

Headline Book Publishing, Cash Sales Department, Bookpoint, 39 Milton Park, Abingdon, OXON, OX14 4TD, UK. If you have a credit card you may order by telephone – 01235 400400.

Please enclose a cheque or postal order made payable to Bookpoint Ltd to the value of the cover price and allow the following for postage and packing:

UK & BFPO: £1.00 for the first book, 50p for the second book and 30p for each additional book ordered up to a maximum charge of £3.00.
OVERSEAS & EIRE: £2.00 for the first book, £1.00 for the second book and 50p for each additional book.

Name ....

Address ....

....

....

If you would prefer to pay by credit card, please complete:
Please debit my Visa/Access/Diner's Card/American Express (delete as applicable) card no:

Signature .... Expiry Date ....